Waiting for Li Ming

Waiting for Li Ming

ALAN CUMYN

GOOSE LANE

To Suzanne, and the memory of hot *jiaozi* on a cold night.

Published with the assistance of the Canada Council, 1993.

This novel is a work of fiction. Any references to historical events or characters, or to real locales, are intended only to give the fiction a sense of reality and authenticity. Other names, characters, places and incidents are the product of the author's imagination and their resemblance, if any, to real-life counterparts is entirely coincidental.

A section of chapter eleven of this novel has been adapted from "Christmas," a short story which originally appeared in *Quarry* (Fall 1991).

The author would like to acknowledge the early editorial help of Mark Frutkin, made possible by the Ontario Public Libraries' writers-in-residence program. Much thanks also to Tim Wynne-Jones and many other friends and family who gave valuable assistance and support, and to Laurel Boone of Goose Lane Editions for her careful editing. The deficiencies which remain are entirely mine. *Xie xie!*

Cover illustration by Suzanne Cumyn after a photograph by Leong Ka Tai originally published in *National Geographic* (July 1991, p.132).

Book design by Julie Scriver.

Printed in Canada by The Tribune Press Ltd., Sackville, N.B.

10 9 8 7 6 5 4 3 2

Canadian Cataloguing in Publication Data
Cumyn, Alan, 1960-
    Waiting for Li Ming
    ISBN 0-86492-146-2

I. Title.
PS8555.U69W35 1993   C813'.54   C93-098514-1
PR9199.3.C86W35 1993

Goose Lane Editions
469 King Street
Fredericton, New Brunswick
Canada E3B 1E5

1

IT WAS A BLAZING EARLY SEPTEMBER DAY WHEN THE WORLD SEEMED to be apologizing for the coming winter. The air was achingly clear, cold in the breeze but hot in the sun, and alive with the colour of the first changing leaves cracking the green of summer. Rudy was content for the moment to stand in the sun and breathe fresh air. He was wearing battered jeans and running shoes and a blue cotton shirt that had been worn and washed nearly out of existence. His brown curls had blown to their usual state and his eyes were a strained blue, tired. But it was soothing to watch the rose-pearl clouds, so vibrant and sharp in that clear air they made the comfortable Gatineau Hills in the distance seem stunning, as much a work of miracles as the Himalayas. Rudy had seen the Himalayas, briefly, and he never thought he would see anything again as magnificent. But here he was home in an Ottawa suburb, on an ordinary day, just any sunny day in the fall of 1988, and God's hand was here too. You didn't have to go anywhere. You just had to open your eyes.

Li Ming should see this, he thought. No — Li Ming *will* see this. But he had had a dream, just the other night, of Li Ming and Dean Chun, the laughing bald man with the one silver tooth in front. He and the Dean were fighting, but there was nowhere to hold on, he couldn't grip the man or take the smile from his face.

The taxi came and Rudy shouldered his backpack into the trunk, which the driver had opened from the inside without bothering to get out himself. Rudy's portable typewriter clunked on the bottom of his pack. Without looking back — his parents were away; there was nobody to say goodbye to — he got in the front seat and immediately felt dwarfed beside the driver.

Rudy tried not to stare, but a year in China among very small people made it hard. The driver's belly nearly pressed up against the steering wheel and his neck was inflated like an inner tube, rubbing against his shoulders and his ears. He looked like an exaggerated part of the seat cushions themselves, bulging out to steer the vehicle. In China the taxi drivers were wiry, whirling sorts whose clothes hung off them like bags, who drove with the horn first and then the accelerator, leaving the steering wheel and brakes for emergencies.

This driver said only four words during the trip. When Rudy was settled in the front seat he said, "Train station?" and when they arrived he said, "Eight dollars." Rudy remembered having a conversation with a young man who drove a motorized tricycle in Laozhou. The man knew no English and Rudy had no Chinese besides *ni hao* — hello — and *wo shi Jianadaren* — I am Canadian — but somehow in a twenty minute ride he had managed to communicate that he had only been in China a few weeks, that he liked Chinese food, especially steamed dumplings, was twenty-five years old, not married, and would not exchange his foreign currency. He had learned that the driver was also twenty-five, had a wife and one child, a son aged three, and he knew that the capital of Canada is Calgary and the greatest Canadian hero is Norman Bethune, who was praised by Mao and revered by every Chinese. They had played this game of charades, the driver going on in Chinese, Rudy yelling in English, while the tricycle weaved in and out of the swarm, sometimes passing on the left, sometimes on the right, sometimes on the sidewalk on the wrong side of the road, if you could think of it as the wrong side. They threaded their way among bicycles, carts, pedestrians, donkeys, swerved to avoid the mad rush of an oncoming troop truck, army green, as old as the republic, and bucked over potholes, the driver using both hands sometimes to make his point, turning to laugh and exclaim, always seeming to know when to look back at the road to avoid disaster.

This taxi now had a radio playing classical music, Mozart perhaps, pouring out of the FM stereo as rich and full as buttermilk, making speech, except for essential communications, unnecessary, nearly rude. The fat driver stroked the steering wheel lightly with his fingers, gliding the car through the mundanity of traffic. His eyes seemed hazed, as if he were in meditation. Rudy saw the man's photo and taxi licence card hanging from the sun visor in front of him. The name was unpronounceable, and Rudy for some reason thought it might be Romanian. He had met a Romanian in Laozhou, Joseph, a coal engineer who spoke elegant French and gave the impression that his country had fallen into a state of unspeakable ugliness and depression. "We are part of Europe," was the extent of what he would say about it. "We are civilized people, really." They had met at a Chinese New Year's banquet put on by the mayor of the city for all the foreigners, and Rudy was amazed to see a room of fifty men and women, only eight of whom — the other English teachers — he had seen before. The rest were all coal technicians and engineers from Poland and Romania and East Germany, who were never allowed out of their guest houses, never went out in the market, in the streets, to the stores or theatre. Joseph had told him he was sent to Laozhou for five years, after seven years in one of the African countries — Tanzania? Rudy couldn't remember — and now he was counting the days till he got home.

The taxi pulled up to the station; the driver stayed with his music, pulling the lever to open the trunk and accepting Rudy's money with the same slightly tranced movement.

Rudy went into his own kind of meditation when he got into the train station. He marvelled at the gleaming open space, the floors devoid of mud, spit, people, dirt, at how everyone actually stood in line to get their tickets instead of massing

7

together in a mob, a scrum in front of every wicket. He took a long moment to consider the computers and fast food and plastic chairs, the special seats with the pay televisions attached, the velvet ropes keeping the lines straight and orderly. He remembered arriving at the Laozhou station and having a man fly past him out of the crowd like a sudden apparition, legless, his trunk resting on a wooden cart, propelling himself on wooden blocks strapped to his fists like knuckles.

Here order, cleanliness, silence. Like a hospital. Rudy sat in a plastic chair beside his backpack and watched a family sitting on a mountain of luggage, the three children swarming in and out of their mother's arms while their father read the paper anonymously, smoking here in the no-smoking section, flicking his ashes on the floor, which still gleamed. Indestructible polish. In China, everywhere, floors so old and trod-upon and ill-cared-for nothing could transform them from the dullest grey or green. Walls paintless, cinderblock buildings, the most depressing architecture imaginable. Air hazy with coal dust, which you don't notice after a while, you just think perhaps it doesn't get sunny here so often, it's part of the climate. Blowing your nose and finding black soot on your handkerchief. Washing your clothes in cold water with only hand soap, and still the water turns black.

The train was a little late. Nobody said anything. By then they were all standing between velvet ropes with their luggage, waiting, calmly waiting. It seemed to Rudy that if a fire had broken out people would have stood there, still, until an official came to tell them where to go. When the train finally did arrive the crowd leaned forward a little, expectantly. Rudy thought of the Chinese crowds waiting for hard seats, penned for hours, and then suddenly set free to run madly, scramble, dash down the hall, around the corner, up the ramp, over the bridge, down the stairs, carrying, dragging baskets, suitcases, overstuffed bags, live chickens, children, all in the rush to get the few seats, a place to rest. The losers, the late ones, would stand the whole way, perhaps if there was room lie down on the floor at night underneath the seats. Li Ming's aunt had come once to visit, six days on the train, hard seat all the way, and then was sick for a month after she arrived. And now the tickets were so expensive. It was easy to think of Li Ming. The hard part, the part that Rudy really had to work on, was not to worry, not to become obsessed with the thousand and one things that could already have gone wrong. The words of her last note were carved in his brain. *I am being sent away. I have to go tonight. I have your address. Wait for me!* And that whole night in the train station. And the banquet — God, the banquet!

"Don't think about it," he said out loud, and the man in the blue uniform who was checking the tickets looked at him.

"Sorry," Rudy said, startled. "Just talking to myself."

On the train Rudy settled into a window seat, but the window was shaded an annoying grey. He wanted the whole day to come in while he watched it roll by. Winter would be here soon enough, there would be enough grey then, and it would last far too long. He would apologize to Li Ming for the grey window, if she were here, and he would just watch her as she stared out at the passing countryside, the green lawns, the individual houses — "Where do the ordinary people live?" she would ask — then outside the city, the bushland stretching far past the imagination of someone from a land that has been levelled, dug, prodded, planted, picked clean for thousands of years. Where are the factories? she would wonder. What, a whole lake wild, with not even a fishing boat? Are there so few people, then, that Canadians let land go unused?

Rudy remembered his several train trips in China as one long ride, the wet fields and dusty towns drifting past hour after hour, with the tinny music and propaganda screeching from the box overhead until eleven at night, then starting again at six in the morning. The crowds of curious passengers watching him, the men all smoking wherever you went, smoke rising to choke off any last corner of fresh air. Some people coming up to practise their English, or try something out on him in Chinese, which he did not understand at all. "*Wo bu dong,*" he would say, shrugging his shoulders. "*Wo shi Jianadaren.*"

"Ah, ah, *Jianadaren!*" they would say, nodding their heads, smiling, clapping their hands sometimes, and then a long stream of Chinese would come out, incomprehensible.

"*Wo bu dong,*" he would say again, smiling.

Now, no one spoke to him, and he spoke to no one, and the day passed in a green blur, and he fell asleep.

In Toronto he had to change trains. On the way into town they had passed factories, plants, warehouses, smokestacks — squatting, massive, muscle-bound buildings smelling of smoke and dust and work. He thought of the train to Shanghai then, which passed industrial works like these, and all the little clay and brick agricultural towns along the way, which somehow were never very different from the industrial works — the same dust, the same dirt and gravel and concrete, not so much utilitarian as depression grey.

On the new car the windows were not shaded, but the day was dying, and there would be a half-hour wait before they would get out of the station on the way west. Rudy took out his notepad and worked on a letter to Li Ming, an act of faith he had maintained throughout the summer. He had to believe that she would write. It was going to work out in the end.

But the connection with Li Ming seemed fragile now, like a single strand of spider's web spun over ten thousand miles. What if she wrote a letter and it got lost, then she might not send another one, thinking he had changed his mind once he had gotten home. *You will go home and marry a blonde-haired girl, that is all! It is my life that is running away!* He could see her still, passing from the shadows into light. If only they had had another chance to talk. There was just the note now. He had to believe in that. But why wouldn't she have written by now?

There was probably a reason, something that Rudy did not understand and that had nothing to do with him and Li Ming. So much that had happened in China he did not understand. Best to wait. He smiled, thinking of her saying, "We have to keep cold heads." If only he knew what had happened to her, where she had been sent, what she was doing. If only he knew for sure that she was all right.

Don't worry, Li Ming, he thought. I will keep a cold head.

Rudy was trying to write a description of the train station for her when someone took the seat beside him. He hadn't noticed that the car was filling up. He shifted his legs and looked at the person busily adjusting her bags at her feet. Her quick, bright smile struck Rudy immediately, a hammer on a bell buried deep in his memory.

She didn't remember him, that was clear. She turned away and looked through her bag for a book. Rudy watched her. It was the smile, mainly, that he remembered, how it expressed itself through her dark eyes, which were very gentle. Older, obviously she was older, but her hair was still the same, long and black and straight. Her face still very white and fresh; she had put on weight, not drastically, but she was no longer a sixteen-year-old runner. What was her name? He had written a poem afterwards, he remembered now. A song. He did that sort of thing back then, met a girl on a bus and then sat up for hours in the night writing a song for her, just because of the way she smiled and the sound of her name.

Janine. Of course.

He couldn't remember the song at all, except that he had written it, but because he had he could still remember her name after seven years, and now all at once he remembered the whole day. Rainy, cold, in October. The end of the cross-country running season, with winter breathing down their necks. He had a meet in Barry's Bay, two hours out of Ottawa, so he had to go to school early to catch the bus. And there had been an accident, a motorcyclist was hit and down on the street, surrounded by people, but the police and ambulance had not arrived yet. Someone was administering first aid; Rudy had lent his coat to help keep off the rain. The young man was conscious but in shock; you could see the bone sticking out of his lower leg, a brilliant, sickening flash of white.

He had had to leave. The ambulance had arrived; his bus was leaving. He asked a friend to pick up his coat for him. And then he was on the bus, thinking about how he could write that accident down in a poem. He might have even tried writing something in his notebook, which he kept with him all the time then, for ideas. The bus went to some other schools to pick up their runners and that's when Janine got on, and sat beside him, and they talked for two hours, the way people will on a bus, telling complete strangers things they would not tell their friends.

"The Same Day." That was the name of the song. It was about seeing the accident and then riding away on a bus and nearly falling in love and that eerie feeling of glimpsing the swirl of the universe in one day. He used that phrase, "the swirl of the universe." Now he wasn't sure what it meant.

And she didn't recognize him. Rudy thought of going back to his letter, the comfort of silence. It was tempting.

"Are you going far?" he asked finally, relieved to get the first words out.

"Saskatoon," she said, smiling at him again. He remembered. They had talked about rock music.

"Saskatoon! How long will it take you to get there?"

"I'll be there by tomorrow night," she said.

"That's a long trip." Rudy had taken similar ones in China, but foreigners do crazy things that natives usually wouldn't contemplate.

"Where are you going?" the girl asked him.

"Bellsbridge," he said. "It's only a couple of hours from here."

She nodded. There was no doubt who she was. Rudy remembered it all very clearly.

"Your name is Janine, isn't it?" Rudy said then, and explained how he knew. She looked doubtful, then slowly seemed to remember.

"Of course, yes!" she said finally, nodding her head. "I know why I didn't recognize you. You aren't wearing your hat."

Rudy had to think for a moment, then laughed, remembering. Yes. It had been raining, and he was wearing one of those Scottish hats his parents had brought home from their trip. His duffer's çap, he had called it. Lost now. But she had seen him in it and that's why she had sat down beside him. She had asked to try it on and she looked cute in it, her long hair flowing out the back and . . . oh yes, the way her face took on light when he handed it over.

They talked about that bus ride now, remembering it as they went along, and the cross-country meet, how cold it was and brutal running up and down bare ski hills, mud and rock and knuckled clumps of grass. She had only been in grade nine then; he was a senior. She was definitely cute. He had kept thinking the whole way along, as she had talked and talked and talked, about how he could ask for her phone number. But she was from another school, and he was too shy, and then the bus ride was over. On the way back he had looked for her, but she had sat with friends, and it was dark, and most people just slept the whole way.

"So now you're going to . . . Saskatoon?" Rudy said to her now.

"I'm going to college there."

"To study . . . ?"

"Uh . . . it's a Bible college."

"Of course!" he said, light suddenly opening up another corner. "Your parents were missionaries, right? I remember you talking about playing with snakes when you were little. In Africa."

"In Rhodesia, yes."

"But wait a minute. I remember you were rebelling against your parents. You were really into rock music. We talked about Bruce Springsteen."

"Yeah, yeah, you're right," she said, and her face took on that light again, the same one that had slept there, preserved in his memory like some old book deep in the library stacks. And then she started talking, the way that she had the last time, the words bubbling out of her, cool fresh water from deep underground. She had been against religion back then, but a couple of years later she had felt a presence come into her life. Jesus. She said it with a little embarrassment, not wanting to sound weird or proselytizing.

"And now you're going to Bible college?"

"Yeah, it's funny," she said. She might have added more, if he had thought of the right question to ask, but he didn't, and she asked him instead what he had been doing. He briefly mentioned university, and then mentioned teaching in China, and she said something that surprised him. "I remember! You were going to be a writer! You wanted to do exciting things so you could write about them!" she said and he looked at her, the red crawling up his neck and flushing his face. Had he told her that? He didn't tell anybody about wanting to be a writer back then. His poems were for secret, for composing late, late at night and then memorizing and having those words running through his brain for days afterwards while the rest of life went on all around him.

"Your parents are really wealthy, right?" she said. "Your whole family is lawyers. But you were going to break away from all that."

"Not wealthy, no," he said, but then he reversed himself. "Well, yes, okay, I guess they are wealthy," and then he told her that indeed he was on his way to do the Creative Writing program at the university, that he'd been accepted when he was in China.

He was a slow talker, everything coming out in a story that more likely than not was going to be interrupted before he could finish, and that was why he usually felt shy to start. But it was easy to talk to her, once he got going. Maybe his year in China had helped him that way, opened him up. He told her all about the story he had read on the plane to China, just one short story that took twenty minutes of a sixteen hour flight, but he had spent the rest of the time thinking about it, turning it over in his head. The author was William Rogers of Bells-bridge University. Some other fellow was teaching the senior seminar, but Rudy had written to Rogers and he had agreed to work with him.

He began to tell her then about China, about his town, Laozhou — trains, coal, dust, the rounded hills and the valley that had been a battleground for thousands of years. The latest huge battle, fought in 1948, was one of the great defeats of the Kuomintang, but it flattened the entire town. He talked about his school, too, the teacher's college, how it was shut down during the Cultural Revolution and became a factory and how you could still see the remnants of the pipes and old cables running through the classrooms, like skeletons. Every detail he thought of reminded him of another and then another but it was not coming out in a coherent way. The stories piled on top of one another until he was filled with the urge to just go away and write it all out and then present it to her, and to everyone else he had been trying to tell. It would be a relief to be settled, finally, to set up the typewriter and let the page take over. She asked a few more questions but she knew nothing of China, probably could not guess at the depth of images behind the things he said, just as he knew nothing of the feelings behind her acceptance, finally, of her parents' faith and vocation. *I felt a spirit come to me,* she had said.

"So you left China to come back and do the writing program?" she said, to keep the conversation going.

"I guess so," Rudy said, thinking of Li Ming, and of Dean Chun, and what he should have said back then, too, and how it wouldn't have made any difference anyway.

"There were some things that happened to people, to friends," he said quietly, "that made me lose faith in the system. Not that I had much faith in the system to begin with. But when people treat one another like that — not with violence so much as with cruelty and jealousy — then you have to wonder what's going on."

Just after sundown the train pulled into Bellsbridge. They had eaten a meal together in the club car, and talked some more, and for the last hour slept. Rudy remembered riding the train to Laozhou that first time, a little more than a year ago, from Nanjing. Everything seemed bleached white from the heat and the dust; he wasn't sure where to get off; had sat upright anxiously for the last hour wondering which little stop it was. What if he missed it? He would just keep riding north. All the way to Beijing? No, they would kick him off before that, or ask him for more money. Nobody spoke English. The little towns were rolling by. Which one was his? He couldn't even pronounce it properly. Lao-joe, the *lao* rhyming with *cow*, but the tones he couldn't get. Finally, at the right stop, the conductor was there, took him by the arm, helped him off personally. And he was immediately surrounded by a mob of white-shirted men. Nylon, short sleeves, the undershirts showing through. Every official from the college, maybe thirty in all, from the president to the party secretary of the Foreign Language Department. Shaking his hand, carrying his bags. *Ni hao! Hao, hao! Ni hao!*

Janine was still asleep when the train pulled into Bellsbridge, her breathing quiet, her pretty face calm and undisturbed. Rudy rose quietly and squeezed by her, nearly stumbled on the last step when it all seemed clear. She stirred a little but did not awaken. He lifted his pack from the overhead compartment and tore a sheet from his notebook: *See you again in another seven years. 1995? An airplane next time? Take care, Rudy.*

Then he was walking down the aisle of the train with his pack across his shoulder, and stepping out into the coolish air of another town strange to him. This time no one was waiting, no one even stared as he walked along, and there was space between the people, so much space his footsteps echoed off the walls of the station.

2

WHEN WE STEP OUT OF THE TRAIN STATION THE SUN HITS MY FACE like the flat side of a pan. It is so bright and dry and dusty I have to stop and let my head clear. The white-shirted men surround me; one small, thin-looking man nearly buckles under my pack. I try to help him but he waves me off.

Swarms of people, in green and blue, mostly, but some in other bright colours. An orange sports shirt, a lime-green dress. Heads turn as we walk along. Everyone, now, looking at me. Suddenly it seems I have grown several inches, am as tall as everybody else, not swamped in the crowd like I am at home. A legless man scoots across my path, not even looking up, on a wooden trolley with squeaking wheels, propelling himself on blocks of wood which he uses to protect his fists. I'm stunned, momentarily, but no one else seems to notice.

A man walks by, pulling a cart behind him. He is like a terribly thin horse, quiet, patient, plodding inexorably beneath a straw hat. He turns to watch me, his neck screwing farther and farther but his expression never changing. I raise a hand to him and he does nothing, his head eventually turning back. A little boy does the spinning head trick, too, but walks straight into a concrete post and starts crying, his mother laughing at him. "What is she saying?" I ask one of the white-shirted men, but he doesn't understand me, pointing instead to the parking lot.

Nobody in the welcoming group speaks English. I don't know what happened; I was assured I would get a translator, but all I have seen so far is polite smiles, nodding heads and shaking hands, and everyone saying, "Harro! Harro!" Even strangers in the parking lot yell it out to me. "Harro! Harro!"

I am led to a gorgeous black car waiting for me in the heat of the parking lot. It looks about forty years old, rounded and gleaming, with enough steel in it to make a battleship. I help the little guy put my pack in the trunk. Then he motions me into the back seat and the door is closed behind me. Inside the seats are grey and feel like worn velour, and there are black crepe curtains to pull across the windows. The driver starts up the engine, turns on the air conditioner, and gets out, leaving me alone.

Like an animal in a cage. An air-conditioned cage, yes, but a cage nonetheless. The people passing by on foot or on bicycles stop to have a look. Who's in the black car? Is it a foreigner? Look, look, it's a foreigner! In the black car. Look! I am watching it all, a silent film behind the noise of the engine and the air conditioner and the thick panes of glass.

Like a visiting dignitary, trapped in a limousine, all alone for ten, fifteen, twenty minutes. Half an hour. What a waste of gas in a poor country! Just so the spoiled Westerner won't be uncomfortable. The white-shirted men have disappeared; I don't know what's going on; there isn't even anybody I can talk to.

So I watch the people go by, behind the glass. I can't bring myself to pull the curtain. They watch me, I watch them. Crowds clot. What's he going to do? The foreigner, where's he from? Look, he has a big nose, doesn't he? And his hair is so light and curly. Why is he just sitting there?

Finally, I reach forward and turn off the ignition, then get out. Some of my hosts are standing together several metres off having a terrific argument over something. When they spot me their faces change, go from serious anger to exaggerated smiles, and their hands shoot up and down again in welcoming gestures. Somebody starts to bring me back to the car, but I say, "No. What's happening? Is there a problem?"

Two men wave their hands, no problem. Can they understand me? A crowd starts to gather around us. *Waiguoren, waiguoren!* they whisper. Foreigner, foreigner!

"What's the problem?" I say again, thinking that maybe they do understand me after all. "Are we waiting for something?"

They ignore me, start talking among themselves. Somebody takes me by the arm, pointing and smiling, back to the car. There's nothing I can do but go with him. It's their country. He opens the door for me and I get in again, and then the driver comes back and turns on the engine, although I say, "No!" gesturing, "Not necessary!"

More waiting. I am suddenly feeling very tired. What can I do? Is it possible I'm the only one at the college who speaks English? What are my students going to be like? But there must be somebody who can manage — they're supposed to be English teachers, for God's sake. But how could they forget to bring a translator? I know I told them I know almost zero Chinese.

"Hello?" comes a voice at the window, a woman. She seems quite young at first, but in another moment she looks older than I am, perhaps in her thirties. "Hello?"

"Yes, hello!" I say, reaching over to open the door. "You speak English!"

"Yes, I speak English," she says, with an Oxford accent that nearly makes me laugh, it sounds so practised and polished.

"You are the new teacher, Rudy Seaborn?" she asks.

"Yes. Yes I am!"

"We are having trouble finding your luggage. It shouldn't be too long. There are just some problems with the train officials. It happens sometimes."

"What luggage?" I ask. "The man put my pack in the trunk."

"Your other bags. We haven't been able to . . . "

"I don't have any other bags. All I brought is in the trunk."

"Ah!" she says, her eyes going wide. "Then that solves the problem." She turns to go almost immediately.

"Wait. Wait!" I call.

"Yes?"

"What's your name?"

"My name is Li Ming," she says, and there are two things that strike me — that she is startlingly beautiful, and that the focus of that beauty is in her eyes, which meet mine with a strange combination of fierceness and timidity, a yearning to know and a shutter to keep out the world.

"Pleased to meet you, Li Ming," I say, but she has already turned to leave.

I do not see her again for two weeks. Instead my translator is Fang, a functionary from the *waiban*, the foreign affairs office, whose English comes out in nervous shivers mumbled behind his hand. He is taller than I am and thin and has been ill, apparently — I don't know what from, we don't get that far in the conversation after he deposits me in my apartment, directly under the ping-pong room of the Foreign Languages Department. There is plenty of space for just me — a bedroom, sitting room and bathroom — and though the floor is rough concrete the rest is fine, the furniture sturdy and serviceable. Much nicer than the conditions I've been used to in the last four years at school. I don't tell anyone this, of course — I am a foreigner, they think I am used to five-star hotels. But here I have a little courtyard and a nice big fence and there is a little building across the way where my meals are produced by my own private cook, beautifully arranged little plates of oddities that taste all right as long as I don't peek into the adjoining kitchen, so dark and filthy it looks like a breeding ground for cholera. Hepatitis more likely.

The students have already started school. I watch them flock to class in the morning, most of the young men in their fatigue-green jackets, their blue cotton pants, some of the young women in dresses with red bows in their hair and knee-high nylons the tops of which show in a way considered terminally unsophisticated back home. Some of them approach me, stammering out their few phrases, their books clutched to their chests.

"When you will teach to us?" they ask.

Good question. I have come at the invitation of the school, through the introduction of a friend of a friend who was travelling in China last year and mistakenly got off the train in Laozhou, not a tourist stop on anyone's map, unless you are a coal miner or a specialist in dull countryside towns destroyed in the civil war and rebuilt in sober socialist cinderblock. But she had four hours until the next train and so she wandered and happened onto the campus of the Teacher's College, where officials offered her a job immediately lecturing in English. It didn't matter what she wanted to say, they told her — she was a native speaker, that was all that mattered. She declined but kept the card of the dean, English translation carefully printed on the back, and gave it to me when I said I wanted to work in a culture completely different from my own.

I have paid my own travel expenses. Or rather, my parents have, a graduation gift. The school pays me state wages, and will pay my return at the end of the year.

Which is fine. Everything is fine. Except that I'm trapped here, alone, with no Chinese, and no translator, and ping-pong balls clunking over my head from ten in the morning until ten at night, and nothing to teach yet, nothing to do except wait for Fang, who doesn't come very often and doesn't seem to know anything when he does come.

There is an endless round of meetings. On Tuesday I meet the president of the college, another tall man but quite old, with an enormous head and a feeble handshake. Fang tells me he has written a famous book on mathematics. We have tea in a big room and eat candies, and several other old men whose names and titles I cannot remember make speeches in Chinese, thanking me I suppose for coming "to help China realize the four modernizations," although Fang's translations are so brief I wonder how much I am missing. On Wednesday I meet Dean Chun, another elderly man, but bald and very round, with a silver tooth gleaming in his grin and private thoughts hiding behind careful eyes. These are only my first impressions. I will not get to know any of these people very well, I realize. The room is different, but once again the meeting is all tea and candies and stultifying speeches, cut to the barest of words by Fang.

"I was hoping we could talk about the classes I'll be teaching," I say, pushing, and then wait for Fang to say something to vaguely represent that idea in Chinese. He does not look confident. "In your letter you mentioned a few possibilities . . . " I say.

Fang and Dean Chun talk together for several minutes.

"You should take time just rest!" Fang says finally, as Dean Chun smiles, and pours me more tea.

Thursday a luncheon banquet with *waiban* officials; Friday a city tour in the same black car that was waiting for me at the train station; Saturday and Sunday alone to wander the streets snapping pictures and bobbing my head and smiling, illiterate and dumb. Crowds form behind me when I walk, individuals cross the street to hurl their three words of English at me over and over; others just stare, mouths open, as if I were a gorilla wandered in from the jungle.

Monday I stay in reading, writing letters, trying to put together some notes for class. What class? When am I supposed to start? If I had a gun I'd shoot those bastards playing ping-pong while I'm going out of my mind.

Finally Tuesday Fang says, "Meet with department leaders.

Three o'clock?" "Fine," I say. "Am I finally going to find out what I'm supposed to be teaching?" "Fine, yes," he says earnestly. "The leaders will to discuss with you. No need hurry."

At three o'clock Fang is there, but with Li Ming this time, to "assist" in the translation, which means — thank God — she does all the translating, and Fang sits back eating oranges and candies.

I am brought to yet another large room with stuffed chairs arranged around the four walls, a large empty space in the centre. Perhaps twenty men are sitting when I get there, and they all stand up for me as I enter. Mostly thick, solid, middle-aged men, with big smiles and no English, though this is the Foreign Languages Department and many of them are English teachers. Another ceremony. I sit down, dismayed, the ubiquitous mug of green tea in front of me, as the speeches begin to rain.

Dean Chun again. Round, bald, smiling, like an elf. "We of the humble Laozhou Teacher's College extravagantly welcome the renowned English scholar Dr. Seaborn, who has come all the way from the wealthy country of Canada to live and suffer our simple life and teach us the Western methods of teaching." Li Ming standing and delivering the translation loud and clear, absolutely deadpan, in an Oxford English accent totally incongruous with this run-down little room full of blue Mao jackets.

I give as ingratiating a speech as I can manage, correcting them of their mistaken notion that I have a PhD, saying how much I look forward to learning from the ancient culture of China, getting to know people and trying out the language (by now they all know I can't string three words together). I sit down again, Li Ming translates a full speech — she must have a quick mind to keep track of all that — and then there is another speech, to which I must reply, and then another, all the men in the room taking their turns, being introduced and welcoming the foreigner in much the same terms as the dean had.

They even have the janitors and security people making speeches by the end. On the way out — I still haven't found out when I am supposed to start — I ask Li Ming how I did.

"You really want to know?" she asks.

I nod.

"You should have kept your PhD," she says. "And it is — what do you say? — a bit of an insult to say you want to learn from ancient China. We Chinese are building a new country. We are learning from you now. Ancient China stopped in 1949."

Ah. I start to apologize when she cuts me off.

"The other thing," she says, "is you must be very patient. Everything happens according to its own pace here."

"But I've been here for two weeks and I still haven't found out when I'm supposed to start classes, or even what it is I'm supposed to be teaching."

"Tomorrow," she says. "Seven-thirty. Room sixteen."

"What am I teaching?"

"The History of Britain and America," she says, and then she is gone.

3

THE LOUDSPEAKER WAKES ME UP AT SIX IN THE MORNING. YI ER! SAN, si! Wu, liu! Qi, ba! calls a strident voice again and again in sing-song, Ed Allen meets the marines, with blaring martial music in the background. The physical jerks. Orwell would have loved it. The first morning I ran out to see what it was and found a soccer field full of students doing jumping jacks in brilliant blue sweatsuits, clouds of cool mist rising from their lips. Their compound is a good quarter-mile away, but the loudspeaker is right beside my apartment.

God. Today I start teaching. British and American History! Who decided that? I didn't bring a textbook for that. I've brought collections of short stories, and manuals on writing, and ESL exercises. If they'd told me earlier I could have used their little library — it was closed after the meeting yesterday afternoon. I know they have an *Encyclopaedia Britannica* in there at least. And I've seen Li Ming sitting at the sole desk, under the window, writing away, pausing to consult the books piled on the corner of the desk and on the floor around her.

1066. Right. That's where we'll begin. The consequences of the Norman invasion. What were they again? I know I studied this in grade nine.

But I don't even know if these students speak English. Maybe it won't matter what I say. Maybe I can make it up as I go along.

I did not bring a formal jacket or a tie. I was told I wouldn't need them here. I wear my one collared white shirt, wrinkled from my pack — did I bring an iron? — and a sweater for formality, even though the sun is already baking concrete buildings that have stayed hot overnight. I bring my little travelling briefcase even though all I have inside it is a pad with a few notes scrawled while I ate breakfast: *William the Conqueror, Doomsday Book, King Harold?*? and *arrow*, with a primitive diagram that represents the famous faked retreat that I think I remember won the battle for William.

It's not a long walk around to the main entrance of the Foreign Languages building, a tired building the yellowy-grey of the dusty grounds surrounding it. The stairs are concrete, sturdy, but the two doors are flimsy wood, painted green around the time of the revolution probably, broken for decades by the look of them — they never close, but lean inward as if introducing the gullet of a cave. I hurry in, aware of already being a few minutes late. The air inside is hot, suffocating. My eyes have to adjust to the darkness. Up the stairs. On the left is the big meeting room where the departmental leaders gave their party for me yesterday. I turn right, down to the end, beside the clunkity-clunk, clunkity-clunk, clunkity-clunk ping-pong room.

Sixteen. The door, also frail, wooden, is closed. I hope it's the right room. I push it open, step in. Fifty-four faces look up.

Then someone yells something in Chinese and they're all on their feet as one, standing to attention like a roomful of soldiers. "Yikes!" I say stepping back, smiling, waving them down. "That's okay! Hi! Good morning. You can sit down."

"GOOD MORNING MR. SEABORN!" they chant in unison, and then they sit down together, leaning forward to see what I will do.

"Second Year Class B reporting Mr. Seaborn sir!" says a very serious boy in the front row, standing again by himself. "I am the class monitor," and I don't catch his name, it goes by so fast.

"Thank you," I say. "Excuse me, your name is — ?"

He says it again and I miss it a second time.

"Sorry, a little slower . . . "

"Chen Liangdong," he says.

"Chen Liangdong," I repeat and the class erupts in laughter, as if I have dropped my pants in front of them.

"I'm sorry," I say. "I thought you said . . . "

"No, no, Mr. Seaborn," the monitor says. "Everything perfect!" They laugh again and wait for me to speak some more.

The monitor — whatever his name is — brings me a class list, but I do not attempt to pronounce another name right away. A little rattled, I just start talking, inventing an outline of the course on the spot. A few milestones occur to me: the Magna Carta, Henry VIII, the Spanish Armada, Cromwell, the American Revolution. I write things on the board as I say them, speak slowly, waste as much time as possible. The students watch with big eyes as I pace back and forth; no one is taking down a note. A young man in the back with shaggy hair leans over, hawks and spits on the floor, the gob drooling out slowly. Nobody notices but me.

"Maybe, before I put too much of the course before you," I say, "I should just get a few impressions from you people, so I can know where you are starting from. Why should we study the history of England and America? What sort of impressions do you get when I mention those countries?"

Silence.

"I mean — America! The USA! What do you think of when I say those words?"

Nothing. Heads lower. Everyone suddenly finds something to write in their books.

"Mr. Chen," I say, going back to the monitor. "Maybe you can start us off. When I say, 'United States of America,' what do you think of?"

Chen rises with great reluctance, his face now alarmingly red, as if I have singled him out for punishment.

He doesn't say anything.

"I'm not trying to test you," I say, to explain. "There's no right or wrong answer. I mean, what is it you think of? McDonald's hamburgers? Big shiny automobiles? Somebody walking on the moon? What?"

No reaction. None. Chen shakes his head, suddenly humble, shy as a little girl.

"Okay, okay. Let's do it this way," I say. "Everybody, I want you to take ten minutes right now and write out, in a few sentences, what your impressions are of Britain and America. The main things you think about when you think of those countries. After ten minutes I'll get you all to read out your answers to me. All right?"

Looks of total panic from most of the room.

"It's no big deal. I mean, I'm not going to give you a mark or anything. This is . . . a western teaching technique. It's called class participation. You'll get used to it."

I sit at the desk at the front of the room and take a few deep breaths to gather myself. My hands are shaking. I haven't the slightest idea how much of what I say they understand. I glance at my watch, then look about the room. The desks are battered and old, many of the windows broken; a large crack runs across most of the blackboard, the corners of which are caked in ancient chalk dust. The walls are dull institutional yellow, the paint neglected; a water stain runs most of the way around the four walls of the room, about a foot off the floor, evidence of some ancient flood. Large round pipes run this way and that across the ceiling, while thick cables burst through the walls at odd points and curl into the air cut and exposed, as if hacked apart with an axe. There are classrooms up and down the hall but not a sound is coming from them; through the closed door I can hear the clunkity-clunk, clunkity-clunk, clunkity-clunk of the ping-pong room.

I give them fifteen minutes for good measure and then I start with the pig-tailed girl in the first desk on the left-hand side, ask her to stand and read what she has written. She seems to stop breathing when I point to her, makes it out of her seat only with prompting from the others. And then she reads in a voice so soft I cannot hear her.

"Louder, please!" I say. "You're training to be a teacher here. Let your voice boom out!"

She repeats her answer exactly as before, and it is only on the third try that I can understand what she is saying.

"Britain and America," she reads, her accent gnarling every word, "are bourgeois liberal so-called democracies that exploit workers and seek to dominate the world as aggressor nations."

She sits down again, her face baking.

The next six say remarkably similar things, although one mentions technology and another disco music, which makes everybody laugh, especially me. "Disco music?" I say and we laugh again, and I realize at least I have made a start, for whatever it's worth.

"Okay," I say, picking up my chalk and pointing to their books. "I might not agree with you — it doesn't matter. I can see we are going to have a lot to learn from each other. Write this down. It's important. We're going to begin in 1066 . . . "

At three-fifteen precisely there is a knock at the door. I have stayed in bed a little too long for my afternoon nap — *shuxi* — and quickly get up and rub the tiredness from my eyes. Already Fang has walked in on me twice when I was still in bed. Somehow the door has a different meaning here; it is never locked, is more an invitation than a bar. It is assumed that people who lock their doors have something to hide.

I walk into the middle room. "Just a minute, Fang," I say, heading for the bathroom. But then I stop short. "Ah, Li Ming." I don't have a shirt on. Somehow, I feel as if I might as well be naked.

"Mr. Fang has been called away for other duties," she says, looking down, red in the face. "He asked me to go with you."

"Wonderful! I'll just be a minute," I say, as cheerfully as possible, retreating to my bedroom. When I come out again, fully clothed, she is standing with her hands behind her back and her face is like the mask of an oriental princess, beautiful and bored, with only her eyes — too dark, too intense — giving her away.

Outside it is still hot and dry, everything wearing a film of white from the dust. I am in my light cotton pants and sports shirt and tennis shoes; Li Ming is in a bright pink shirt and long blue polyester pants that must be cooking her legs on a day like this. We start walking together slowly.

"Mr. Fang said that you wanted to take photographs."

"Yes."

"You can take excellent photographs on Laozhou Shan."

"I know. I've been there. Fang took me."

"Ah. Then I will take you to the Monument to the Martyrs. It is the sixth tallest war memorial in China."

"Yes, Mr. Fang took me," I say. "I got a good picture of it from down below all the steps."

"Then I could take you to the sports stadium which hosted the Jiangsu Province Games last year."

We walk down the lane past the Foreign Languages Department. I nod at three girls who are my students. They are standing together in white blouses like petals, reading from a textbook to one another. When they see me word passes between them like light passing between mirrors, and they all look up simultaneously. "Hello, Mr. Seaborn," they say together, then dissolve into giggles as I pass by.

"Hi!" I give them a good wave. "*Ni hao!*" I add, just to see them flutter into laughter once again. They don't seem like college students to me, more like high school students, but even younger and more naive than that — like high school students from the forties, perhaps, long before pink spiked hair, black lipstick, cadaverously pale faces.

"Actually," I say, "I was hoping to go down a few of the back streets behind the college. I want pictures of ordinary life in China. Some common scenes for my friends back home."

Li Ming nods without comment. She is not like the giggling college girls, although at times she looks hardly older than most of them. She seems focused, intense, more serious, perhaps troubled. We walk around the corner, past acres of basketball courts, towards the front gate. The boys have all stripped off their shirts, so that you can't tell who's on what team — they are one brown, sweating mass following the ball. Some of them pause to watch me but mostly I pass unnoticed. I stop at the corner of one of the courts, kneel down, and zoom in on a young man dribbling. His shoulders relaxed, his head up, he isn't tight like so many of the others. He carries himself like a real basketball player. With the slightest move he flashes past his man on the left and springs suddenly into the air and shoots the worn leather basketball softly through the hoop that has no net. I get a picture of him releasing the shot, his black hair moppish, his wrists extended, fingers pointing to the basket.

"*Xie xie!*" I call out to him when he sees me with my camera. He nods to me, then calls something out to Li Ming, who does not answer. He smiles, turns back to his comrades, then says something again to Li Ming. A joke of some kind which she laughs at, briefly, before donning again her official face. Encouraged, he approaches and they talk for some minutes. I can't understand a word of it, and yet it is a universal sort of language, the way the young man is trying to impress her, and the way she is standing there hardly saying anything, trying to stay unimpressed.

"I think I got a good shot," I say to her when we are on our way again. "Who was that?"

"Nobody," she says, not looking back, though he is looking at her even as he scrambles for the ball.

"Do you play basketball?" I ask, to keep the conversation going.

"No," she says.

"I thought everybody played basketball here. I can't believe how many people are out every afternoon. And not just the really good players, either. That's the thing that's so impressive. Back home you'd only see the really good players come out. But here everybody participates, just to have fun. I think it's terrific."

"There isn't so much to do," Li Ming says.

"So, you make your own fun. That's great!"

She just looks at me without comment.

We pass through the college gates. I say, "*Ni hao!*" to the old man sitting there and he lights up, his face being sombre most of the time. Grey whiskers, the usual blue pants and white undershirt and blue Mao jacket, buttons undone because of the heat. He says "*Ni hao!*" to me and then fires something off to Li

Ming, who answers him with a brief staccato burst and he nods. I assume he has asked where I am going.

Out on the sidewalk. As usual the street is a steady current of bicycles, their bells ringing like incessant birdsong. Almost immediately a young man passes in front of us pulling a fifteen-foot concrete pillar behind him on a cart. I have to change lenses quickly to get it all in, but luckily he is not moving very fast, especially as he approaches the hill just ahead.

"That's something that you don't see at home," I say to Li Ming. "The sheer physical labour that you have here. These guys must be in terrific shape."

"They are paid very well," she says. "But their life expectancy is not high. Perhaps forty-five years."

We walk in the same direction as the moving concrete, and I notice at the foot of the hill a group of men have parked their carts, each one with a similarly enormous pillar on the back. They are sitting on the curb, smoking and talking. Then, as we walk up the hill, we are passed by four men pulling one cart, their heads low as they strain. I get a picture of them, feeling guilty as I press the shutter button, as if I should go and help them. But perhaps a hundred people are on the hill, most walking their bicycles, all ignoring this monumental labour. If those men let go of that cart it would kill dozens, I would imagine, as it rolled back down.

We take what looks like a back street. It doesn't really matter, everything is new to me anyway. The road winds among little stone houses, private to the street, clustered around courtyards. I get a picture of a small boy sitting on a tiny stool, wearing a People's Liberation Army uniform, complete with peaked hat. I get another picture of an old, old man sitting on the same sort of stool, his back against a wall, his eyes closed, asleep, his face so dark and wrinkled he looks like a field after fall ploughing. And I get a picture of a rooster poking his beak around a corner, looking for food, his leg firmly tied to a post with a string.

"How long have you been at the college?" I ask Li Ming.

"Three years."

"And you teach the basic English course. What's it called?"

"Intensive Reading."

"What's that like? I'd like to sit in on one of your classes someday."

"It is extremely boring."

"But it's the most important course, isn't it? Doesn't everybody take it every year?"

"The leaders like it a great deal because that is the way they learned. I would be very embarrassed to have you in my class. We get through perhaps one paragraph in forty-five minutes. I have to speak in Chinese quite a bit or else we will not get through even that much. The students like it because it is easy. The only problem is that nobody learns very much. You are lucky. Because you are a foreigner you can teach whatever you like. Everybody likes the foreigner's classes."

"You think so? So far it's hard to get a feel for it — I'm not sure just what I'm getting across. I think I'm mostly a novelty for them."

She looks down at her shoes and I get the distinct impression that I have said something wrong, perhaps been too familiar. Or perhaps she has not understood an expression.

"You must have had foreign teachers," I say. "Your English is excellent."

"I learned from the radio."

"That's all?"

"Every night I listened to the BBC. And then I started to dream in English. I would like to learn Russian, and German, and Japanese. But I have to get my English better, first."

The streets wind in and out of one another. We come upon a cluster of shops and little dwellings. An old woman calls out something to Li Ming and she replies, and the woman nods and tells her little grandson, who is hiding in the doorway. I think I hear the word *Jianada* in the exchange. I motion to my camera and the woman seems to nod, so I kneel down and take their picture, the woman and the boy. She does not smile, though, as I expect, but remains grave, her eyes narrow. After I click the shutter I thank her, feeling embarrassed, and we walk on.

"Should I have taken that?" I ask Li Ming. "I thought she understood."

"You should bring a copy to her," Li Ming says.

We continue through the warren of backstreets, but I become camera-shy. The people are too close; I'd never find them all again to give them copies; it seems rude to photograph them as if they were in a zoo. I don't take a picture of the little girl studying in her red dress, sitting at a tiny table; I don't take a picture of the woman bent near double, some sort of sack across her shoulders, her back seemingly hooped under the weight; I don't take a picture of the father with his new baby in his arms, showing him the big-nosed foreigner.

"Where are we, Li Ming?" I ask after we have been walking a long time, and the narrow streets have wound themselves into larger ones again.

"The college is in that direction," she says, pointing opposite to where I'd have gone on my own.

"Can I take your photo?" I ask.

"Me?"

"I'll give you a copy. Just by the wall here."

"I will take your photo for you. For your family."

"My camera's a little tricky to work. Just stand there. Beautiful."

With the telephoto lens her face fills the frame. Her eyes are lowered, but she lifts them, slowly, dark and full. Her face is a little flushed from the walking; her hair a little blown, free; she does not smile, really, but does not have to, looking proud and confident and striking, and it isn't just the light, either.

"You could be a model," I say, advancing the film. "You wouldn't want to be, but you could."

"Let's go back," Li Ming says.

 Waiting for Li Ming

4

RUDY WOKE AT DAWN WITH THE SOUND OF THE FIRST TRANSPORT truck rolling along Bridge Street, the main road that led through Bellsbridge and then continued on inevitably, as if pulled by gravity, towards the industrial and financial mass of Toronto. He dressed quickly, his body stiff from sleeping on the thin mat. The floor was cold, too, since he had taken out the carpet, a filthy relic from a previous tenant. He drank the last of the orange juice, rubbed his sleepy eyes, then walked out of the apartment, his keys jingling in the pocket of his sweat pants.

Outside it was brisk, the air still but cool. He felt as if he was walking into a painting, the way the new sun glinted off the shop windows and the green spires of the old tower that was the university library. Everything was closed, quiet, asleep, except for the trucks rumbling through now and again, most of them loaded with Japanese cars from the new joint venture on the edge of town.

Rudy crossed the bridge, left the road and followed a municipal path beside the river, which was so calm in the morning the water didn't seem to be moving. Sluggish and brown and polluted, in this light, at this time of day, the river looked pure again, silverish almost and full of life. Rudy saw two large carp brooding near the shore, vacuuming the bottom; a frog murmured in the reeds, and then suddenly a blue heron rose from the bulrushes, majestic, prehistoric-looking, almost out of place. Rudy stood still and watched until the heron was a speck in the distance. Three large grassy knolls blocked out the sounds from

Bridge Street, and somehow the river didn't smell the way it would later in the day, when the air was warmer.

Rudy thought of the low hills around Laozhou. Rounded bumps rising perhaps a few hundred feet and covered with thirty-year-old cedar trees, more or less evenly spaced. At this time of the morning those hills harboured small pockets of quiet people playing tai chi and *chi gong*. There were paths throughout the forested hills, of course, the area having been settled for thousands of years. And along the paths were occasional terraces, the ground packed hard and built up like small theatre stages, ringed by rocks. Surrounded by trees, the terraces were hidden until you happened upon them. Rudy thought that some of them, at least, had been used for artillery platforms during the war. Now they were used for meditation and quiet exercise, people stealing into the hills for an hour of solitude and silence away from the eight hundred thousand other souls who packed the small town.

Rudy's tai chi spot was not so secluded as those hidden terraces. It was a grassy, nearly flat opening beside a swing set and slide. But facing east he looked over the river and felt the sun directly in his face as it rose between two large willows on the opposite bank. He did his warm-up quietly, feeling the blood finally running to his fingers. He wished he had worn gloves. Master Wang had worn them well into the spring, even when it had really begun to warm up. He wished too, of course, that he had been able to speak Chinese, to pump Wang with questions, to get a sense of the way the man thought and spoke. He knew very well how the man moved and thought of him every time he did a work-out, the slide of Wang's shoulders being the slide of his own, the deep sit with the straight back, effortless, the way he held his hands with the fingers slightly spread, relaxed but ready, steel behind velvet. He remembered the first time that Wang had showed him the *liu he ba fa*, how impossibly smooth and complex it had seemed, faster than tai chi, more ornate than the Yang style he had been doing, with the arms whirling, wrists curling, hands ever circling in upon themselves.

He had that memory imprinted in his brain and tried to bring it to his muscles with every work-out, not the exact steps so much, which his body knew now, but the spirit of his teacher's movements. Concentration, grace, a willow tree bending in the wind, a whip snapping in the air. He tried to keep his breathing controlled, deep, noiseless; he tried for balance on every step; and most of all he tried to make it look easy, inevitable, the way Wang made it look. Like that blue heron rising from the weeds and flying away up over the trees.

On the way back after his work-out the traffic was heavier along Bridge Street. Shops were beginning to open; Lee's Pepsi-Cola Restaurant was filling up with its breakfast crowd; primary school students were playing in the playground before the bell. On the bridge Rudy stopped a moment to look at the river from this angle, thinking of the sorry excuse of a river in Laozhou, the flat, muddy, stinking backwater that had once been part of the main stream of the Yellow River. Still, on every day of the year you could see men fishing there with their long bamboo poles, and women doing their laundry, talking and scrubbing. Once when he was walking along the back routes he had come across a factory outlet spewing metallic purple and green liquid into a stream that went directly to the river, the main water source for the town.

Rudy turned to walk back and was nearly hit by a jogger who had to swerve suddenly. Her ankle turned and she would have fallen off the sidewalk onto the road, which was thick with traffic, if Rudy hadn't quickly grabbed her around the waist and pulled her in.

"Oh!" she cried, hopping a few steps away, then pulling up and holding her ankle.

"Are you all right?"

"Shit, it hurts!" she said. It was Lou, short for Louise, a woman from the department whom he had met only briefly. A playwright, perhaps in her early thirties. She was in black running tights and yellow windbreaker and had her red hair tied back like a large bush behind her head. "Oh it's you!" she said when she recognized him.

"Twisted ankle?"

"Sure feels like it. God!"

"Can you walk?"

She tried, hobbling, and he supported her shoulder. "I'm really sorry," he said. "I didn't hear you coming at all."

"That's okay, I should have seen you," she said. "I don't know what I was looking at. My feet or something."

"You look at your feet when you run?"

"I get too tired to look anywhere else," she said.

"I should help you home. You should put some ice on this."

"It's this way," she said, pointing back across the bridge. "Were you out running?"

"No."

"Just walking?"

"I do a bit of a work-out. In the park, down by the river."

"Aerobics?"

"No. Not exactly," he said. "I used to do a lot of running. Before I went to China."

"Yeah?"

"Yeah. But the air there is so filthy, you go out for a run and you come back feeling like you've just smoked two packs of cigarettes."

"Oh God. Cigarettes!" Lou said.

Rudy looked at her.

"I'm trying to quit," she said. "Don't mention cigarettes!"

They walked for several minutes, leaving Bridge Street and heading back into one of the old neighbourhoods full of large brick houses. Whole streets had been renovated and looked prosperous, while the houses of other whole streets had not and looked faded, crumbling, fifty years older. The two, arms around the other's shoulders, were a good height for a three-legged walk, falling into it more or less naturally. When they were nearly at her house he asked her, "What's that scent you're wearing?"

"What?"

"That scent."

"I'm not wearing any scent," she said. "I was just out jogging."

"Oh," he said, retreating. Could her sweat smell like that? Or maybe her shampoo or something. It was instantly familiar.

"The night I arrived in Hong Kong," he said, "we came in through the tail end of a typhoon. The winds were still whipping badly and it was very late and sheets of rain were coming down. There I was in such a foreign town, trying to call a taxi . . . "

"Excuse me," she said, interrupting him. "This is my house."

"Ah, very nice," Rudy said. It was on one of the not-fixed-up streets, a small white bungalow with green trim and a big porch in front. They climbed the stairs slowly and Lou stopped in front of the door, fiddling with a key that was on a chain around her neck.

"Anyway," Rudy continued, "I'd never been to Asia before. I had the address of a hotel in Kowloon, but I had no idea how far it was or how to get there. So this one taxi driver comes up and I tell him where I'm going and he says it'll cost a hundred dollars. Oh God, I thought, I can't afford a hundred dollars for a taxi ride."

Lou finally got the door open, and there was a terrible yapping. It was the smallest dog that Rudy had ever seen, a brown Pekinese puppy that made enough noise for three German shepherds.

"Down, Oswald, down!" Lou said, several times, kneeling gingerly to embrace the little thing. "Down!"

The yapping continued inside. Oswald ran ahead of them,

skittering and sliding over the newspaper sheets that had been laid over most of the floor. He ran into the kitchen, back again, through the living room, back again, and then to the bedroom and back again, scattering newspapers wherever he went.

"I just got him a week ago," Lou said.

"You don't like taking him running with you?" Rudy asked.

"Oh God no! I'm self-conscious enough as it is. Can you imagine me running with this little guy beside me? The whole town would be staring!"

Lou sat down on the sofa in the living room, untied her shoe and peeled back her sock. "You left me in Hong Kong," she said, not looking up.

"Right," Rudy said, thinking of her scent. "At the airport. All alone, at night, in a strange city, and the first taxi driver tells me it's going to cost a hundred dollars to get to my hotel. Christ, I thought, how much is the hotel going to cost? So I told him forget it, and he took someone else, and I waited. The weather got worse. It got later. There were no other taxis, and I start thinking — a hundred dollars? That can't be right. And then I realize, of course, that it's a hundred dollars *Hong Kong money* . . ."

"God, this is really swollen," Lou said, interrupting again.

He knelt down to feel her ankle. "I'll get some ice. Is the fridge through here?"

"It's a mess," she said. "Don't look."

It was a mess. Newspapers were scattered on much of the floor, some with deposits, some just wet. Several meals of dishes were on the table, counter and sink. Rudy tiptoed carefully to the fridge for the ice and then rummaged through several drawers before he found the plastic bags, a jungle of them, in the closet. He filled a double bag with ice and brought it back to her.

"Is it a disaster in there?" she asked.

"Oswald has left his mark."

"Oh God," she said, "I shouldn't have let you in. This house is only for very close friends. I like to spare others." She put the ice bag on her ankle, cringing immediately.

"Just hold it there," he said. "You'll get used to it in a minute or so. You should ice it for twenty minutes on, twenty minutes off. Have you twisted an ankle before?"

"You know," she said, "I've been running for four days now. I got this outfit and new shoes and everything. My girlfriend gave me this book that has three chapters on the runner's high, how it's just like drugs, etcetera, etcetera. And all I've gotten from it is fucking pain, excuse my language."

"It takes a while," he said. He got up and went back to the kitchen. Oswald suddenly re-appeared from wherever he had been, yapping and nipping at his ankles. Rudy bent down and grabbed him by the scruff of the neck.

"In the old country, little Pekinese," he said quietly, "yappers like you are eaten for snacks. Your cousins are taken to market on bicycles, tied upside down, their mouths sewn shut so they won't bite the feet of their owners. They have to hold their heads up or else their noses will drag on the ground, or get clipped by the spinning bicycle spokes."

Oswald yapped again and ran away, back to Lou.

Rudy started cleaning up the newspapers. "Oh Rudy, please!" Lou called. "Don't do that. Please, you're embarrassing me!"

"It'll only take a minute," he said, rolling the papers together, then stuffing them in a garbage bag. He had to hunt through the packed closet before finding the mop, wedged in the back behind the plastic bags. In a few moments he had mopped the affected parts of the floor, and then spread new sheets from a pile of papers in the corner.

"That's fantastic," Lou said when he came out again. "You don't do windows, do you?"

"No. I don't do windows."

She was sitting back with Oswald, temporarily quiet, in her lap. She looked quite pretty with her hair freed. Rudy smelled it again, whatever it was she was wearing.

"Anyway," he said, returning to his long-lost story. "There I was, still at the airport, waiting and waiting, cursing myself for having let that first taxi go. Then finally another one came along and I was ready to pay him anything, I was so tired. A hundred dollars, he said. Fine, I said. I got in. And it was the most magnificent taxi ride I have ever had. We whizzed through this foreign town, the streets black as obsidian, polished with the rain, the neon burning against the black sky, and the fresh air streaming into my lungs after sixteen hours of breathing recycled air over the Pacific. The most magnificent odour filled the cab. It was coming from a single white jasmine, just picked, which the driver had tied to his mirror. That was my introduction to the East, that jasmine. It's funny how the smell made it all come back to me in a rush. I don't know if it's your shampoo or what. It couldn't be the car factory, I don't think."

Lou was blushing. "I don't think I wear anything with jasmine."

Rudy suddenly felt uncomfortable. He hadn't meant it to be anything. It was just a story, from one writer to another, one which in fact he had modified. What he hadn't said was that the jasmine was Li Ming's scent as well.

"The funny thing is," he said, "the next day I took another taxi back to the airport for my flight to China, and it only cost me *fifteen* dollars. But this guy didn't have any jasmine in his car, so I figured that was the difference. A little piece of heaven for eighty-five Hong Kong dollars."

"Will you stay for some breakfast?" she asked, taking the ice bag off and feeling her ankle. "I think that's twenty minutes, isn't it?"

"I should get going," he said, rising suddenly. "I'm sorry about your ankle. It may take a few weeks."

"Don't be sorry. Thank you for all your help. And cleaning up the kitchen. God! Oswald thanks you."

"You're very welcome, Oswald."

"I won't get up, okay?" she said, brushing the hair from her eyes.

He did a little exercise as he was leaving, something he had started doing some years ago when he began thinking of himself as a writer. If she were my character, he asked himself, how would I write her? There was an attractive sort of disorder to her — her hair, her house, the accident — that made him feel she was the kind of woman whose life was at best serendipitous, in the low times chaotic, if not completely out of control. How could he decide that from just those few impressions? It didn't matter. That's how he would write her. He made a mental note that there was no sign of a man in the house. But she was not the kind of woman who would go for too long without one. Her physical presence was obviously full of the love of life, of sexuality . . .

She would be the one the man fell in love with, he thought. Whoever the man was. And if it were a story.

5

SHE COMES WITH THE MAIL IN THE MORNING, POLITE AND CRISP AND, without saying a word, seemingly put out, as if these duties are somehow beneath her and slightly distasteful, or perhaps it is not the duties but me. I thank her too profusely and trip over myself trying to be friendly but nothing seems to warm the chill. If she were angry at me then I wish she would say something, get worked up, explode, but that does not happen either. In a pattern we repeat she asks, professionally, if I would like to go to the market later and I reply, warmly, that yes I would, and she nods her head both in a sign of agreement and at the same time as if adding up the extra duties I have caused her but about which she would never dare whisper a complaint.

The market is a place I can return to day after day, just to look at the creased, brown faces, the intelligent, laughing eyes, the lean bodies bent from hard work. The stalls of Chinese cabbage, of apples, bananas, snow peas, lotus root, of pork and dog meat, of yams beside carp beside rice beside beer, homemade, light yellow in glasses with lids on top to keep out the flies. The bin of black eels, writhing, still alive; the other stalls full of weird vegetables and creatures I have never seen before, never heard of, that Li Ming can find no English word for. And the crowds milling mostly on foot, with cyclists slowly threading their way through, loath to stop completely and have to dismount. The hand-held scales, the children in blue playing tag, the tired men and women sleeping on mats on the pavement back in the shadows, having been on the road pulling the cart at four in the morning to bring the goods to town.

But today we are off to buy a bicycle. It is hot still, and dusty, though September is draining away. The men in the streets are all wearing white shirts and blue pants and heeled sandals with sheer nylon socks that would be thought of as feminine back home, and they carry little black cases I can only think of as purses. I mention these cultural differences to Li Ming and she tells me that on the contrary Laozhou men are quick to fight, have sharp tempers and have probably been taught *wushu* — martial arts — since this is an area famous for fighters in China.

"Do they do tai chi here?" I ask, as we are walking along, but she does not understand. "Tai chi," I say, doing some of the hand movements from the set I learned in Ottawa.

"Ah! Taiji!" she says, flogging me with the Chinese pronunciation.

"I asked Dean Chun, when I arrived, if I could get a teacher," I say. "But he said that only old people do tai chi."

"We have at our college a very famous teacher of *taiji*," she says. And then, with uncharacteristic generosity, "If you like, I will bring him to visit you."

"That would be wonderful. I really would like to learn some more, especially since I am here."

"He will look at what you can do, and if he likes you, perhaps he will agree to teach you."

"I could pay him, of course," I say, but she shakes her head gravely.

"You could not pay Master Wang to teach you."

"No?"

"In China, if you want to learn *wushu* you must petition a master for a long time, in order to gain his favour. You must convince him you will be a worthy student, have a good moral character, and will dedicate the rest of your life to following the art. A teacher like Master Wang would never accept money to teach *wushu*."

The bicycle store is actually the Number One Laozhou Department Store, which has three floors crammed with the oddest assortment of goods I have ever seen: machine parts on a shelf with badminton rackets across the aisle from fabrics, with farm tools colliding into make-up and ping-pong paddles and purses. And every aisle elbow-squashed with people pawing the merchandise, trying to get the counter-person's attention, squirming, pushing, turning to get by. Old ladies in Mao jackets, young women in bright dresses and knee-high nylons, young men with droopy mustaches in blue sweatshirts and old canvas running shoes, the treads worn completely smooth.

The bicycles are on the main floor, arranged in a long line and protected by a metal railing. You enter only if you are going to buy a bike. Li Ming marches us in with an extra authority she seems to don whenever she enters a store like this; she stands taller, takes on the expression of someone not to be trifled with.

"It doesn't really matter," I whisper to her as we approach the salesman. "They all look the same to me. Let's just buy one and get out."

No such luck. We look at a Flying Pigeon but it is too ex-

pedal like a wounded limb as she disappears into the swirling bicycles of the afternoon.

In the evening I am visited by a young man who seems familiar, though it's only after he has sat down and refused tea twice, only to accept it the third time, that I realize he was the one playing basketball who spoke so long with Li Ming that day we took photographs. His name is Jiang and he is mostly bones and nervousness as he stammers out the phrases he has learned in his English training. It is a difficult conversation, with a lot of strained laughter and hand motioning. He is a young Chemistry teacher, knows his English from science books, has never talked to a native speaker before. And I am tired after a long day, especially after having to go back to the shop to have a man hammer the cotter pin back into my pedal while the crowds gathered once again to see the curiosity. I am not sure how long I can go on with "How you like our China?" and "Chinese food good, yes?"

I look at my watch several times, yawn obviously, get up to go the bathroom. When he does not take the hint, I am about to make up an excuse when he says, "You very lucky . . . have translator Li Ming."

"Maybe," I say.

"Very brilliant student," he says, nodding his head seriously.

"Her English is first-rate."

"Yes!" he says enthusiastically. "Best in college!"

"Have you known her long?" I ask, then again when he has not understood.

"We went . . . school . . . "

"Together?"

He nods his head, yes, and then says, gravely, "Li Ming . . . very beautiful girl. Hard . . . but beautiful."

"What do you mean?"

"Hard like . . . animal . . . "

 Waiting for Li Ming

desperate to just get out of here. But even with the decision made it still takes forever. There is the money to be handed over and the receipts to be made out and then the forms to do for the licence and then the tires have to be pumped up, and through it all the crowd stays and grows, watching every detail as if they had suddenly been presented a Martian.

When we are finally on the street and riding in the dizzying stream of bicycles on our way home, my right cotter pin falls out and the pedal clanks to the ground. Li Ming looks back to see me wobbling, my right foot with nothing to push on, and then for several seconds continues to ride, as if refusing to believe what she has seen.

"Li Ming!" I call, losing my balance.

"Li Ming!"

Reluctantly she returns, her face flushed red. I give her my lopsided grin, which charms most people, then reach down to pick up the pedal. "Well, I guess you were right about the . . . "

She doesn't let me finish, launching instead into a torrent of Chinese that nearly strips the paint off my broken-down bike. Her hands gesture like knives slashing and her eyes are dark centres of resentment and I stand looking at her too stunned to speak. It lasts for perhaps only thirty seconds but like an earth-quake rattles everything within reach, and even when it is over nothing is the same as it was before.

"I am sorry," she says, finally, with great control, when the dust has settled.

"What did you say?" I ask her.

"Nothing."

I look at her.

"What is it? Tell me! What have you got against me?"

"You will have to go back to the Department Store to get your bicycle fixed," she says.

"To hell with the bicycle!" I say. "What just happened? Why are you so angry at me?"

Her reply is to turn and ride away, leaving me holding my

pensive. "This bike is cheaper by thirty yuan in Shanghai," Li Ming says to me. We have a look at the Long March. "Not very reliable," she says to me, "but not so expensive." We go back to the Flying Pigeon. A crowd gathers, pressing against the railing, jeering at the salesman, pointing at me, the *waiguoren*.

We look at a Flying Leaf. "Not as good as a Flying Pigeon," Li Ming says, trying the brakes.

"Looks all right to me," I say, getting out my wallet.

"But the pedal is broken," she says, pointing, "and there will not be a replacement in until, perhaps, next year."

We go back to the Flying Pigeon. Li Ming has a lengthy conversation with the salesman. The crowd grows even greater, several boys in the middle now pointing to me, calling something out, laughing.

Asking me something, then waiting to see my response, then cackling with laughter when I don't do anything. "Harro!" someone yells. "Harro! Harro!"

"Hello," I say, looking up, smiling, but they laugh at me behind the railing as if I were on display. "Li Ming," I say, touching her sleeve. "Li Ming."

She doesn't respond. She is in a heated argument now, gesturing with her hands, yelling almost into the salesman's face, then pointing back at the Flying Pigeon.

"Harro! Harro!"

"Li Ming!"

I can't breathe. The air is being sucked out by the crowd and their faces seem to be up against mine and I have to get out, somewhere, just back onto the street, Li Ming . . .

"I'll take the Long March!"

She turns back, surprised.

"It doesn't matter!" I say. "Give him the money. I want the Long March."

"He has come down ten *yuan* on the Flying Pigeon," she says, startled.

"No! The Long March. I want the Long March!" I insist,

"You mean untamed? Wild? A wild horse?" I say, acting out the motions of a bucking bronco. I expect him to laugh but he doesn't — he looks at me with great earnestness, with the eyes of one who has been hopelessly in love for a long time.

"Hard," he says again, and then, with an abruptness that is cultural he rises suddenly, sticks out his hand, and leaves.

It is not something we refer to again, and yet after her explosion things *are* different. There are times when she is friendlier, more human, and her good mood does not seem to be fuelled entirely by guilt. Other times she is as cold and sharp as ever, but in control still, perhaps conscious of not losing face again. It's not my fault, I tell myself; it isn't me. There's something else that's twisting her inside.

But she follows through on her promise to talk to Master Wang. On the day he comes to visit the crowds are back, gathering from vapour when he arrives, so that in the time it takes for an introduction and for Li Ming and Wang and me to walk out the door to my little courtyard there are suddenly twenty people standing by the gate, peering in.

Wang is a little man, perhaps in his fifties but it is hard to tell. His step is very light, his face smooth, his eyes darkly radiant. He speaks only a few words at a time and waits for Li Ming to translate. He asks almost immediately that I perform my tai chi for him, and then stands still, watching.

My tai chi is very new and at the same time rusty. I have felt self-conscious about trying it here, in the country where the sport was born. I imagine I must look like someone from the tropics who is visiting Ottawa and trying on a pair of skates for the first time, wobbling on his ankles, his arms waving erratically while seasoned skaters nimbly glide out of his way and then turn to watch the spectacle.

And a spectacle it is, evidently, even funnier than the bicycle buying, the foreigner trying to do tai chi for Master Wang.

Almost every move is funnier than the last but I won't give them the benefit, will not look at them, will not stop, will not give them the satisfaction . . .

Except I lose the sequence as soon as I think of something else. So I fudge a move and then my body goes into the "single whip" and then "wave hands like clouds," that is easy enough, although Master Wang is shaking his head just a little, as if talking to himself, and the monkeys in the crowd erupt in laughter again. When I go into the kicks and wobble, red-faced, they scream and slap their sides and pantomime my clumsiness. But Master Wang's face never changes; he watches me as if we were alone. And in a glimpse I notice Li Ming as well, very serious, looking on as if there is something to be seen beneath the awkwardness.

I finish, finally, the most wretched set of my life, standing still and flushed with effort and embarrassment. He watches on as if there should be more, as if looking to see if the tai chi extends into the way I walk. Then Wang whispers a few words to Li Ming.

"You have shown great spirit," she says simply, his words, but maybe hers too. "Master Wang says, if you want to learn *taiji*, he will teach you."

And so the routine changes. Two afternoons a week Wang comes to my little courtyard and teaches me, very slowly, a short set of tai chi, while Li Ming translates and the crowd at the fence watches, laughing less and less as my balance, my flexibility and feel for the movements improve. The other afternoons Li Ming and I still go to the market, or go out photographing or ride our bikes into the countryside. Gradually the days turn colder, and then as my movements get better Wang starts teaching me more, a longer set that is more complicated, takes great concentration. The harder I work the more he teaches, and I come to realize that is his way of praising; otherwise it is correction after correction after correction, and then on to the next series of movements.

For three days I see nothing of Li Ming. I come across her finally by accident in the tiny library at the Foreign Languages Department, sitting by the cracked window leaning over an ancient typewriter. I stand for a few minutes watching her tapping away, then peering at her notes and tapping some more. I clear my throat but she doesn't hear me. I approach and she doesn't look around.

"Li Ming."

She looks, finally, her eyes strangely unfocused, as if she is reluctantly returning from somewhere far away and does not quite remember where she is. "Ah, Rudy!" she says, getting halfway out of her chair. "Do you need something?"

"No, it's all right," I say.

"You want to go to the market?"

"No."

"Master Wang has arrived?"

"No — nothing, thank you! Sit down. I just wanted to see what you're doing."

"Oh, it is nothing," she says. But of course it is not "nothing"; it is the text of a linguistics paper she has written, which she has been asked to translate into English and deliver at an international conference in Xiamen.

"There is little chance I will be allowed to go," she says matter-of-factly.

"Why?"

"Because of who I am," she says, "and who the leaders are." Her fingers, though, are resting on the keys, as if made impatient by this interruption.

We talk a little more and then I leave her, and when I pass by the same room several hours later she is still there typing in the gloom, by the drafty window, her feet squarely on the floor.

"I've brought you some tea," I say.

"What? Oh, no — no need. Thank you."

"Take it. Don't be so Chinese."

"I am Chinese."

"I know. Nearly finished?"

"Do you need me to help you?"

"No, I'm fine."

"Is Mr. Fang there?"

"I'm fine. I'm just visiting. Take some tea."

"You are very kind."

"And you look exhausted. When is this conference?"

"In March," she says. "Which means I have to get the paper done now, so the leaders will have no excuses to refuse me."

"I don't know how they could. A person with your determination. You are going to succeed."

"I'd say my chances are not very good."

"I would say you are wrong."

She looks at me holding out the mug. Quietly, she takes it, closing her eyes as she drinks the hot liquid. It is starting to get dark outside; her window light is fading.

"I got a letter from my father today," I say, by way of making conversation. "It's full of hockey scores. He's a nut about the Toronto Maple Leafs, who always lose, I'm afraid. It's terrible. Does your father have an obsession like that?"

She looks at me very oddly, then shakes her head. "My father is dead," she says.

"Oh," I say. "I'm sorry. Was it . . . was it recent?"

"No," she says, lowering her voice just a bit. "Not recent."

I nod.

"He was arrested in the Cultural Revolution," she says. "He was a biologist, and he subscribed to Western journals. They put him in re-education camp. I was the one who had to bring his rice to him every day. I was only six years old. I brought it in a little tin that kept the rice warm. I wasn't allowed to cry, but I always did, walking home." Her face is strangely blank as she tells the story, her eyes just slightly down. "One day when I went one of the others told me not to come back anymore, because my father was dead. On the way home that time, I did not cry."

It's an extraordinary story, and I am stunned for a moment that she is telling me, as if I have somehow passed a test I did not know I was taking part in.

"So you see," she says, after a pause in which the colour comes speeding back into her face, "what's important is that I keep going."

"Yes," I say, not wanting to lose the moment and yet not being sure how to proceed. But maybe it's time to take a risk. "My country," I say, "has never seen a time like your Cultural Revolution. We can hardly imagine what it must have been like."

She nods. I probably shouldn't say anything more. She doesn't want to talk about it. I give her a chance but she stays quiet.

"Anyway," I say, to ease my way out. "I should get going."

"It isn't over," she says quickly, in a low voice.

"Sorry?"

"The Cultural Revolution . . . isn't really over," she says. "There are no more dunce caps, no more Red Guards . . . but the fear is still here. Those things can always come back. It isn't what it seems . . . on the surface."

"What do you mean?"

"We should not be talking like this," she says and I suppose it is true, but it is the first real talking we have done, and she knows that too.

"Everyone finds you so interesting," she says, looking mainly at her fingers, the analytical part behind her eyes finally saying what it thinks. "When you walk down the street you are like a celebrity, and you come from a land that is magic to us, so free, where people can do what they want. We have grown up . . . in little boxes. And we are so big now the boxes are too little, we are squeezed inside them. That is what it is like here. Everyone is in a box that is too small. But by everything you do — the way you walk, talk, look around, look people in the eye, by the questions you ask — you show that you are not from here. You have not grown up in a box that is too small. So you have no idea how hard things are. You think everything is easy."

"Was that hard, what you just did?" I ask her. "Was that hard to say?"

"Everything is hard," she says, looking fiercely into my eyes, to see what lies there.

6

WILLIAM ROGERS, RUDY'S WRITING PROFESSOR, A SHORT THICK man nearing fifty with hands too big to be comfortable on a type-writer, came into the seminar room distracted and shaken. It was only the third week of classes; Michael Adams, the writer who was supposed to lead the group, had missed the opening two to illness, and now he seemed to be away again. Rogers put down his briefcase and sat down, then rubbed the edges of his eyes with his thumb and forefinger, and paused, as if waiting for things to come into focus again. When the room was silent he announced that Michael Adams was very ill and would not be back that semester to lead the class.

"What's the problem?" Lou asked from the corner.

"I'm afraid he has AIDS," Rogers said quietly. "His health has taken a very bad turn recently. If anyone would like to visit him, I'm sure he would appreciate the company." And he gave the room number at the hospital.

At first no one said anything and then everyone talked at once, except for Rudy, who did not know the man, and for Lou, who sat slumped in her seat, white and silent.

Lou was first out the door, disappearing before the others left their seats. Christopher and Amanda, two of the other graduate students Rudy had become friendly with, walked out together, quietly.

"Are you going to visit him in the hospital?" Rudy asked. They were out of the building now, on the street. It was raining and Amanda, a very pale, nearly elfin girl, gave him a thoughtful look from under her red umbrella, pressing her handbag to her chest.

"Yes. Definitely," she said.

"It's an awful thing," Rudy said. They kept walking. Christopher, in his early thirties, wiry thin and losing his hair, had actually forgotten to open his umbrella and was walking with his collar turned up, his head getting soaked, the umbrella closed in his right hand. Rudy began to say something, but decided not to.

"Go in for a beer?" Rudy asked, as they were approaching Lee's Pepsi-Cola Restaurant.

"I have to catch a bus," Christopher said, the rain dripping through his mustache.

"I've got some work to do," Amanda said.

Christopher stayed at the bus stop and Rudy and Amanda walked on in silence. The rain worsened. Thick, cold drops splashed against Rudy's hood and ran in streams off Amanda's umbrella. As they approached Rudy's apartment he asked her if she wanted to stop in for some tea. She said no, then hesitated.

"Chinese tea?" she asked. He had told her how much he hated green tea.

"Earl Grey."

"Okay," she said.

They stepped down the short flight of stairs into the basement where Rudy's apartment was, then stood in the hall for a moment dripping while Rudy searched through his pockets for the key.

When they went in he turned on several lights immediately. On a dark day like this the apartment was buried in a cavelike gloom, even though he had fixed it up as much as he could. Amanda did a quick tour, saying nice things until she peeked into the bedroom.

"Where's your bed?" she asked.

"Oh, that's it on the floor. I haven't got a real bed yet."

"You sleep on the floor?"

"There's a mat there. I'm getting used to it, actually."

Amanda shuddered. "Is that what you slept on in China?"

"Oh no — I had a real bed in China. A beautiful mattress, down comforters. I just haven't gotten around to getting one here yet."

Rudy put on the tea and brought Amanda back to the living room. "This is my room for company," he said.

"Do you mind if I smoke?"

"No," he said, and went back into the kitchen to find a dish for an ashtray.

"Did you have any . . . idea about Michael?" Rudy asked when he returned, handing her the dish. "I mean, did you know he was . . . "

"This is the first I've heard of it," Amanda said. "I don't think he was gay, if that's what you're asking. God, we're already talking about him in the past tense."

She sat in the stuffed chair in the corner. Rudy sat on the sofa at the end closest to her, making room by moving some books that he'd piled there. Then when he was settled, there didn't seem anything to talk about. Finally he got up to serve the tea, and they drank more or less in silence, as the rain streaked down the two windows that looked up onto the street, and cars splashed past with a whoosh of water. Amanda snubbed out her cigarette.

"Michael . . . really helped a lot of people, a lot of writers," she said finally. "He's very warm and caring, an easy person to get to know. I can think of about seventy-five other people who deserve to get AIDS more than Michael Adams." She said it ironically, her green eyes looking far away, and then meeting his.

"There are new treatments," Rudy said, but abandoned the line when he saw the way Amanda was looking at him. The situation, the prospects, were horrible. There was no getting around it.

"Lou looked pretty upset," Rudy said. "Maybe we should go over, or give her a call."

"I'd leave her for a while," Amanda said.

"They're really close, are they?"

Amanda put down her teacup. "I'm pretty sure they were lovers," she said. "I don't know for certain. I hope not. But I think they were."

It snowed the next day. Large, wet, freaky flakes tied up traffic on Bridge Street, turned the sidewalks to slush, weighed down cedar hedges and clung in heavy clumps to the leaves of the trees that had not stripped themselves in time for the first flex of winter. Rudy was two steps up Lou's front stairs when Oswald started barking from inside, feverish and frantic, throwing himself against the door. Rudy swore under his breath and put the plant he was carrying down on the mat. Then he took out a pad and pen and wrote: *Lou — I thought that this cactus needed a . . .*

He didn't mean to bother her; he just wanted to make a gesture. But Lou opened the door and Oswald bolted forward until he reached the end of his leash and was jerked back, landing paws in the air like a cartoon figure and scrambling up again, with never a break in the yapping. Rudy looked at him from his kneeling position, the pad on his knee. "Smooth move, Ozzie," he said.

"What's this?" Lou asked.

"Hi. I, uh, my apartment is really dark, and I thought maybe you could find a place by the window for this Christmas cactus. It's just starting to bloom, but I really don't think — "

"That's very sweet, Rudy," she said. She was dressed in a sheepskin coat, with her boots on and mitts, and she had put on make-up and tied her hair back. "Ozzie and I were just going for a walk. Will you come?"

"Sure. I guess," Rudy said, standing awkwardly.

"I hope you haven't damaged the cactus by carrying it all the way here in the cold," she said, taking it from him and bringing it inside.

"How are you doing?" he asked her, when she came back.

"I'm depressed," she said.

Rudy nodded.

"It's barely October, Rudy, and it's snowing! I can't handle winter this early."

"It'll melt," Rudy said.

They started walking along the back streets, their footprints silver and wet in the quickly melting snow. "Listen, I'm in a real state right now," she said. "Let's not talk about it. Let's just walk, okay?" And so they did, in silence, for half an hour, circling through different neighbourhoods and approaching Lou's house again from the other end of the street, away from Bridge Street.

"Thank you, Rudy," she said when they came to her walk. "I needed that."

"You saw him?" Rudy asked, his hands in the pockets of his coat. Lou knew that he meant Michael, and nodded.

"How does he look?"

"He looks grey, Rudy. He looks like he's going to die." On the last word her tears flooded up suddenly and Rudy embraced her awkwardly. They stood, her head on his shoulder, Oswald whining now at their feet.

"I'm sorry," she said, wiping her eyes.

"Are you going to be all right?"

"Yes. Thanks."

"No," Rudy said. "I mean are *you* going to be all right?" He couldn't find the right way to say it.

"What?"

"I talked to Amanda. She said — "

"Oh for Christ sakes!" Lou exploded, and he was sure for a moment that she was going to hit him, she seemed so angry.

"I'm sorry," he said. "I didn't mean . . . I was just worried."

"You mean curious?"

"No," he said. "Worried."

"I'm going for the tests this afternoon. It'll be a week after that. We had sex three times. He used a condom. Is there anything else you want to know?"

"No," he said. "Lou — I'm sorry."

"These fucking writers!" she said. "You know? When something awful happens, they really want you to go into the details. It's all material, right? Am I right?"

She was up the stairs in a rush, and the door slammed behind her, bringing down a small wet slide of snow.

7

I WAKE IN THE DARKNESS, BEFORE THE COCKS, BEFORE THE EXERCISE music, feeling buried beneath the heavy comforters. An animal hibernating in the warmth of its own fat and fur. But I am in trouble, I can feel it even hidden here, alone, half asleep. I am in trouble. Because when I am sleeping she is in my mind and she stays there when the alarm goes off, and she is there still when I pad to the bathroom and watch my breath cloud the mirror. I am talking to her as I shave, using the last of the lukewarm water from yesterday's thermos. I smile for her, briefly, as I put on my clothes, imagining her in my bed, rolling over sleepily, looking up, saying my name. Her bare shoulder peeking over the blanket. Almost golden in the shadows.

Big trouble.

She is at the door, then. Wearing her plain padded jacket. Tired face. The sun isn't even up yet. There is just that faint glow that starts the dawn.

"You are ready?"

"Yes."

"Mr. Fang is unable to come. He has a meeting today. He says to say that he is very sorry."

"That's quite all right," I say. "You look tired."

"My body is awake. My mind is still asleep."

I laugh. "In Canada we would say that you are not a morning person."

"In China, everyone is a morning person."

Down the lane, past the basketball courts, quiet now. Frost on the ground. Silence. The academic buildings bare skeletons, tired brick and concrete, sieves to the wind and cold, the walls shivering for lack of proper clothing. The naked dirt of the grounds crunching beneath our feet.

"This is our driver, Mr. Shan." I shake hands with a burly, smiling man who does not speak English. His head bobs, he opens up the door of the Toyota cruising van, all glass and gleam, a fantastic expenditure for our poor little school.

"You got the van? For only three of us?"

"For the foreigner, nothing is too good!" she says ironically.

The van is so quiet it feels as if we are riding a bubble on a calm lake. We pull up to the college gates and the driver has to get out and wake the gatekeeper, who pulls aside the bar and waves sleepily as we leave. Li Ming sits in the front beside the driver; I sit in the next seat back, a huge panel of newly washed window before me.

Quiet streets, but there are people out even now, peasants

coming in from the countryside, pulling their carts to market. We drive up the hill quietly, the glow now growing in the east, the sky there light blue, darker all around.

Li Ming passes me a wrapper of moon cakes she has made herself. They are traditional this time of the year, sweet white hockey pucks that flake and crumble as you bite into them. There is also tea and dumplings — hot meat and vegetables in a doughy sac, dripping gravy when you bite into them. We eat quietly, the three of us, as we pass the lake, square, man-made, tinted silver in the cool air. A small man stands in the frost by the shore, dressed only in a bathing suit, doing breathing exercises. I see him for a moment, and then the van passes on.

With the tea the colour comes back to her face. She looks at me almost warmly and I compliment her on her baking, and she, naturally, says no, the cakes are not very good. "When my mother makes moon cakes," she says, "you cannot leave the table until you are shaped like a moon yourself!"

It takes no time at all to be completely out in the countryside. But there is no such thing as wilderness here. Every bit of arable land is used in some way; it's only the hills that have more than a token line of trees, and the land here is mostly flat. We are on a dirt road, narrow and dusty, the fields sometimes lined by loose stone or brick fences, sometimes by rows of tall trees. The whole countryside still has a sheen of frost that will melt swiftly once the sun is fully up.

We are travelling quickly but we hardly notice, the van is so new and comfortable. Because few people are on the road the driver doesn't have to use his horn very often. We sweep through a little town, if that is what it is, a collection of stones that passes for housing, and then the most beautiful stone bridge crossing a darkly silver river, a junk moored just down there, by the shore. With the sun peeking behind it is suddenly a classic photo, the cover of *National Geographic*. I grope for my camera, packed away in my little bag. Of course we are past in an instant. I almost speak up, say, Stop! Back up! Wait! but the moment is gone, and I think, I'll get it on the way back, or, There will be many more chances at such pictures. Of course there won't be, and I know it. The moment is there, and you either catch it or you miss it.

Onward. Back into the countryside. On the right, huge quarries, whole cliffs showing naked against the lightening sky. "Are those the coal mines?" I ask Li Ming.

"I'm not sure," she says.

"What do you mean? They are some kind of mine, aren't they? A stone quarry, maybe?"

"Perhaps," she says, shaking her head. "I am from Shanghai. I don't really know this region."

"So you've never been to Qufu before?"

"No. I was just assigned this school. I had never been to Laozhou before. I will probably never get out."

"If you can bake moon cakes like this, you can go anywhere!"

"Pardon?"

"Nothing. Sorry. It's too early for those kinds of jokes."

I have another moon cake and turn back to the countryside, which has changed again. The driver seems to know instinctively where he is going. As far as I can tell there are no signs on any of the roads. Junctions suddenly appear; we go from narrow dirt stretches to wider pavement and then back again, sometimes confronting forks, waiting a moment before deciding, left or right. He is not following a map.

"Has he been here before?" I ask Li Ming. She turns to the driver, and they have a long conversation. Then she turns back to me.

"No," she says.

"What do you mean, 'No?'"

"He has never driven to Qufu before."

"But you just talked to him for fifteen minutes. What else did he say?"

"Qufu is the birthplace of Confucius."

"I got that from the guide book. What else?"

"He was just asking about you. Where do you come from. Why are you so small, when the other foreigners are much bigger than you."

"What did you say?"

She laughs, but I keep on her. "What did you tell him?"

"I said that you are a gentle man. And so you do not need to be big."

"Ah," I say, nodding, smiling. Was that a compliment? But she looks away, back out the window, leaving me trying to think of what else to say.

It comes upon me then, a certainty that I don't want to feel. We are on a straight stretch and the van has slowed because there are more people out now. A river of people, on foot, on bicycles, pulling carts, leading donkeys, riding tiny motorized tractors that look as if they have been welded together out of parts scavenged from generations of dead vehicles. The stretch of the fields surrounds us, and I look back and the sun is risen, the flat low light bathing the frost-touched landscape in liquid gold. I am watching from inside the bubble, and then I am aware of the music, building, like the background to a movie, strings weaving in and out. Pachelbel's Canon. The driver is playing it on the stereo system of the van. I am in the middle of the unchanging Chinese countryside, with the sun rising behind me and an ocean of humanity suddenly out on the road, in the fields . . . and there is no way to photograph this, because it is not just the light or the view but everything, this sudden heavenly panorama of life on the other side of the planet, where I live now.

And I am watching too the beautiful face of Li Ming bathed in this light, and my certainty is that I cannot know her, that like this countryside and these people there will always be a distance, a gulf, a bubble of cultural glass and steel between us.

The certainty burns and then, like the light, fades into the usual and is almost forgotten as we roll on.

Days later I walk into the guest house at the Technical Institute, the big university outside of town, and I am treated to a blast of real foreigner heat which wraps my body like an electric blanket. The woman at the desk barely looks up, and I walk past quickly, so there won't be any uncomfortable moment when she feels she has to do her job and ask who I'm coming to see. Whenever she does get a chance to ask, I tell her, she pretends to phone up, and then she says Madeleine is not in, which is not true, it is just part of the funny politics going on. Thank God I teach at a small institution, happy to have a foreign teacher and not equipped to survey my every move the way they feel they have to here.

Up the stairs, down the hall, through the doors into the foreigners' wing. Her door is open.

"Hey!" I call out. "Any foreigners here?"

"I'm in the shower!" Madeleine yells.

"Great! I'll come and join you!"

"You hold your breath, mister. I'll be out in a minute!"

I take off my jacket and slump down on her sofa in the little sitting room, close to the heat. I should have brought my towel — I could use a nice bath. Madeleine has an extra one, but I hate to keep borrowing hers. I pick up a *Vogue* magazine which someone has sent her and flip through the lingerie ads. As soon as I open it garish perfume floods the room. All the way from New York. Ruffles, legs, and muscular young men scowling in their underwear. What would Li Ming think if she saw this?

"Hi!" Madeleine says as she comes into the room, her hair up in a towel, the rest of her in a big, blousy sweat shirt and well-loved blue jeans.

"Any hot water left?"

"It was just running out towards the end. I think they've turned it off again."

"Why is that? Do they know I'm coming or what?"

"That must be it. How are you? You look a bit pale. Are they feeding you properly?"

"I'll have to get you on the case. Mom, Part II — The Wrath of Madeleine."

"Well, you come to visit me more often and I'll beef you up. What's that you've got? Oh my dear, my sister's Vogue. I have a whole shelf of important twentieth-century novels here. Why did you have to go straight to that?"

"Your sister's Vogue?"

"She seems to feel I'm deprived of higher culture. I never look at it."

I give her a big laugh and she puts on her little kettle for tea and I ask her about her husband, Jeremy, who is back in the States, and her son at college, who is reading Proust and falling in love with someone new every two weeks or so. I'm not quite sure why she is here while her family is back there but there are a lot of unusual foreigners in China, I'm finding, and it's best to just take delight in who they are.

"Are those . . . are those brownies?" I say, spotting them on the counter by the kettle. "You didn't get them sent out — ?"

"I made them, young man!"

"Madeleine, you made brownies? God sent you here, all the way to the other side of the planet, so that you could make brownies for me?"

"Is that why I'm here?"

"It must be." I get up and bring the tray over to the little table by the sofa. "I'm just going to put them down here and look at them while the water boils. How's your, uh, plumbing working?"

Madeleine laughs and laughs, wiping a tear from the corner of her eye. She goes into the other room and returns with the towel off her hair and a brush in her hand, doing battle with the unruly greying mass. "The realities of being a foreigner," she says. "Let's get right down to it. Hot water, food, and are you still constipated? Well . . . yes. How about you?"

"Still running like thin soup," I say. "Do you think . . . do you think the water's boiled enough yet?"

"It hasn't been ten minutes."

"Well, I'll just . . . look at these a little longer. God, chocolate fudge brownies!"

We talk about classes then, and students, and writing, and Emily Dickinson. When Madeleine talks about any of these things she flushes pink with excitement, her eyes become wide, and the lines around her face soften like the light at sunset.

"I've taught all over the United States," she says. "In all kinds of colleges and schools. I even taught high school once, in Philadelphia, inner city. Talk about a burn-out place. But I found it even there, and I've certainly found it here. If you just look hard enough, it doesn't matter where you are. There's a spark, and if you blow on it . . . A student I had in Philadelphia, a little girl from a destitute family in one of the worst neighbourhoods — she went on to do her PhD at Columbia in twentieth-century feminist literature. And I've got a student here who's thirty-seven years old, spent most of her adult life working in a lightbulb factory. But her father had taught her English and she listened every night to the BBC broadcasts, and the essays she writes me — they are so moving, I can't tell you. There was one short description she did about saying goodbye to her brother at the train station, when they were both being shipped out to the countryside, in opposite directions, hundreds of miles apart. How controlled they both were, showing only the slightest emotion, even though they knew they might not see one another for years and years, and in fact didn't see one another again because he died the next year of hepatitis. She describes how they held back because the crowd was there, and you didn't know who you could trust. No one was sure if crying

at the station was allowed. And not a correction on the page. Absolutely flawless English."

"I think the water's boiled," I say, getting up to pour it into the pot, the green tea leaves swirling to the top and then slowly sinking.

"I've told you about my friend, Li Ming," I say.

"Did she get her permission yet to go to that conference?"

"No, not yet. She's working on the leaders one by one. She says that she has three of them now who agree she should go, but there are five more who are against her, and it has to be unanimous or else no one will vote for her. She has the paper nearly translated. I was helping her a bit with it."

"What's it about?"

"I'm not sure."

"Oh."

"It's about some special class of Chinese verbs. That's as far as I could get. I never took linguistics. It seems to have a language unto itself. But the Chinese sure like it."

"They'll go for anything scientific," Madeleine says. "Industry, technology, concrete, linguistics. Good male yang stuff. You know, she should be applying for scholarships abroad. I bet with her knowledge of Chinese linguistics she could get an invitation to one of the really good schools."

"The question is . . . would the leaders let her go?"

"I don't see why not. If she comes back with a PhD in linguistics from an American school then the college would look really good. She's a terrific student."

"I don't know if it's that simple," I say. "But I do think this tea is ready, and I can't possibly wait any longer to try out these brownies. Oh . . . Madeleine . . . *ohhhhhhh*. That's . . . oh, God . . . oh!"

The brownies don't last very long. The talk does, for hours and hours, about books, mainly, stories that we love. Madeleine has forgotten more books than I've read, but she doesn't forget a good one, and she talks on and on about Anthony Trollope,

John Donne, Yeats, Synge, Lawrence, Thomas Wolfe, and Henry James. I talk about C.S. Forester's Hornblower books, about Larry McMurtry and Alice Munro and William Rogers, his thin, thin book.

"You should show me some of your stories one of these days," she says.

"I will," I say, nodding. "When they're ready."

It gets late quickly. I have a long dark bicycle ride ahead. Madeleine has some papers to mark. There's something else I want to say.

"So you're worried . . . about your son, are you?" I say. "With all these different women?"

"It's just a phase I think he's going through. You know, when you're young all those hormones are bouncing through your body. He's got a heart like a hotel."

"I, uh, I think I might be . . . in a bit of trouble myself."

"What's that?"

"Well, I guess I've mentioned her a few times. Li Ming."

"What's the problem?"

"I, well, I can't stop thinking about her."

"What do you mean 'thinking about her'?"

"I mean . . . thinking about her."

"Oh. Thinking about her."

"Yes."

"Oh."

Madeleine looks at me in her motherly way and wipes her hand across her brow.

"Forget it," she says.

"What do you mean?"

"I mean forget it. Or, let's put it this way. Think about her all you want. Don't *do* anything about it."

"Don't do anything."

"Exactly. This isn't . . . the south of France. If you wanted romance, that's where you should have gone. Not communist China. *Nobody* here is going to take kindly to a foreigner making advances to a Chinese girl, probably least of all Li Ming. I mean, think of the position you would put her in. She would be shunned so quickly. God knows where they'd send her. It would be *extremely* irresponsible . . . "

"Madeleine . . . "

"And they'd kick you out of the country so fast your head would be — "

"It's not that bad — "

"Do you understand what I'm saying?"

"Yes, Madeleine."

"I'm not your mother. I'm not being an old prude. But what you're thinking of is absolutely — "

"I understand, but you're exaggerating. That's the old China, Mao's China. This is a different place. Deng Xiaoping is in charge. It's an Open Door Policy. Everything's changing. It's not such a big deal, a foreigner and a Chinese girl."

"Rudy," she says, and I expect debate, but her face is set and very troubled. "You have it wrong. This is an old society. What you are thinking of is very serious. Don't start, all right? Trust me on this. Do you hear me?"

"Yes."

"So what are you going to do?"

I smile at her, but she grabs my arm. "What are you going to do?"

"Nothing."

"Good. It's not that I want to give you advice — "

"Thank you, Madeleine," I say, giving her a hug in the doorway, and then walking away, along the darkened hall, down the stairs, past the receptionist, who looks away since officially I did not enter in the first place. I push open the heavy doors and the air outside is cold, very cold.

"Hello? Are you in? Hello?"

"Hi! Li Ming! Come in!" I call, getting up from the sofa.

"It's very dark in here. I wasn't sure you were in."

"I'm just waiting for the electricity to come on," I say, closing the door behind her. "Some tea?"

"No, thank you."

"Are you sure? I still have some hot water in the thermos."

"No. It's all right."

"Okay. That's two. This is my last offer. Will you have some tea? You look very cold."

"Fine," she says, smiling. "I will have some tea."

I pour her a mug and put the top on, and she uses it to warm her hands.

"Don't you have any candles?" she asks.

"Yes, I do," I say. "I just forgot to light them. You know how you're reading by the window, and as the light fades your eyes slowly adjust? And it just gets darker and darker?"

"Yes."

I look through my desk, then pull out and light my two candles, which I place, one on the desk, one on the side table. The candles suddenly make it seem darker, night-time, in the shadows beyond the glow.

"I have some mail that I forgot to bring to you," she says, pulling a couple of envelopes out of her bag.

"Wonderful! You wonderful, wonderful person!" I say. "It's been four days now. Look, there's a letter from my mother, and one from my friend."

Li Ming puts down her tea and rises. "I should go," she says, "and let you read your mail."

"No, please, stay for a bit. I can read it later. The candlelight is not . . . it's hard on the eyes. Have you heard anything?"

She sits down again, on the edge of the sofa. "There is no news," she says.

"The leaders haven't made up their minds?"

"They had a meeting this afternoon, but I do not know what they decided, or if they even talked about my case."

"God, you are so patient!"

"No," she says. "I am not patient. If I were patient then it

 Waiting for Li Ming

would all happen easily. But the leaders think I want things too quickly. I am not Chinese enough. I am — "

"A Western bourgeois liberal?"

"Perhaps," she says. "I do not know the phrase in English." Then she repeats it, as if it is something important to learn.

"That's it. I read it in every second story in the *China Daily*. That and *unity and stability*. You could do a linguistic study of Chinese political euphemisms."

"I am sorry?"

I tell her about political euphemisms, and she shakes her head. "I do not think I could do a study on that."

"No, no — of course not!" I say. "I mean — I said it as a joke. No, of course not."

She is looking towards the door.

"You see," I say, "there was an Englishman who predicted this sort of thing, after the war. The Second World War. George Orwell. Actually, he saw it being used all the time during the war. Propaganda. Official truth. And he predicted that governments would use euphemisms — he called it 'doubletalk' — more and more. In fact, he said they would become so good at controlling information that eventually the people would believe whatever the government said, even if it contradicted common sense, because people . . . would be trained not to think for themselves. It wouldn't be safe anymore. You'd wait to see what the official government policy was. And if it was a reverse of what they said yesterday, well . . . people would just forget what was said yesterday."

She nods her head just once and does not say anything, her way of not contributing to a conversation she wants no part in. So I start filling the air with talk of Canadian politics, whatever comes to my head out of the latest *Maclean's* magazine, but as I'm talking I'm thinking about her body, her strong, tidy limbs, the delicate curve of her breast not quite hidden there beneath the layers of clothing, the flat warmth of her belly and how golden it would look in the candlelight. When she forgets herself her face radiates great beauty, like a lake emerging beneath a ceiling of mist.

"I must go now," she says, suddenly conscious of the way I'm looking at her. "Thank you for the tea."

"You're very welcome. Thank you for the mail. Goodbye, Li Ming."

As I open the door for her I catch a glimpse of young Jiang standing outside my courtyard, looking in. Li Ming sees him too and lowers her head and I'm not sure what it means that her pace is so quick, that he stands there looking at her so long after she passes by.

But when she's gone the apartment is suddenly empty; the candlelight is cold and the hours of the evening ahead seem like a long stretch of desert, even when the lights come back on and there's a pitiful glow in the twin coils of my little electric heater.

8

RUDY WROTE FOR SEVERAL DAYS, GOING OUT ONLY TO BUY GROCERIES, to attend his few hours of classes, and to exercise. The cold deepened. He moved his little typing desk closer to the radiator and wore two sweaters inside the apartment, which made him feel as if he was back in Laozhou. No mail came from Li Ming — it was a slow death daily, checking for that airmail envelope that never came — and no one called or stopped by to see him. But he wrote in a quiet, sustained fury, and read when he took his meals, and talked to himself much of the time.

Late one afternoon, coming back in the gloom from a cold walk by the river, he found a note in his box. It was hastily written, in red, on a torn lined sheet of paper. It said: *I'm sorry for what I said. It's been a hell of a week or two. We'll talk soon. Lou.*

He tried to call her but her line was busy. For half an hour it was busy. He made himself some dinner and read from a book of Orwell's essays, then tried her number again, but she was out. He padded around the apartment, flipped on the television set, ran through several channels and then turned it off. He wished he had his photographs. He had left them all at a discount processing place in Hong Kong and had still heard nothing from them. He found the receipt in his papers and typed out a curt letter, making a mistake on the word "Sincerely" and then ruining it with the white-out, trying to type over the correction before it was quite dry. So he typed out the letter again and snapped it in an envelope and tried Lou's number but she was still out.

He tried the television again, found a nature show about the slaughter of elephants in Africa, stood it for only a few minutes and turned it off. He could not concentrate on Orwell. He put on his warm jacket and boots and went out to the end of the block and mailed his letter to Hong Kong. The wind tore through his clothing and the ice beneath his feet was frozen like steel. He got back and then didn't try phoning again and ended up at his typewriter. When he looked at the page there was Li Ming, filling it . . . but when he looked away there was only an emptiness that scared him, that twisted inside in such a familiar way, like an old virus he had fought so hard to defeat, now returning fresh for another round the moment he let down his guard.

Lou called a few days later. Rudy was re-reading *Nineteen Eighty-Four* and thinking about Orwell at his life's end, scraping up the energy to put down this last, bleakest vision. And now here was Lou and her news, whatever it was, literally life or death.

He asked her how she was and she said fine, and there was a longish pause while he waited for more.

"This whole thing with Michael has just put me through the wringer, of course. Considering all that — "

"Did you — ?"

"What?"

"Never mind. It doesn't matter."

"I got my tests back."

"Yes."

"God, it's horrible, Rudy. It's just . . . it's the worst thing I have ever had to go through. I mean, I thought my divorce . . . "

She was crying. Rudy took a deep breath. "It's okay, Lou," he said. "It's okay. Do you want me to come over?"

"No."

She was still crying. "Listen, Rudy . . . I have to go. Bye. Thanks."

Rudy listened to the dial tone for a minute, then flipped through his book by the phone and called Amanda.

"Hi, Amanda, listen — I think you should go over and drop in on Lou. I was just talking to her on the phone."

"God, what's happened now?" Amanda asked.

"Well, I'm not sure, I think she just got her tests — "

"That I know about," Amanda said curtly. "There isn't anything else, is there?"

"No," Rudy said, uncertainly.

"She told you she's all right?" Amanda said. "She tested negative."

"Ah," Rudy said. "Good."

"But it scared the shit out of her," she went on. "It would anybody. I should probably go over there. Is that what you were calling to say?"

"Yes," Rudy said. "I guess so."

"Okay," she said, and Rudy put down the phone and stood awhile in the kitchen, thinking.

9

"YOU MUST PRACTISE DILIGENTLY," LI MING SAYS, TRANSLATING WANG'S words. "Every day, as much as you can. And when you go back to Canada you must teach. If you don't believe in yourself enough to become a teacher, then I will not teach you now."

I nod, tired. It has been two hours already this afternoon and I'm not getting it. I never do, straight off. When he first shows me it looks effortless and extremely complicated at the same time. He doesn't like to break the series down into separate moves; I have to stop him so he can show me bit by bit, and even then I'm slow to get it. But he knows me. He knows I'm going to go off and stay with it hour after hour until it's into my body somehow. If not elegant, then there. Elegance I can work on later.

"This move here," Li Ming says. "With your hands sliding apart. Think of water running down a rockface."

When she comes to translate these sessions for me she wears a mask of concentration, as if she too is learning these movements. It makes me try harder.

Wang shakes his head, no, then shows me again.

"Sit lower," she says. Wang slaps my bum in, pushes down on my shoulders. Then they run on in Chinese for a long time, while I stay in my sit, my legs beginning to shake.

"What did he say?"

"He said you are too stiff. You must do those flexibility exercises. Like he showed you."

"I do them!" I say. "Listen, it took me twenty years to get this stiff. Give me a little time. Don't tell him that."

Wang asks her, what did I say?

"Tell him I will work harder."

I work harder. We do three waters down rockfaces, then into a jabbing move with the right hand, and something fancy, whirling with both hands before jabbing again with the right. I have to go over it piece by piece. First rockface, step, hold the ball; second rockface, step, hold the ball; third rockface, then up again with the hand . . .

Wang shakes his finger at me, no. He looks at the ground, disgusted. Then goes through the series. It really is water coming down the rockface. But I can't sit that low. And I'll never be as graceful . . .

He pantomimes something, rubbing his stomach.

"Master Wang says the feeling must come from there. There should be strength from the hips as you pull the hands apart. And keep your back straight. You are hunching over."

Keep your back straight, turn your hips, feel it in the belly. Now what's the fucking move? I've forgotten!

"Master Wang says you must do this with seriousness, or he won't teach you."

I do it again. And again. And again. Then he shows me the next series. Hands become snakes, shooting forward, then back, with a ripple in between. I try it, forget the very first part, have to ask him to repeat.

He points to his temple, then shakes his head. Li Ming starts to explain but I say, "That's okay. You don't have to translate."

He shows me again, and I try it with him. Turn the right hand over, shoot it out, left hand, the other direction, then a hesitation, and a ripple down both arms . . .

"Not so stiff!" Li Ming translates. Wang shakes his finger at me, no . . . and there is laughing now from behind me.

It is the crowd again; I can never seem to escape them for long, whatever I'm doing. Thirty or forty people this time, some of them my students, most of them from other parts of the college, standing by the gate of my little courtyard, looking in at the foreigner learning *wushu*.

"Oh Christ!" I say. "What do they want? Why can't I do anything in private?" I try it again. Shit, I can't remember anything. What was the move? Wang shakes his finger at me, letting loose a long string of remonstrations.

"You cannot do *wushu* in a foul mood," Li Ming says. "You must have harmony between your spirit and your body. Don't mind about who is watching. Concentrate on the movements. What is outside does not matter."

He shows me again. The hand turning over, shooting out, and then the other hand in the other direction, and the ripple passing down the left arm, through the shoulders, down the right . . .

I try it again and again. Get stuck at every little point along the way. Plod. Start over. I have to think everything through rationally, make it make sense, get it in my head . . . then in my body. Wang gives me a little time to practise, then we go on, four, five, six more moves in a row. The left hand chopping over, but how does that foot get over there? Wait, stop! I have to look at it from this angle. Okay, the right foot sideways, and then the hands go up in a circle and the left foot swings over. So you're facing this way now, and as the arms come down you sit and then come up, and the hands whirl . . .

No, I need to see that over again. How do they go? Slowly. The left hand moves in this direction, then the right goes that way, they come around, and now you're stepping over here, and . . . how did that hand get there? I have to see it again. Let's back it up. The right hand shoots out . . .

When I look up the crowd has gone. It's getting dark, time for dinner. Somehow another hour has passed. Wang would keep me going even longer. But Li Ming has been standing in the cold, patiently translating, trying not to smile when I do something awkward. It is just this moment. I'm standing with my foot in the air, my arms curved in a defensive circle, Wang beside me, doing it correctly. This moment, when I'm in the middle of it, learning step by step. Every fibre tingling, every bit of attention taken . . . until my mind wanders and I think of what he has told me before, about how these movements are learned slowly and methodically, day after day, like layers of lacquer brushed on and then left to harden, brushed on and left to harden, then carved and smoothed and painted and polished.

Is this how Li Ming comes to love? I wonder, as we all stand here, waiting for me to learn.

Lou was in the hall. Rudy left the department office, turned right and there she was, talking to what looked like a first year student, going over her paper. Rudy hung back, found a bulletin board to read for a few minutes, and then when he looked up again the student was leaving. She did not look happy.

"Tough case?" he asked.

Lou gave him a small, reserved smile, brushing a reddish tangle of hair out of her eyes.

"She has a hard time expressing herself. Except when she thinks she's been ripped off — then she has no trouble at all."

"How are you?" he asked.

"Fine. You?"

"As usual."

They nodded at one another.

"I'm . . . uh . . . I'm just going in to see Rogers. About my stuff."

"Good luck."

"Yeah, thanks. I'm . . . uh . . . I don't know how long it will take. Will you be around in . . . half an hour or so? Maybe we could . . . "

"I don't know," she said.

He waited for her to say something more, but she didn't.

"Oh."

"Have a look in the grad room," she said. "I've got some marking for a while."

"Okay. Sure."

The meeting took an hour and a half. Rudy left Rogers's office dazed, the fluorescent lights of the hall giving everything on the periphery of his vision a dull, misty look. Every part of his body felt heavy, as if gravity had singled him out for extra duty.

There was no one left in the grad room except Lou, sitting at the far desk, her pen in the corner of her mouth, papers surrounding her. She didn't hear him until he was nearly upon her. "Oh God!" she said, looking up, her eyes startled wide with fright and laughter. "You were gone a long time."

"We had a lot to go over."

"And — ?"

"What?"

"How did it go?"

"Fine," he said, sitting down on the edge of her desk. "I'm exhausted."

"What did he say?"

"Everything," Rudy said. "Twice. Three times. He made about eight thousand corrections."

"Eight thousand?"

"Maybe it was only eight hundred. I don't know. I can hardly remember what he said, I'm so dizzy. All kinds of little things that he pointed out. Just quicker ways of saying things. And other places where he wanted more details. Then he wanted me to show him the plan of the novel. Well, I didn't have one, so I told him pretty well what was going to happen, and he had a lot of good questions about that. Some points he wants me to nail down. So I know where I'm going."

Lou nodded, warm and full of life.

"What are you smiling at?" she asked.

"Nothing," he said, shaking his head. "It's just a dumb thought."

"What?"

"Nothing."

"No, I like dumb thoughts. What is it?"

"Well," he said. "I was just thinking of all those artists over the ages who paint bowls of fruit. I guess it's an exercise that you do in school, to get a feel for shading and three dimensions. But just, well, as I was looking at you — you look beautiful, you know, sitting there in your red sweater with the green scarf tying back your reddish hair — I was thinking, if I was going to paint a bowl of fruit, I would think of you, just the way you're sitting . . ."

"I look like a fruit?" Lou asked, screwing her face up in mock outrage.

"Well, now, you playwright," he said. "You're twisting my words. I did not say you look like a fruit. I said you looked like a bowl of fruit. A bowl of fruit and a fruit have very different connotations. I only meant it in the kindest sense . . ."

"Oh, so now you're being kind," she said.

"Perhaps not kind," Rudy said. "Perhaps stupid is a better word."

"Come on," she said, touching his arm. "It seems like forever since I've had a chance to kid around with someone. Thank you for saying that I look like a bowl of fruit."

Rudy slid off the desk corner and took a long, low bow.

"Can I interest you in some alcohol to deaden your wit?" he asked gallantly.

"Thank you, no," she said, cleaning up her papers. "But you can walk me home, good sir."

"My pleasure."

Outside it was dark, cold, still. The sidewalk squeaked beneath their boots and the cars were splattered with road salt that looked old and hoary, fake frost.

"So, he made eight hundred corrections?" Lou said. "How do you feel after that? Okay?"

"It's funny," Rudy said. "It didn't feel like he was making corrections. I felt he wanted . . . as much as I do . . . to make the piece as strong as it could be. Like he knew I have this really good story to tell, only it isn't coming out quite right yet. And all the time he was talking, part of me was thinking of what else I could write, you know. What other scenes I had left out. So when it was over, I walked out of there with my head full of story. It wasn't anything he said, in particular . . . but I could go off for six months probably and I still wouldn't get down on paper everything I thought of in his office."

"Sounds like you've got a real rapport with him."

"Yeah, I think so," Rudy said.

They talked about other things for a while, then they approached Lou's house, quiet and asleep on the dark street.

"I'd ask you in, but I have to get ready for work," Lou said.

Rudy nodded. "What's your work?"

"Oh, very glamorous," she said. "I sling drinks at the Wild Boar, which I spell a little differently. It gives me a bit of money to pay Josie towards her mortgage."

"So you're just renting here?" he asked.

"House-sitting more like it. Josie's a PoliSci prof. She's gone to Geneva on sabbatical."

"Well, anyway," Rudy said, "It's great to see you . . . looking so well."

"In the dark, wrapped up in a winter coat," she said, smiling.

"Whatever. You know what I mean. Is he . . . you've been visiting him a lot?"

"He's about the same," she said, quieter, looking down. "Maybe a little better. The nurses are all falling in love with him. There's something about a terminally ill young man . . . Oh well, I don't really want to joke about it. But . . . it's just made me realize we could all go tomorrow. I don't know why we don't realize that all the time anyway. I mean, we've grown up in the shadow of the bomb. Did they have those nuclear drills when you were in school? When the alarm would go off and we'd all get under our desks and close our eyes?"

Rudy shook his head.

"Well, we did. For years I thought it was going to fall any day now. I don't know why we all aren't chasing every emotion, living life right out on the edge like Romantic poets or something. But we just kind of forget about the black side over there and plod on, step after step. It's too short, you know. It really is."

"I know what you mean," Rudy said.

"Do you?"

"Yeah, I think so," he said, shuffling his feet.

"I've got to go," she said. Suddenly she leaned in and kissed him quickly on the cheek. "You look very cute in that woollen hat!" she said.

He just looked at her, startled.

"Get going! You've got six more months of writing to do, while you can still remember it!"

"*Hao, hao! Ganbei!*" Dean Chun says, showing his glass, his eyes shining silvery like the alcohol.

"Oh God," I mutter, but smiling. He pours more into my glass, then the bottle circles the table. The dean proposes a toast, lifting his firewater high.

"To eternal friendship between Canada and China," Li Ming translates.

"*Ganbei! Ganbei!*" the dean says, grinning maniacally. He tilts his glass at me.

"You must drink it in one go," Li Ming says.

"I know. Like the last one."

The dean downs his with a swift jerk, closing his eyes and then laughing uproariously as he shows the empty bottom. The other men cheer, applaud, point to me. "*Ganbei*," they say. "*Ganbei!*"

I drain it. It goes down like fish hooks. I close my eyes and feel the pressure in my temples, then show my glass and try to smile without throwing up.

On with the next course. I don't know how long we have been at it. This is probably number seven. "What is that?" I ask Li Ming.

She confers with the dean, who explains it confidently, as if he himself has cooked it.

"It is a chicken dish with ginger and lotus root," she says.

I nod at the dean, showing my appreciation.

"You are the guest, so you should eat a great deal," Li Ming says.

"I'm trying. I don't know how much longer I can keep this up. How many more courses will there be?"

She looks down at her own little dish, which is almost empty, while mine is overflowing with bones and delicate morsels I couldn't manage to swallow. *She* has the hang of these dinners, not me. "I think perhaps not more than ten or twelve more," she says.

The dean's chopsticks flick into the big centre plate like deft claws and pull out a gigantic piece which he plops onto my plate before I can defend myself. He grins, showing all his teeth, stained and crooked, except for the silver one in the front.

"What did he say?" I ask Li Ming.

"He says you are young and can eat a great deal more!"

I nod, trying to find my sense of humour. Then I pick up the strange piece with my chopsticks and turn it around, looking for an opening.

It's a very odd piece, mostly bone from what I can tell. But I am obliged to try. Then just as I am biting I catch my tongue on something sharp and pull back, look at it again. Two little eyes stare at me like the eyes of a tiny cooked vulture. I nearly drop it.

"Li Ming?"

She is talking to one of the other guests, a professor from the Mathematics Department.

I bump her a bit with my elbow.

"Li Ming," I say in a low voice. "I'm not quite sure what to do with this."

She turns to see what the problem is. "It is the head," she says.

"I know it's the head. Just pretend we're talking about something else. But how do I eat it?"

She puts her hand over her mouth, stifling laughter. "Just put it down on your plate," she says. "If you cannot eat it."

"But it's some delicacy or something, isn't it?"

"Doesn't matter," she says, laughing, then reaching into the centre plate with her chopsticks. "Have something else!" She passes me another piece and I casually let the head fall on the huge pile of bones that is accumulating in front of me.

"*Ganbei! Hao, hao! Ganbei!*" comes the call again, too soon, almost bringing the contents of my stomach to my throat.

Another round. I lean over to Li Ming. "I'm not sure I can do this," I say to her.

"What do you mean?"

"I mean I've been drinking all night. I don't think I can keep on much longer."

"Perhaps only six or seven more courses," she says.

"I don't know if I can last six or seven more *minutes*."

"*Ganbei! Ganbei!*" cries the dean, tilting his glass, proposing his toast.

"To eternal good relations between all men on the earth," Li Ming translates.

"To the greatest good will and harmony between friends!" I say, tilting my glass.

Liquid shards of glass lacerating my throat. My stomach rises. My bum lifts from the seat. The air screeches from me as if I've been kicked in the gut.

My brain starts to implode.

 Waiting for Li Ming

I show my empty cup.

The dean laughs and laughs and laughs, rubbing his hand over his balding head. Li Ming grips my elbow. I don't know why, but it makes me feel better. More food arrives. Black eggs, buried for four months, staring at me now, waiting for revenge. I have a taste. Nothing. The alcohol has burned out my senses.

"I would like to toast the enduring and unending good relations between the students and faculty of the Laozhou Teacher's College and the people of Canada!" I say sometime, raising my glass, feeling warm with good humour, the banquet roiling inside me. I have to go the bathroom something horrible. Only the soup left to go. I tilt my glass. Not so bad. Like slowly drinking a headache.

Li Ming is saying something. I have to turn to her. "What?" I say, too loud.

"The dean says that you can go now, if you like. Unless you are still hungry."

"Still hungry?" I say. Laughter clutches my belly.

"Can you eat more?"

I can't even talk any more, it seems so funny. The dean laughs along with me, all the guests are laughing, they have no idea why. Still hungry?

We take our leave. Somehow I control my bladder. We have our coats on and are walking in the cold night air across the compound.

"My friends and I will see you home," Li Ming says.

"No no no no no," I say, giddy with the word. "I will see *you* home!"

I stumble for some reason and her friends, two big guys who appear suddenly from out of the night, clutch my arm.

"You are the guest, so we must see you home," she says.

It takes no time at all, half a thought. One look down at my shoes, another at the cold moon, and we are there.

"I don't know. Are those the same stars as at home?" I ask.

"Have you got your key?" she says.

"Key, yes. Key! But, those stars. I don't remember any of them at home."

"I don't know much about stars," she says. Somehow she has the key and opens the door, turning on the light, so bright it makes me woozy.

She speaks Chinese to the men, who very cleverly understand her, and then they are guiding me into the bedroom.

"Can you manage?" she asks from the other room.

"Yes. Yes!" I say, falling over onto the bed as a joke but missing it, and then I'm on the floor, cold, like a bathroom floor on one of those nights . . .

The two guys help me up. I start to peel off my jacket. Then they take off my shoes and I am in the bed with the comforter over me, and it is so dark, but I can see her perfectly as she peers around the doorframe into my room, her black eyes, the way her hair hooks back behind her ears.

"Are you all right?"

"Yes. Wonderful," I say. "I should walk you home."

"No, thank you," she says, and her smile is a quick flash of white.

"You walked me home. I should walk you home."

"Another time, perhaps."

"Yes. Okay. Another time," I say.

"Good night."

"Good night, Li Ming." Her feet tread lightly beside the heavy feet of the others, and the light in the other room falls shut, and I am lying here, warm, needing to go the bathroom. But in a minute. It is a fine thing just to be still, thinking of what it would be like to be married to Li Ming.

10

AFTER THE FIRST PROBLEM WITH THE PEDAL, MY LONG MARCH BICYCLE is steady through frost and mud and rain and my laziness in never cleaning it. It weighs about twenty pounds, has one gear, a wide comfortable seat that keeps my back upright, traditional handlebars with handbrakes, and fenders, a rack on the back, a kickstand, chainguard and bell. Every other bicycle looks exactly like it. You can put almost anything on it, including an entire family, with father driving and mother on the handlebars and son sitting on the rack.

Li Ming rides recklessly ahead of me. She looks so demure and shy, but when she gets on a bike her right thumb constantly strokes the bell while she weaves in and out, pedalling furiously. When trucks roar up she ducks out of the way at the last possible moment, then squeezes in behind them after they have gone past, darting through the openings they create. I try to stay with her for a while and then fall back, keeping her purple jacket in sight as it flashes through an intersection, flirting with collision. I know she is cursing under her breath like some stress case on the freeway.

We ride down a long, tree-lined avenue and at the far curve, approaching the Monument to the Martyrs, she waits for me, at peace now that she has stopped. I am several minutes behind her, which she finds funny. Already the rest has restored her. "If you ever come to Canada," I say, gliding up behind her, "I'll have to teach you a whole new style of riding a bicycle."

"What style?"

"It's called defensive driving. It assumes that in a collision between a troop truck and a bicycle, the truck will win."

"No collision," she says, pushing off again.

Now we are riding down a dirt road between the winter cabbage fields, long, low greenhouses opened in the sunshine, covered with plastic sheets at night, heated by coal. The ground is frozen but food still must be coaxed from the soil. Almost no one is around. In a few minutes we have ridden from the middle of the swarm of humanity out to open spaces, silence, fresher air.

Along another road now, paved but farther out. Past a few carters, past the lonely Laozhou Zoo, where the lion and the bear are kept in concrete bunkers; the monkeys huddle together in the cold. I went just once and it was so depressing I will not return. Around the corner, and then we walk our bikes into the cedar forest, standing them together and locking them. I have seen pairs of bicycles like this before in the woods, have ridden by and assumed, usually, that a young couple has come here to be alone. In the warmer weather, in the shadows by the fence under the basketball hoops, the silhouettes of young lovers holding hands, kissing. Now Li Ming looks at our bikes together before we start up the hill.

"We should not stay too long," she says.

Rudy heard the barking before the bell but still was surprised. He had to look up from his typewriter, refocus his eyes, figure out where he was.

"Hi! Just a moment!" he called out, pushing back his chair. He nearly upset a pile of manuscript papers he had placed on the cardboard box he was using for a deskside table.

Lou was standing in a pocket of cold air in the hallway outside his door, dressed in a battered combat jacket, a woolly scarf around her hair. Oswald was leaping and spinning at the end of a well-chewed leather leash.

"It's not too late, is it? I'm sorry, Rudy, were you asleep?"

"No, not at all," he said, though rubbing his eyes as if he had been. "No, I was just working."

"Writing?"

"I've been at it too long anyway. What's up? Come on in!"

"No, listen, maybe this was a dumb idea. But I didn't have to work tonight and I was just out for a walk and the moon is . . . it's about the biggest moon you'll ever see. It looks pregnant." She started laughing suddenly, then said, "I mean, I was passing by and just thought I'd ask if you'd like to join me and Ozzie. It's cold, though. Maybe you should just . . . "

"Wonderful idea," he said. "Just a minute — I'll get my coat."

"I didn't mean to interrupt — "

"You're not, really," he said, going through his closet.

"You're probably just in the middle of — "

"No," he said. "It's time I took a break."

He was ready very quickly. "Okay?"

"Aren't you going to show me around your apartment?" she asked.

"Oh," he said. "Okay. It'll take a second and a half. This is the hall here. And around here is the living room, yes, and this is the kitchen . . . "

"You have a lot of plants," she said.

"I know. And they're all dying. There isn't enough light here. How's the cactus doing?"

"Fine." Lou kept looking around. "Is that the bedroom?" she asked.

"It's . . . in a mess," Rudy said.

"Where's the light?"

"It's really not . . . "

Lou found the light switch. "Oh," she said.

"I just use it for sleeping in."

"But where's your bed?"

"There's a mat . . . "

"On the floor here. Is that your bed?"

"Well, it's funny, but — "

"Doesn't it get cold at night? I mean, a futon at least is a couple of inches thick . . . "

"I've gotten used to it," Rudy said, shrugging his shoulders.

"It's none of my business anyway," Lou said, snapping off the light and pulling Oswald back. "Did I tell you how big the moon is?"

I let Li Ming go up the path ahead of me. She's a strong woman, with a straight back and a simple way of carrying herself. We're climbing a steep part right at the beginning, the steps laid down who knows how long ago, worn smooth by passing feet and slipping water. It seems weird to find these steps — in the middle of what amounts to wilderness here — leading up the highest hill in the region, but from what I can see people don't come here now. These steps were worn smooth by another society, not the one that built the factories I can see as I turn around and look down into the valley.

"It is a long way up!" she says, turning to rest at a clearing where we can look back over the winter fields of the flat plain where so many armies have collided in the history of this old place.

"Are you all right?"

"Yes, fine!" she says.

"Do you come up here often?"

"No."

"I just found it the other week," I say. "I've climbed almost all the hills around here now. I guess there's nothing to do but climb them over again."

"It is not a very exciting place," she says.

"Not like Shanghai?"

She laughs. "Not at all like Shanghai."

"How many people are there in Shanghai?"

"Perhaps . . . twelve millions."

"I don't know how you could live there."

"It was not always that many. Now, you are right. My friends ride the bus two or three hours to get to work in the morning. It is too big. But at least people . . . are part of the world in Shanghai."

"What do you mean?"

"In Shanghai . . . the fashions are much better . . . it is much more cosmopolitan . . . But in Laozhou . . . "

"Do boys and girls openly walk hand in hand in Shanghai?" I use an objective, sociological tone.

"Yes, sometimes," she says, a little off balance. It would of course be forbidden in Laozhou.

I smile. "It's funny for me," I say, backing off, "to see men walking hand in hand, like they do here. In Canada, if you saw two men walking hand in hand, you would assume they were homosexual."

Li Ming brings her hand to her mouth as she laughs, her face going very red.

"I don't mean to . . . shock you, or say anything wrong," I say.

"No, not shocking," she says. "Very funny!"

"Yes, it's funny," I say, looking at her, how she can go into giggles like a young girl, and then look at me sometimes as if she is older, more beautiful than the moon.

"It's gorgeous, isn't it?" Lou asked.

"Yes," Rudy replied. They were walking now down a dark street near the river, the moon a large, chilly silver dish set in black velvet.

"I love winter nights like these," she said, "when everything is so still, and you can hear the crunch of the snow beneath your boots, and the cold air wakes up your cheeks, stretches them tight. I remember cross-country skiing once, by moonlight, on a night like this. Way out in the woods, it was like we were in outer space. Everything had this bluish tint to it, but it was so light, with the snow and the moon, that we could see just fine."

Lou started laughing, like ice warming in water and crackling.

"What?"

"Nothing."

"Oh."

They walked on, Oswald subdued in the cold, not pulling at the leash or yapping or even looking up for that matter. They left the road and took an icy path that led to the park by the river. The playground was ghostly still in the dark, the swings and the slide sheened in ice like silvery bones, while the river was white, covered in snow except for the black, ominous middle. Further on, the bottom of the bridge was a black shadow which gradually turned to gold as the eyes lifted higher to the streetlights and the traffic up top.

They came to the end of the park, then followed a path that wound its way through a thick wood into a clearing where the moon was close enough to show its wrinkles.

"You know what I was laughing about before?" Lou asked.

"What?"

"That night when I went skiing in the moonlight. I had just remembered. We went for miles and miles, and got kind of lost, and then around midnight we came upon this lodge in the middle of the woods. It was there for skiers. We started a fire and had a little mulled wine that we had brought. My husband, Gary, was with me. We ended up making love on this picnic table which we pulled up beside the fireplace. The floor had too many splinters in it. And all the time we were waiting for somebody else — some other midnight skiers — to blunder in.

So we didn't even take off our clothes. Our pants were wrapped around our ankles, and then I heard this sound, it was a twig snapping or something, and my feet . . . " She started laughing again. "Maybe I shouldn't be telling you this."

"You've got this far," Rudy said. "Don't stop now!"

She was laughing harder. "I can't!" she said.

"Oh, come on!"

"Well, my feet were planted on the table, you see, and I was on the bottom. Then I heard this noise and I was so scared I went rigid and did this back arch — " She dissolved into laughter again, which started Oswald yapping at her ankles.

" — I used to do gymnastics, you see, so I have a very flexible back. And I did this sudden arch, and Gary flew right off of me . . . right *out* of me, and landed on his back on the ground. He almost got a con . . . " She couldn't continue, she was laughing so hard, and now that Rudy was laughing too they set one another off.

" . . . He almost got a con . . . "

"A what?"

She bent over, trying to breathe.

"A . . . what?"

"A con . . . *cussion!*" she said, rolling on the snow as if wounded, with Oswald licking her face and barking in the moonlight.

We reach the top and already the afternoon light is dying. There are ruins here, some sort of simple concrete building, just three walls now. Looking out the empty sockets of the windows, though, we can see a magnificent view of the whole valley as we face the different directions.

"Hey! What's this over here?" I ask, taking a path down a short, steep slope. Li Ming follows and together we peer into a small cave which has inside it a carved and painted golden

Buddha, with small pots in front of it soiled with the remains of joss sticks — incense, not too old.

"People come up here after all," I say.

"From the countryside," Li Ming says, her arms folded across her chest.

"Your family is not religious?"

She shakes her head. "My father was a scientist," she says simply, as if that explains it.

"My father is a lawyer," I say. "We aren't religious either." We turn back and I take her hand to help her up the slope. It's a casual gesture, casually accepted, but I'm extremely aware of her strong, sure grip, somehow warm through the thickness of our gloves.

We cross the main path and look out at the valley on the other side, and then climb down another slope to a concrete platform that looks as if it might have supported an artillery gun in another era. Li Ming sits on a rock beside it, pulling her jacket tightly around her for warmth. I sit beside her and if I could would put my arm around her. But I don't know what would happen, what her reaction would be.

"What did your father do in the Revolutionary War?" I ask her, but she shakes her head. "He never talked about it," she says. "I was too young when he died."

We sit in silence and I try to think of a better topic, but the more I think the less there is to say. And then it becomes obvious that we have nothing in common. We come from different cultures and are different ages and I've dragged her all the way here to the chilly top of a deserted hill, and she has come only because it is her function as my semiofficial translator.

She looks off to the west, away from me. What is she thinking now? If I were a Chinese man, and if she loved me, what would we do now? Would I lean in and turn her face towards mine and would we kiss? Or would I slip my hand across and hold hers and would we sit together talking about something else and pretending nothing out of the ordinary was happening? Or would I petition her family for her hand before anything could happen?

I think of asking her about Jiang, who is so obvious in his feelings, who hangs around her so much and whose company she does not entirely avoid. I would have heard if they were engaged. But what does she feel about him? How to introduce the topic? Or maybe, since she doesn't mention him, maybe he doesn't matter. It feels otherworldy to be sitting here so close and yet with the distance between us immeasurable, either far wider than I imagine or far smaller, but I don't know which. What is she thinking? If only I knew that. I would know then to take her hand or turn her face towards mine or give up completely, know there is no hope. If only I knew!

But then she says, "We should go now," and we're walking down the hill with the opportunity, if that's what it was, unravelling before me with each jolting stride, each silent miscommunication.

They approached Lou's house in silence, the cold and the dark and the hour having subdued whatever conversation was left. She had left a light on in the living room and drawn the curtains so that the house looked warm, lived in, private.

"Will you come in for a bit?" she asked. "I think I have some hot chocolate."

"Yes. That would be nice," Rudy said.

The warm air inside hit him like a sleepy embrace. He shed his outside clothes, then walked in his stocking feet to the fireplace.

"Have you got any wood?" he called. She had gone into the kitchen to look after the hot chocolate.

"No," she said. "It would be nice, wouldn't it? It's too expensive, though."

"Doesn't matter," he said, joining her in the kitchen. "Where are all the newspapers?"

"It *has* been a while since you've been here," she said. "Oswald has become a very advanced dog. He's much more intelligent than he looks!"

Rudy warmed his hands over the element on the stove, feeling the pleasurable stab of life returning to his fingers.

"Do you mind if I say something?" she asked then, going over to stir the pot. She stood very close to him; he could feel the cold air still cloaking her skin.

"It depends," he said.

"On what?"

"On what it is."

"Oh," she said. Her eyes were very green in the kitchen light, brilliant and clear.

"Well," she said. "I'm going to say it anyway."

"Okay." She wasn't moving away. She was still stirring. The air around her wasn't cold any more.

"You seemed . . . kind of distant to me this evening. I really . . . am happy that you came along. I know I just dropped in on you. But it seemed like you were . . . somewhere else."

She looked at him too long, making him feel flushed and vulnerable.

"I guess I'm still thinking about my writing," he said.

"What about it? What are you thinking?"

"I don't know. It's . . . complicated," he said. "You'd have to know the whole story. But you know how you're in the middle of a scene and even when you stop writing the scene keeps on going? Or you're out for a walk somewhere and all of a sudden the story is happening in your head? The things you see all around you — they suddenly fit exactly with what you're writing about. All kinds of details. It's like this orchestra playing in your head. And you're thinking about — "

"What?"

"Well, something occurs to you. You're remembering a scene and suddenly you know something you didn't know at the time, but you should have."

Lou asked him a question then but he didn't hear it, was thinking of Li Ming, so he simply nodded his head and hoped it wasn't important.

When the hot chocolate was ready they brought their mugs into the living room, which seemed cold now. Lou took a blanket out of the closet and draped it over their legs as they sat on the sofa, each on an end with their feet up. He happened to take her feet in his hands because they were right there and started rubbing them because they were so cold.

"Mmmmmmmm, that's wonderful," she said, lying back, closing her eyes. Everything seemed remarkably natural, as if they had known each other for years.

"So how is your play going?" he asked.

"It's on hold," she said without opening her eyes.

"Oh."

"I'm waiting for some kind of feedback from Rogers. And everything's been crazy the last month or so. I can't really think straight with Michael and everything."

She went quiet for a moment as he continued working her foot, which was long and narrow, with a beautiful high arch just made for the flat of his thumb. He rubbed her ankle then and tendon, and started up the sleek part of her calf.

"That feels absolutely divine," she said. "Don't stop. Promise me you won't stop."

"I promise," he said.

The room got warmer again. He squeezed the muscles of her calf, felt the stubble on his fingertips, then ran back down to that arch. He took off her sock and squeezed out each toe individually — they were long too, and cold. He warmed them in the palm of his hand, and then pulled each until the joint gave a little pop.

"I can't tell you how magnificent this feels!"

He moved on to the other foot, which was cold too, but warmed noticeably as he rubbed and squeezed. Her face looked very beautiful in the soft light of the lamp, her eyes closed, her cheeks still red from the night air, her hair at once a pillow and a frame. He thought of Li Ming's face asleep, how it curved so beautifully in the shadows.

"I should go," he said then, suddenly but trying to sound calm.

"What?"

"It's getting late." He took a large gulp of his hot chocolate, which he had hardly touched.

"You're not going to do more work tonight!"

"No," he said, rising. "But tomorrow's another day. I like to . . . be steady, you know. If I stay up too late one night, then the next day . . . "

"What time is it?" she asked. She still hadn't gotten up. But she had withdrawn her feet beneath the blanket, which he had abdicated.

He looked at his watch. "It's after two," he said.

"God. I thought it was about midnight." She pulled on her socks and stood as he walked to the door and began re-layering himself for the walk home.

"Thanks again for a wonderful evening," she said, somewhat formally. "I didn't mean anything about your being . . . distant. What I said, I mean." She was suddenly tongue-tied. "It's great that you're writing. That's the important thing. And now I know you have great hands. For feet-rubbing, I mean."

"Any time," he said, gallantly tossing his scarf over his shoulder. "I'm glad you dropped by. It was great to see you." He reached his hand out for the doorknob. She was standing quite close again, looking at him expectantly.

She wanted him to kiss her.

He knocked some snow awkwardly off his boot with the toe

of his other boot. She was still standing there, with her eyes bright even in the darkness of the hall.

He didn't want to leave. That was the terrible thing.

"Good night," he said awkwardly, pulling open the door and then plunging into the cold.

11

MY ROOM IN THE MORNING IS A MEAT LOCKER, MY FACE AS NUMB AS a side of beef. But the rest of my body is too warm beneath the covers to want to move. Grey light. No sound. Nothing. I turn over, ease in and out of sleep.

The floor is too cold when I get up. Stone. Frozen. I slip my feet into my tongs, also cold, grab my dressing gown from off the door. Pad into the other room, pausing briefly by the tiny heater I have Western-bourgeois-liberally left on all night.

Snow overnight. The sudden white softens, lightens the grey. Wet snow, though thick, already melting. November.

I continue into the wintry vault of the bathroom. Snap on the light. Flip up the toilet seat, feel the warm fullness flow from me. Still sleepy, I take my shaving bowl from the shelf and bring it past the partition to the hot water box which is bolted high above the huge, frozen bathtub I never use because it is far too big and the room too cold and the hot water box too small to heat more than an unsatisfying fraction of either the tub or the room. As with the electric heater, I have lazily left the hot water box plugged in overnight instead of rising half an hour early to turn it on. It doesn't have an automatic turn-off; it just keeps heating the water until after this many hours it comes out close to steam. This is my small way of contributing to the poverty of this country, I am thinking, having been raised in a heritage of great waste. But also — this is my treat. Life is hard enough for me here. I will be easy on myself in this way.

The hot water streams into my bowl, and then I temper it with the ice-cold from the tap and carry it back to my sink. My luxurious sink with the mirror and the toilet beside. What an emperor I am. What privileges.

My breath comes out in vapour; the cold draft from the floor goose-pimples my legs. Quickly the shaving water turns cool. Good thing I haven't a heavy beard. After shaving I rinse my face in the cold from the tap, towel off quickly, then think what the hell — I might as well wash my hair.

But it would be suicidal to take a shower under the super hot water of the heating box. Better the ice water of the tap. I shed my robe and quickly kneel, naked, onto the chilly bathtub. A deep breath, shampoo and towel ready, and . . . *unnghggg* . . . I stay under the cold for perhaps a second and a half and then turn off the tap and frantically rub my head, warming it with the towel to make it bearable. Quick, on with the shampoo, which lathers poorly, of course, but well enough for my purposes.

My body quivers with the cold, as if I am outside, naked, kneeling in the snow. I turn on the tap again and plunge my head under for an unutterable two seconds, then rub furiously with the towel and rise, shrieking, sprinting for my robe and the warmth of the little electric heater in the other room, which is not warm enough, something has happened just in the time I have been in the bathroom, it is failing somehow . . .

Damn! The power is off. Seven-thirty in the morning and the power is off! I feel like that man in London's "To Build a Fire" when he realizes it's too late, his limbs are frozen and he can't manipulate the matches and he's going to die in the cold.

I grab the other towel and dry my head as best I can and run on the spot, do jumping jacks, *yi, er, san, si, wu, liu, chi, ba!* and high kicks, flinging my arms and legs out, anything to get the blood moving. Watching the colour of heat drain from the insulating blocks of my precious heater, from delightful orange to dull, cold, dead white.

I put on as much clothing as I can carry. Thick socks, two pairs; my long underwear and then my thick sweat pants and my baggy corduroys; a t-shirt and a turtle neck and a sweat shirt and my big woollen sweater, grey with coal dust and all the warmer for it; my down vest and jacket and hat and mitts. Warm boots. Then across my little compound, into the little dining hut, even more of a concrete tomb than my apartment, the wind whipping through an open wound in the wall; dark, of course, because the power is off. I sit at the rickety table and stare for a moment at breakfast: a plate of cold, greasy fried bread; another plate of cold eggs fried in rapeseed oil, burnt around the edges; a tall glass of vaguely warm super-sweetened coffee.

There is no time to indulge in self-pity. Survival is at stake. Like it or not, this is fuel — the fried bread goes down first because it's the best, even cold, and then I slime down the eggs and drink half the glass of coffee and bolt from the room, yearning for somewhere warm.

There is nowhere. Bulky in all my layers, I stretch and jog on the spot in my little living room, waiting, hoping for the rush of heat through me and thinking all the time, how do people do this? How can they face these long months of winter with the cold grabbing at your throat like this? It's colder back home, yes, but at least we have *heat*.

I need help with it, in the same way that I need help with Li Ming, to know what she expects and what I'm supposed to do. How do people manage love here? How do they make it through the cold? I don't know.

I have to find yogurt. That is my assignment, to bring yogurt to the foreigners' party at the Technical Institute. Apparently there is a stand somewhere to the south, at one of the corners by the big department store; Li Ming, although not able to come, has given me directions. I am on foot, amazed that the snowy streets are full of cyclists who like me have grown in layers with the growing cold, some wearing white face masks to stay warm. An old man wearing ancient sneakers and thin socks, his lower leg a bare fetlock splashed with mud, pulls a cart past me, and I walk up the hill past the park where the vendors huddle over their portable coal ovens with warm sweet potatoes, long sticks of fried bread, noodles, rice, flat cakes of some sort. Sunday, the one day off for most workers, who still have places to go despite the snow.

An arthritic bus moans past me jammed so full of people their arms and shoulders are sticking out of the few windows that are open, crammed up against the glass of the many that aren't. Slower, slower, grinding its gears until finally it reaches the top, a tired dinosaur, and then the engine cuts out entirely as it coasts down the hill, picking up speed, the driver honking to warn the cyclists out of the way. At the bottom of the hill it eases into the bus stop without a touch of the brakes. It's the way people drive when there is a shortage, a war, a tightening belt. Quickly more people wedge on and the tubercular engine coughs into new life. As it pulls away I notice the slick tires and the way the rear of the bus lists to starboard under the cumulative weight of years of people jammed near the door.

A half hour later I find the yogurt stand. An old woman, bent round and wrinkled like an orange peel left in the sun, stands behind the cart, a scarf over her head, a white apron tied across her large front, which must be mostly padding because the arms at the end of her jacket are brown sticks, bare and hard. A silverish glaze over her eyes makes me wonder if she is blind, or, if not, just how much she can see. I take out my piece of paper.

"*Wo yao mai wu ping. Dou shao qian?*"

Waiting for Li Ming

A torrent of Chinese comes back at me. All I can do is repeat my phrase.

She starts gesturing to the bottles. I nod vigorously, hold up my hand, five fingers. But no, that's not right, there is a different numbering system of fingers here. "*Wu ping!*" I say, gesturing to the bottles, which are made of pale ceramic, shaped like small old-fashioned milk bottles.

More torrents. Her voice rises. She is not quite looking at me, but she must know I am a foreigner. I hold out my money. "*Duo shao qian?*"

No good. Her voice gets louder. I look around. A crowd starts to form. I say my phrase again, trying to make somebody understand. An argument starts. A man beside me yells at the old woman, who yells back, shaking her hands in the air.

"*Wo yao mai wu ping. Dou shao qian?*" I yell, and pass my paper around. But it is written in pinyin, romanized Chinese, not in characters. People shake their heads. Who writes in pinyin? More arguments. The press of the crowd starts to close against my chest. Where did the air go? We are outside, but where is the air? I should just leave. We don't need yogurt. I should just go.

"Excuse . . . uh, me," and I turn and see that it is Jiang, the young man so much in love with Li Ming. "Mr. Rudy . . . be assistance?" he asks.

"Jiang, hello! Thank you!" I say. "I just want to buy five bottles of yogurt."

The crowd has gone suddenly silent, listening to me speak the foreign tongue, and Jiang nodding his head, smiling, able to understand a bit at least. He turns to the old woman and delivers two staccato blasts of Chinese, like bursts from a semiautomatic. She turns obediently, takes out the bottles, and then delivers another burst back at him.

"For . . . one bottle," he says, motioning with his fingers. "Eighty *fen*. Plus . . . uh . . . deposition . . . ah . . . thirty *fen*. One bottle . . . one *yuan*, thirty *fen*."

"You mean one *yuan* ten *fen? Yi yuan, shi fen?*"

"*Hao, hao!*" he says, smiling, nodding his head. "Sorry. One *yuan,* ten *fen.* For five bottles . . . "

We get the money sorted out and I put the bottles in my shoulder bag, hoping the tops, cardboard plugs with paper tied over them, will stay. The crowd cheers; I smile, nod, say, "*Xie xie!*" all around, especially to the old woman and to Jiang, who asks if I need more help. I tell him no, thank you.

The crowd parts for me but they do not let me disappear. I start walking towards the corner and the whole surge stays with me, watching the foreigner. Nervously I cross the street, threading my way along the crosswalk as bicycles school through, barely slowing for pedestrians. I just want to melt in, be nobody, but the crowd stays with me, a bulky shadow, nervously looking away when I look at them. I walk faster but there are too many people on the sidewalk, not enough space, nowhere to go.

"Excuse me!" Jiang says, appearing once more at my side. "Where you going?" I tell him, pointing and gesturing in the direction of the Technical Institute until he understands.

"I go with you?" he says finally. "Practise English?"

I nod my head, there being no escape, although I am tired, it is Sunday, I am not sure I have the patience for threading through the barbed wire of another second-language conversation. We walk on, struggling through the weather, where I am from, Norman Bethune the great Canadian hero.

"Take bus?" he says suddenly.

"What bus?"

"Number 21 . . . Technical Institute . . . is go there. Yes?"

"Does it?"

"I will help you!" The bus stop is over-crowded and I have no heart for it but can't seem to find a way out. I stop with Jiang and join the crowd, which is lumped along the curb like an enormous pile of sand waiting to spill over.

I ask him many questions then, and he tells me about his hometown, which turns out to be Tangshan, the city that was hit so severely by an earthquake in 1976. He acts out the walls shaking and coming down, how everyone ran around pulling people out. I think he tells me that his sister died, so I tell him that I am sorry, very sorry. He shakes his head, misunderstanding I think (or I have misunderstood), and says, "No — not your fault!"

The bus pulls in sight then and the crowd compacts in anticipation. There is no line; we are in a mass, preparing to squeeze through the two small doors. Slowly the hulk rumbles into place with the same list and balding tires as all the buses have, the doors open, and we press together against the opening so that the people getting off have to fight their way out. No one gives ground; we squirm and butt and shoulder our way on or off. Jiang, so skinny and experienced, slips several bodies ahead of me and makes it onto the steps of the bus and then is swept inside. He turns as the doors are forcing their way closed, the last arms and legs pulling in. "Hurry! Hurry!" he yells, but I wave, shake my head. "I can't make it! See you! Thank you!"

Sealed, pressure-packed, the great rolling can of people slowly pulls away and I squirm out of the crowd with this funny feeling of both relief and loneliness. I am so far from home, it seems to me. Interesting and kind-hearted as Jiang is, it's Sunday, I'm tired, I just want to be with my own kind. Kind, kynde, kin. Family. Friends.

The next bus stop is about a quarter-mile along. As I approach it I see Jiang waving to me, smiling, overjoyed. "You must be . . . more strident!" he says, coming up to me. "Try again, yes?"

"No, no. It's okay. I will walk."

"Then I walk with you!"

"No, really, it's okay. Thank you. I'm certain I can find the way."

"We have . . . free conversation. You mind?"

Suddenly, yes, I do mind, I mind very much. I can't stand having all these people around me all the time. I'm from a culture which values privacy, and anonymity, and space. I don't like being helped all the time. I'm an independent person. This is my day off! Leave me alone! The thoughts race through my mind in a torrent of bad temper which, of course, I keep to myself, swallow down, walk on. Why is it Jiang? Why not Li Ming? Why can't I just have a half-hour to myself?

We fall into step and struggle through the inevitable topics of How you like Our China? Use chopsticks? Learning speak Chinese? and Where China you visit? Unconsciously I speed up until we're almost jogging, and my stomach starts to hurt but I don't want to slow down. Unfortunately Jiang seems to have better wind than I do and there's no losing him. Down the long avenue, past the dingy grey stores, the lines of bicycle racks with the old ladies collecting two *fen* for parking, the sidewalk carts and the huge billboards which I can't read — one with a traffic policeman in a green uniform pointing a white-gloved finger, another the silhouettes of a one-daughter family walking hand in hand into the sunset, several more with pictures of electrical parts, carburetors, shiny grey dynamos. Past the sudden, comical chirping of a great flock of caged birds hidden behind blue covering cloths, their owners, almost all old men, sitting, talking, listening to a symphony like the tangle of notes from tuning instruments before the conductor arrives. Through it all Jiang sticks to my shoulder buzzing like a cicada until I am knotted inside with anger, ready to boil almost, to yell out, "Please — just leave me alone! I want to be alone! Can you understand that?"

I want to yell, am about to yell . . . and then it happens. We are out of the city now; the Technical Institute is in the distance, visible but still a quarter-hour away. "You should . . . be careful, Mr. Rudy," he says.

"What do you mean?" I ask.

"Be careful — uh, you should to be careful of . . . Li Ming."

"In what way?"

"I think — " he says. "Perhaps, uh — things different in western country."

"What things?"

"Here people — all talk," he says.

"About what?"

"If foreigner spends . . . much time . . . he and Chinese girl — "

"What do you mean? What are you saying? Are you accusing — ?"

"Just — maybe you not understand," he says. "Here . . . man and woman . . . together . . . alone . . . very serious. People talk. Very serious! Not like in western country, I think."

Then why would she come with me alone? I wonder, but do not say it, the answer dawning on me slowly in the same way that I have been so slow all along.

I say, "Thank you. Yes. I understand," and we walk on, the pieces now fitting together in a way they never seemed to when I was looking at them so hard. And then I catch Jiang looking equally hard at my face to see what thoughts might lie behind the mask I hastily try to assemble. He is someone to worry about, I realize now, someone who is watching and interested, and who would talk if there were anything to say.

12

"HELLO RUDY. I WONDER IF YOU ARE NOT BUSY NOW."

"No. No, of course not, Li Ming. Please come in."

"It is not too late?"

"No. I'm just doing a little reading. Please."

She comes in tentatively, closing the door behind her, shut-ting out the cold air. She is wearing her old cloth jacket and thick knitted mittens, very red, and a woollen hat pulled over her ears.

"Sit by the heater. Let me take your coat."

Surprisingly she gives in, sliding off her coat, shaking out her hair, settling by the two small coils of electrical warmth.

"I want to talk directly," she says, folding her hands and looking down at her shoes. "I think that is the phrase."

"About what?" I say, sitting down at my desk, off to the side of the heater.

"I am just wondering . . . if you are not happy . . . "

"What?"

"If you are . . . unhappy in some way."

"Why do you say that?"

She looks at me with frightened eyes. "You have a very hard face these days," she says.

I don't know what to say, much less how to soften my face.

"I'm fine," I say, as gently as I can. "Everything's all right. How are you?"

"Well," she says. "It does not matter how I am."

"Of course it matters how you are. Have you heard — ?"

"I do not like to think about it. If I think about it too much I feel sick in my stomach. I have heard nothing."

The curtains are open. Li Ming catches me glancing at the black glass, opaque from this side, open light from the other. Anyone could see in. The thought flickers through my mind.

"I must go," she says, rising abruptly.

"You just got here!"

"I must go," she repeats.

"Li Ming — are you in some sort of trouble?" The words leave my mouth before I have thought about them.

"No trouble," she says, shaking her head.

"Is it because of me?"

"It is nothing for you to worry about."

 Waiting for Li Ming

"What is it, Li Ming?"

Her eyes are lowered. "I must go now," she says.

"*What is it?*"

"I have many faults," she says.

"What?"

"I think only of myself. I have a very bad temper. I am proud and do not humble myself as I should. I am too ambitious and do not pay enough respect to my elders. I have thoughts that are very dangerous."

"What are you talking about? What thoughts?" I look again at the open curtains, the windows staring in like large black eyes.

"I must go now," she says, turning to the door.

I take her arm, harder than I mean. She turns abruptly and her face is taut. I let go, step back, then pull the curtains closed.

"Just tell me what we're talking about. What has happened?"

"I have been told by the leaders that I am spending too much time with you," she says, her voice thin. "So if you do not see me . . . it is not because . . . "

"What is it the leaders think?"

She looks down.

"It's not true!" I say. "You told them it's not true! *I'll* tell them! This isn't fair — I'll tell them, honestly, who should I speak to — ?"

"Rudy," she says gently, with an unexpected smile, "There is nothing we can do. Mr. Fang will take care of you. His English is getting better."

"But I won't stand for it! You're being wrongly accused of something, and I'm losing a good translator and a great friend. Honestly, Li Ming, you're the best thing about China as far as I'm concerned. If they take you away . . . "

It is just something I see in her eye, for such a short time that I am not really sure afterward if I was imagining it or not. It is not something I even want to think about, because I love her, because she is so beautiful, yes, and changeable, and trapped. But there is a moment of weakness showing, a turning, so that I know she is not fighting any more, at least not in the way she was. The authorities have blocked her; she cannot advance from within; she must stay in her little box.

Stay, or else break the box and step outside. She has nothing to lose and I am the one, perhaps, to help her lose it . . . I see it in a glance and then, as I pause to think, am unsure again.

She walks away with her shoulders rounded beneath the cold, making me want to hold her, prop her up, blow on the fires I know are inside her.

Rudy became a hermit for some weeks, writing, rewriting, thinking, rethinking, working on his academic papers when nothing more would come from his China memories for a while. He missed a writing class because he was in the middle of a section he didn't want to leave. At least that's what he told himself. The next week, when a chapter of his was up for discussion, Lou was away. Rudy was relieved and disappointed at the same time. He didn't call her afterwards. She didn't drop by. Whole days passed when he didn't speak to anyone.

Then in early December he used the department Christmas party as an excuse to leave his typewriter for a while. But the department had a strangely deserted look to it, and as he walked down the hall Rudy wondered if he had got the wrong date. He hadn't, but by being on time he could see that he was uncomfortably early. The party was in the graduate office, where streamers hung from the doorframes and walls. Most of the desks had been pushed to the sides, but three in the middle of the room formed a table for potbellied bowls holding punch and eggnog, surrounded by plates of Christmas cake and other delights. But only one other person was in the room, a burly older man with a lumberjack beard and a mouth full of chocolate fudge. He came over immediately, but his first words were lost in his chewing.

"I'm sorry," Rudy said, extending his hand. "I'm not sure we've met yet."

"Jack Creighton," the man said, finally swallowing most of the fudge in his mouth. "Linguistics."

"Ah!" Rudy said and introduced himself. With no discernible prompting Professor Creighton began a detailed description of his new book, *Linguistics in Corporate America*. It was all about trademark law, as far as Rudy could make out, and it was sprinkled with anecdotes about important cases, most of which involved corporations that didn't consult linguists before launching a new international product and then to their chagrin found their product shunned because the name meant something totally different in another language.

"It's an attempt to get linguistics out of the ivory tower," Creighton said. "I'm hoping to really popularize it. If it goes, then I could see a newspaper column come out of it, a sort of regular feature that would automatically generate a new book every few years, you see. I could call it 'Word Search' or something. I have a few trial columns written already, but I'm just waiting to see how the book does."

"So you're thinking of getting out of teaching, then?" Rudy asked.

"Oh, heavens, no!" Creighton roared. "God no! I could never get out of teaching. My life and soul is in teaching!" Rudy was not certain that he was being ironic.

He told Creighton about Li Ming and how he was hoping that she might apply for the department next year, and the professor nodded his head enthusiastically. "Yes, by all means, yes!" he nearly shouted. "I love the Chinese. I passionately love the Chinese. They have such a profound history, much more innovative, soul-inspiring than ours. When Chairman Mao died, I have to tell you, I wept, I surely did, because there was a poet statesman for the millennium, someone who seized the reins and took a poverty-stricken, crippled giant and then remade it in an image of his own soul . . . "

"But . . . " Rudy began.

"Don't tell me about the Soviet Union!"

Rudy looked at him, confused.

"I don't for a minute believe in Gorbachev and his so-called reforms. He's a very canny fellow, you know. He used to head up the KGB. I don't for a minute think that he believes in McDonald's and Coca-Cola."

Rudy cleared his throat. "No, I was thinking about — "

"He sees what's wrong with the West. He knows we're hung up on BMWs and Rolexes. The home of the throw-away camera and soup kitchens for the working poor. He's a very bright man. He's not buying into our problems. I don't believe it for a minute. You can't tell me that capitalism is working!"

Several others were arriving now, including Christopher accompanied by a young woman, tall and vaguely blonde, wearing a striking hat, black with a round flat brim cutting across the line of her eyebrows like the rings of Saturn.

"No, I think he's lulling the West while buying time to get the old hardliners out, and then he'll replace them with true socialists. Some new blood, men who are for the people, not just for themselves. The West is going to be very surprised when they see what a truly Communist country can do!"

Rudy nodded several times during the ensuing monologue, and then ducked out on the pretext of getting some eggnog, after which, without looking back, he approached Christopher and his date.

"Ah, Rudy, good fellow!" Christopher said. "I saw you trapped in the clutches of Dr. Creighton. Have you met Karla?"

"Pleased to meet you," he said, and Karla dipped her eyes, large and doelike. Karla was studying art theory. Christopher was having a hard time completing a Shakespeare paper, now eight months overdue. Christopher's friend Amanda came in alone and immediately steered away from them, her bright eyes on the furthest graduate student still in the room, the avant-garde poet Lyndon, whose yellow hair spiked like a sunburst two and a half feet above Amanda's head.

Rudy expected to see Lou somewhere. He didn't know what he was going to say to her, but part of him was on edge, waiting for that moment of meeting eyes. Karla seemed to be waiting for something as well, but for what he couldn't tell. She whispered in Christopher's ear now, he flushed, she giggled up against him, and he smiled and shook his head in some sort of happy outrage, then whispered something back.

Rudy excused himself and drifted over to Amanda. She and Lyndon were quietly discussing the abnormally cold weather.

"So you had an engaging conversation with the Hat Lady?" she said, as Rudy approached. "Oh look, she's whispering to Christopher. Look how she pastes herself to him. Oh, not too close! You could knock the brim of your hat!"

Lyndon seemed happy to stand and listen, saying little even when asked a question. He was unexpectedly gentle, given the spikes coming out of his head.

"You haven't seen Lou lately, have you?" Amanda asked.

Rudy confessed that he hadn't seen anybody lately.

"She's been in a real state, of course," Amanda said.

"Why is that?"

"Because of the news. From the doctor."

"Did something happen with Michael?"

"Well, that too, of course. They moved him out to that home in Toronto."

"Oh. I didn't know that," he said.

"A hospice for people with AIDS. It's very crowded these days. He was lucky to get in."

"I bet." Rudy sipped some eggnog. "So she was in a state about that."

"And about her pregnancy."

Rudy sputtered eggnog up his nose.

"Don't tell me you didn't know!" Amanda said.

"I didn't know."

She shook her head in delight at having been the bearer of such news and in the same motion handed him a paper napkin. Lyndon kept quiet, looking as if the conversation were still about the weather.

"When . . . when is she due?" Rudy asked.

"The middle of May," Amanda said. "She's just starting to show now. What a shock! Can you imagine — pregnant three months and she didn't even know it! You can't really tell, but she's been wearing baggy clothes lately."

"So you've talked to her?"

"Several times." Amanda nodded her head, and then her eyes roamed. "Oh, they're leaving!" she said. "So soon! The party's going to die now the Hat Lady is gone!"

Rudy watched the two of them go. Karla's arm was around Christopher's thin waist; the brim of her hat shielded her eyes, leaving a slice of high cheekbone and stray strands of blonde hair to catch the light.

"That woman reads too many *Vogue* magazines," Amanda said.

Rudy carefully sipped some more eggnog.

"You haven't asked me who the father is yet," Amanda said.

"Is it Michael?" he asked.

"Wouldn't that be horrible?" she said. "But that was over at the end of term last year. It's Gary."

"Who?"

"Her ex-husband!" she said. "Honestly, you have to keep up. They collided at the end of August. That's her word, by the way — *collided*."

Rudy continued to nod his head, but the room seemed to have tilted and be spinning. Not quickly, nothing he couldn't adjust his weight to. But moving nonetheless.

"I don't see why any of us have to read novels," Amanda said then. "I mean, really. If you just keep your eyes open, there's no need at all."

13

RUDY APPROACHED THE HOUSE CAREFULLY, AS IF COMING UPON AN area of pain and suffering where a plane has crashed or a train derailed. But actually it looked the same, still under snow but with the porch quite bright and gay even in the grey light. The walk was shovelled, a light was on inside, Oswald barked maniacally as soon as a foot pressed upon the steps.

"Rudy!" Lou said, thrusting open the door before his hand came up to knock. "Merry Christmas!" and she enveloped him in a huge, unreserved hug. "It's so nice to see you! Where have you been?"

"Nowhere," he said. She didn't look any different. But it was true, she *was* wearing a baggy dress.

Her house was warm and he was inside taking off his winter clothes before he knew what it was he wanted to say.

"So you've been working hard?" she said, taking his coat.

"Sort of."

"I liked your chapter. I'm sorry I missed the class." She paused to look at his expression. "Oh," she said. "You're angry at me."

"No," he said, standing in his sock feet.

"I meant to call you. I really did. But there was so much going on."

Rudy nodded. "Yes, I know. It doesn't matter."

"But you could have told me," she said, her voice suddenly sharp. Her hands were on her hips; Rudy wasn't sure how the moment had turned so quickly, or what exactly she was talking about.

"Told you?"

"Yes!" She was looking him straight in the eye. "You know, some things have happened to me, and I've kind of made a pact with myself that now I'm going to be very straight with people. So often, if there's something bothering me, I just go on, try to smooth things over. Whatever. But I really want to say things to people now. People I care about. Just so they know."

"What are we talking about?" Rudy asked.

"About Li Ming!" Lou said. "I've been going along thinking one thing, and then I read in your work about this great love affair and I think, oh well, it's probably just fiction, he made her up. After all, you never mentioned her to me in all the conversations we've had, some of which have been pretty personal. If there was someone he was in love with, he would have mentioned her, I was thinking. And then I talk to Amanda and she says, 'Oh, of course, it's his fiancée!' Now, maybe you're going to tell me that you just forgot about her. That would be a very male thing to do, wouldn't it? And I was thinking, that night, when you didn't . . . I was thinking, well, it must be me, I'm too old for him or something. You know?"

Rudy had no idea what to say. He had hardly said a word to Amanda. She had just asked him one time if there was a real Li Ming. Again, he had the strange feeling that the room was spinning around him.

"Come on in, have a seat, tell me," she said. "Really, I didn't mean to dump this on you. I mean when I saw you. I was happy you came by. But I was so pissed off at you!"

Rudy sat on the sofa and waited, but his head didn't clear. She was in the stuffed chair across from him, piercingly quiet.

"I . . . uh, Amanda said you were pregnant!" he blurted.

"Am, present tense. I am pregnant. What a source of knowledge that woman is!" she said.

"Well, congratulations!"

"What of it?"

"Well, it's pretty big news. Isn't it?"

"Yes it is. But we're skipping a topic here. Li Ming. Your fiancée."

Rudy told her a bit about Li Ming's circumstances, and how he would try to get her a scholarship for next year, and how hard it was to be so far apart. Lou listened intently, her hand on her chin. She looked full, flushed, beautiful. Holding a new life.

"You should be true to her," she said, matter-of-factly, when he was finished. "People should be true to one another. It's taken me a long time to figure that out. But if you're true then things will work out well. If not, then you'll end up like me."

Rudy nodded impartially.

"I don't mean knocked up, or anything. I suppose Amanda told you how it happened?"

"She mentioned a collision."

Lou laughed. "That's a good way to describe it! Gary and I collide every so often. I haven't told him yet. I haven't even told my mother yet. Although I did tell Amanda, so probably everyone knows by now anyway. Do you still do foot rubs?"

"Yes," Rudy said.

"That's great," she said, sliding over to the sofa, "because I really need one. I don't know if it's the hormones or what, but my legs get really sore, even when I'm not doing anything."

Rudy rubbed his hands together to warm them, then took her right foot and ran his thumb strongly along the arch. She was wearing thick blue knee socks, which he didn't bother taking off, and a corduroy dress which was smoothed over her legs.

"So . . . when did you find out?" he asked.

"About what?"

"About being pregnant!"

"Oh that," she said. She was lying back with her eyes closed, concentrating on the rub. "Do you do tickles too?"

"Sure," he said.

"That's good, because I need a lot of rubs and tickles. If I'm going to go through with this all on my own, which it looks like

I will. I mean I will, and it looks like I'm going to be on my own. So I'm going to lean on my friends."

"Any time," Rudy said. Oswald made an appearance then, coming by to bark and lick at Lou's hand, which was hanging down by the carpeted floor. Lou picked him up and tussled with him, shaking his ears and shoulders. Then she put him down again and he sniffed at Rudy, then scooted off.

"When did I find out?" she said, remembering his question. "It seems like months ago. But it's just been a few weeks, I guess. I was feeling shitty, and I thought, God, I really do have AIDS, that test just didn't find it. You know how that feeling is? I guess you don't. I was getting sick and I felt so tired and it had been so long since my period and my legs ached — I have a very irregular period . . . yes, oh good. That's nice."

Rudy was squeezing her calf, rubbing her tendon.

"So I went back to my doctor. Oh God, Rudy, I was just in tears. You can imagine it. There I am holding myself together in the waiting room, looking around at everything — the cheap prints of snowy rural scenes on the wall, the year-old *Chatelaines*, the mother with three snotty kids just trying to keep her eyelids open, she's so tired. And I'm thinking this is it. I'm going to die. I'm going to shrivel and die like Michael, and it's already started happening, and I'm thirty-five and I haven't even done anything! He was forty minutes late, Rudy, and I was getting worse and worse, and when my name was finally called I just sort of sobbed once and then got hold of myself, until I was in his office, when I fell apart completely. Weeping on his desk, honestly, it must have been fifteen minutes before I could even tell him what was wrong."

He was rubbing her knee now, above the sock, gently under the thick fabric of her dress. He kept his eyes on her face, which was expressive even though she told the story with her eyes closed.

"My doctor — Doctor Dunsworth — is a bear. He has a black beard and thick black hair and you can see that he has to shave his neck right down to his chest to hack back the growth. Anyway, the poor man, he probably gets one hysterical female a day. Maybe he gets one hysterical male a day, too, I don't know. But he has ten minutes to spend with a patient and there I am sobbing on his desk, and he keeps checking his watch to see how long I'm going to go on, and asking questions and patting my back and looking at his watch again. Finally, bit by bit he gets the information out of me, and I tell him I'm absolutely positive I have AIDS, and he says, 'But you tested negative,' in this patronizing, dismissive way, and then he says, 'Why don't you have a pregnancy test?'"

Rudy started to move back down but she said, "Oh, the thigh, you have to rub the thigh. Give it a good squeeze. Yes! Oh, yes!"

Rudy was very happy to rub the thigh. The only problem with the thigh, though, was that it led upwards. He watched her closed eyes as he rubbed, wondering if her signals were really as crossed as he imagined. Be true to Li Ming? Rub my thigh? Physically it would have been very easy to slip his hand a few inches further. He wasn't sure which way he wanted the hand to go; nor was he sure that *she* knew which way she wanted it to go either. He scanned her face but she was inscrutable . . . or was she just distracted?

"I gave myself the test the next morning," she said. "You can buy them at the drugstore. The little swab thing turned blue. I didn't believe it. So I waited a whole extra day — you have to get the urine first thing in the morning — and then I tried it again and it turned even bluer. The writing class I missed was that afternoon."

Reluctantly, Rudy retreated and moved to the other leg, scanning her face still for some sort of sign. Was she disappointed? Relieved? A bit of both? Or had she even noticed? He stayed below the knee on this leg and she didn't say anything one way or the other, and in a while he was feeling both uneasy and comfortable at the same time — uneasy because he was so comfortable, touching this woman in so familiar a way. This must be what it's like to be married, he thought. You sit on the couch and rub her feet and talk and the time slips by.

"How are you going to . . . support a child?" Rudy asked.

"You know," she said, opening her eyes and sitting up, but being careful not to draw her feet out of his grasp, "I've hardly even thought about that. Amanda asked me, when I told her, if I was going to keep the child, and I said yes, of course, as if there was no question about it. I mean, I've had an abortion before — I was seventeen, it was a very bad scene, I left home right after. That was like a different life. But this time, I don't know, I just thought, this might be my last chance. Or I felt that. I know I didn't *say* that to myself, but — I guess it's what I'm feeling. My marriage busted up and my life is rocky to put it nicely but I want a kid, and if I don't have this one, there might not be another chance. How I'll do it — well, day by day, I guess. I don't know. I just feel inside that this is the right decision."

The sadness in her voice reminded Rudy of something he had forgotten about. "Last year I used to ride out to the Technical Institute," he said, "a beautiful, big university on the outskirts of my town. I had some friends there who were teaching English, other Westerners. Anyway, in the middle of the winter a baby girl was left in a box by the bus stop outside the university gates. Nobody would take her. She froze to death. The Western teachers heard about it and asked what was going on — why did nobody even take her to an orphanage? Well, nobody wanted to be responsible. They have a One Child Policy. Everybody wants a son, and if you pick up somebody else's abandoned baby girl, then you've lost your own opportunity. People just looked the other way."

"There are so many couples here who would love to adopt a Chinese girl," Lou said.

"It's extremely hard to do. You have to live there for two years before you can apply."

"But they've got so many people. Why is it so hard?"

"I don't know," Rudy said. "That's the thing about China. There's so much you just don't know."

"If I was in this position in China — I mean if I was a single mother, how would I be treated?"

Rudy thought about it. It was warm on the couch; it felt good to look out the window at the snow. "You wouldn't be in this position in China," he said. "You would routinely have an abortion. It would be too difficult for a single mother, there would be tremendous pressure from the family and the state to get rid of it. Or you would still be married. You might not live in the same town as your husband. In fact, you might only see each other every couple of years. Maybe that would make it more bearable. How is your family going to react to this?"

"It's going to take a bit of gentle dealing to tell my mother," Lou said, shaking her head. "She already entirely disapproves of my lifestyle."

"And your father?"

"Oh God, he skipped off long ago. I have no idea where he is and probably wouldn't recognize him unless he introduced himself. If he could recognize me."

"That must feel strange," Rudy said.

"The strange thing is I feel like I'm on this ride. All these bizarre things happen, but . . . the ride just keeps on going, you know? We get in such stupid corners . . . but then we go on. My abortion happened seventeen years ago. Almost another lifetime. My father left — God, he could have abandoned several whole other families by now. Or maybe he's settled down. Maybe he's a model guy. Who knows? But the ride keeps going. If you wait, something else comes up. We make do."

"Now you're sounding very Chinese," Rudy said.

"How's that?"

"They're a people who make do. Through revolutions, floods, famines, earthquakes, more political disturbances than we can contemplate. They make do. They simply dig out of the rubble and keep going."

The sunlight slowly faded from the window. Lou told about her mother, who raised the three children on her own while working as a teacher, and how she hated retirement now, never having had the time before to develop hobbies or new interests, just worked and raised her family, all day, every day.

"So what she does now — she calls us up on the phone. Constantly. She develops these little stratagems, these reasons why she absolutely must talk to us right this instant. Like this morning she called to ask me if it was the law now that you have to have photos for your driver's licence. So I said — 'I think so. I have *my* picture on my licence. But why don't you just phone up the Ministry of Transportation?' It took fifteen minutes to get through that conversation, and then she had to tell me everything that David is doing. David — my brother — escaped to Uranium City, which means he only gets called twice a week instead of every day. The next thing I know I've been on the phone for half an hour, and I haven't even brushed my hair yet!"

Lou asked about Rudy's family, and he thought a moment before answering. "When I was little," he said, "I thought my father was the tallest, strongest, bravest man in the world. And my mother was the kindest, gentlest, most beautiful lady, and they had this love that was going to last forever."

"And then you grew up," Lou said.

"And then I grew up, but . . . she's still the most beautiful lady, and he's still strong and brave and certainly taller than me. They go all over the world together; they really are great companions, and tremendously in love. I never . . . got disillusioned with my parents."

"That must be why you're so disturbingly well-adjusted," Lou said, giving him a little kick. "Especially for a writer."

Later on Lou heated up some old spaghetti and they ate together in the small kitchen, the overhead light reflecting brightly off the yellow walls. Again Rudy had the strange feeling of being uneasily comfortable, sharing a meal — a home-cooked, leftover meal — with this woman, and talking and being together as if they had a long history, a shared life.

"What do your parents think about Li Ming?" Lou asked, near the end of the meal.

"They don't know yet," he said.

"Don't know what?"

"Anything," he said, wiping his mouth with the paper towel that served as a napkin.

"They don't even know there is a Li Ming?"

"I've told them about my wonderful translator, sure. They know the name. But I guess I've been waiting before I hit them with any sort of bombshell."

"Waiting until she's here and you're married, you mean?"

"No," he said, choosing his words carefully. "I am waiting . . . until . . . I hear from her, I guess."

"Until you hear from her?"

Rudy nodded.

"You haven't heard from her?"

Rudy shook his head. "The last time I saw her was May."

"And you haven't written?"

"I've been writing constantly. I just don't have an address for her."

"And she hasn't written you?"

"No."

She looked as if she wasn't sure what she was hearing and didn't quite know if she should ask.

"You see . . . I'm pretty sure we decided to get married," he said. "But events . . . ran ahead of us, I guess. She was sent away, and we didn't get a chance to talk. But she wrote me a note, said she had my parents' address and asked me to wait for her. So that's what I'm doing."

Lou nodded. "How long are you going to wait?" she asked.

Rudy concentrated on his spaghetti. "I don't know," he said

finally. "But, anyway, about my parents, what I'm trying to do with this book is use it to explain to them . . . properly . . . how our love came to be. I want them to read it, and then they'll know."

"I'm sure you could write it in a letter and save a lot of time," Lou said.

Rudy scraped the last of the sauce onto his fork and finished it off. "You're probably right," he said. "But . . . the other thing I'm trying to do . . . is get my parents to approve of . . . my choice of careers."

"Writing?"

"Yes. Nearly everybody in my family is a lawyer. My cousins, my sister, my father, his father. It goes way back. Except for my father's younger brother, the sort-of actor. The biggest part he ever had was on a toothpaste commercial, in which he played, ironically, a family man, dressed in a suit, trying to brush his teeth while the teenage daughter is rushing in and out and the son is playing rock music and his wife comes in with curlers in her hair. It played for about ten months in the early seventies. I was famous for a while in my school, because that was my Uncle Lorne who always got toothpaste on his tie when the dog jumped up on him. It was the only time in his adult life Uncle Lorne ever wore a tie. To hear my father tell it, anyway."

"So what's the point?"

"The point is . . . I can't just announce to my family . . . that I *want to be* a writer. I want to present a manuscript, and have them read it and be moved by it, and then I'll be able to say, I *am* a writer. And I only have this year to do it."

"You don't put much pressure on yourself, do you?" Lou said. Rudy shrugged his shoulders. "I guess you don't," she said, pushing her plate aside. And as they continued to talk it occurred to him again how natural he felt, sitting in this woman's kitchen, eating her food, sharing their common life.

"I wonder," he said, later, over coffee, sitting back and feeling warm and tired.

"What?"

"Are you going to go to those classes where they teach you how to breathe and exercise and stay calm? Childbirth classes."

"I haven't really thought about it."

"If you do," he said, "I wonder . . . maybe you'd like someone to go with you. I mean as your partner. To help you through."

"To help me through the classes or the birth?" she asked, smiling.

"Both, I guess," he said. The request was out so quickly, and then it was lying on the table for both of them to examine. It would be a good experience, he thought of saying, but didn't. "I don't mean . . . I'm not . . . ," he said, struggling, and then she was laughing, and he was laughing too.

"You mean you don't want to marry me?" she said. "An instant family could be going cheap!"

"That's not what I meant," he said, smiling, trying to back out but not trying to either. "I mean . . . you know what I mean. As a friend."

She took a long moment to clear the giggles, and then drank some more coffee and looked at him seriously and started to laugh again.

"Rudy Seaborn . . . I would be honoured," she said, reaching across and squeezing his hand.

It was a sisterly sort of gesture, and he looked at her in a brotherly sort of way, and then in his mind he saw her clothes peeling off slowly, her fresh warm skin emerging and her hair shaking down around her shoulders and the patch of deep black between her thighs — or would it be red? — and the heaviness of her breasts. He bathed in the reverie for a moment and then he looked down at the table abruptly, as if there were something there that needed attention, quickly, before it got out of hand.

14

DOWN THE BACK ALLEY, A DIRT ROAD WITH THE RIVERS OF MELTING snow carving channels along the cart ruts. Women out scrubbing laundry by the pump. Talking away, their hands raw red, not even noticing me as I walk by with my hood up against the drizzle. A young man splashes past on a motor scooter, too noisy, drowning out the bicycle bells. A little girl with a brilliant red bow in her hair, sitting in the doorway of a little stone house, printing something in a notebook. Lips pursed, not looking up, feet set at resolute angles, the notebook on her lap. Her shoulder hunched over it to keep off the rain.

A chicken ranges by another doorway, tied on a string. A huge pig looks up, grunts as I walk by. A grandfather sits smoking a pipe. Grey sky; brown puddles; the syrupy strains of "Auld Lang Syne" come from the college loudspeaker, on the other side of the high wall that separates the worlds. The intellectuals and the peasants. The students and the masses. The college and the back alley.

Out now into the countryside, my leather boots splashing in the puddles. It's late afternoon. The electricity is off; my apartment is a clammy cave until after six, when the power comes back on. So I am best to take some air. My teacher Wang has stopped our lessons for now, until the better weather comes. The three hundred and ninety movements of the *liu he ba fa* spin in my mind, little sequences spilling out from time to time. I have to practise it every day, make sure it does not get lost. He said he would come back in the spring and teach me more, but only if I remembered and perfected what he has taught so far.

I'm not really sure where I'm going, but my feet take me past the zoo and towards the high hill at the curve in the country road, where Li Ming and I went before. I don't know why I go there, in this cold rain; it's far out of my way, a much longer walk than I need to fill the time until the power is restored. But it reminds me of something that we shared, makes me feel maybe a little closer. I can imagine her with me, walking quietly, not saying anything, but we are relaxed and sharing the feel of the road beneath our feet, and the cold kiss of the mist and, as we enter the woods, the cool dark shadows of the cedar trees, all the same height, the forest floor beneath picked clean of firewood and herbs, anything useful.

I notice a bicycle leaning in the shadows just off the road where Li Ming and I parked ours that time before. I take a look: black, stubby, the carrying rack over the rear fender. It could be any one of a billion. And yet, it looks like hers. My heart gives a leap. It looks like hers; it must be hers; she must be here.

It's amazing how quickly the thought crystallizes. In an instant I'm absolutely certain that she is here, up on the hill. And then as I start walking again, up the stone steps of the steep slope, the certainty melts. The coincidence would be too great. But perhaps, because we came here together — or am I just wishing? Anyway, why would we both choose such a dismal day, and so late? And yet as I climb I become more and more curious to see who it is who parked the bike at the base of the hill. Somebody is up here on a terrible day. Why couldn't it be Li Ming? Why couldn't we both have the same unconscious thought at the same time?

It's nearly dark when I turn the corner and round the last slope that leads to the top. In the distance, against a purpling sky, the outline of the abandoned concrete building, three walls, no roof, windows hollow. I stop. Silence. I wait until my breathing slows from the climb, but my heart keeps racing. This is not the time to be here. Someone else is here, but it is not Li Ming. I have made a terrible mistake. I try to relax, to calm myself, to turn slowly and become water and flow very softly and quietly back down.

It's not dark enough for stars. There's no moon. I stop, listen. Still no sound. Someone is up here but there is no sound. I feel utterly alone perched on the side of this steep hill, face smack against the universe. The city is down below; the college, I can see in the corner of my vision, past the trees, is now lit for the evening, until ten o'clock when the lights in the academic buildings are all shut off. I've been in the Foreign Languages Department when that happened — one moment there was a party for National Day and the next it was as black as the universe and we were feeling our way out of the concrete cave, down the steep stairs, our steps and voices and nervous laughter echoing along the corridors.

I leave the trail, walk softly into the woods with *wushu* steps light and hollow and soundless, feeling the ground intimately with my feet, working my way slowly over the round of the hill. There, to the left, something catches my eye. I walk towards it. A clearing . . . what is it? I have to get closer. A concrete cylinder perched against the side of the hill, and there, some kind of turret . . . of course, a pillbox from the war, like the one on the other side that Li Ming and I sat on that time, but more private, sheltered. From here there is an uninterrupted view of the whole valley. I step on top and sit cross-legged on the cold concrete, the tail of my jacket tucked under against the wet, and look out over the valley where there are no armies now, no tanks, no artillery, no men about to be ploughed back into the soil. Then, from far below, finally a sound — the roaring of the lion from the darkened zoo. It's not a brave sound at all, but mournful, tired, old. Just the one loud moan, as if that is all he is allowed, and then silence again.

Slowly the stars come out. Not many, but one or two pricking through the cloud cover. And then the moon, suddenly emerging from behind a wall, full, bright, huge and cold. From my perch it seems exceptionally close; I think I can see craters, wrinkles, the old wounds of rock. It seems impossibly bright, and yet when I look away the rest of the world is in darkness.

It seems I stay a very long time, but perhaps it is only a quarter hour. I try to imagine the big guns pounding out of the concrete bunker below me, but tonight the stillness is so complete it's hard to believe it has not always been that way. I don't know what has led me here, either, but I cannot believe I have come by chance. It feels like a spot of great power, of magic. One that is very hard to leave.

When I do finally stretch out my legs and climb down, I notice, in an eerie half-shadow of the moon, that the iron door to the pillbox is closed but not locked. I test it with my fingers, feel it give way, pull a little harder. It creaks and moves several inches. I push it back closed. If there are ghosts inside, I have no urge to know them.

Suddenly I am cold and tired and hungry; it's late and I'm a long way from home. I stumble clumsily back through the woods, breaking branches with my feet, catching the slap of cedar boughs in my face, stumbling several times over unseen slippery rocks. I scramble up a slope of loose rocks and then am back on the trail, which I descend recklessly with long jolting strides. My breath comes out harsh, loud, ragged; there is no pretence any more of being quiet. I just want to be down, off the mountain, back home in my concrete room.

At the bottom, finally, the ground solid beneath my feet. I feel calmer, walk with less commotion through the stretch of clean forest that leads to the road. When I get to the edge I pause, turn, check. The bicycle is gone.

On my long walk back the moon slides behind its curtain; the clouds become grey; the night seems lighter than it was. I hear no animal sounds as I pass the tired zoo; I'm too tired and hungry and cold myself to take much notice of the life in the back alley that runs alongside the college for perhaps a quarter mile. It's a relief to return to the front gate, to re-enter the safe compound, to cut across the empty, black basketball courts and climb the small hill. I fumble for my key and switch on the lights and turn on my little heater, feel the glowing warmth of home.

When I have warmed up I cross my little compound and collect the dinner that has been waiting for me all evening, now cold. *Jiaozi*, triangles of spiced meat and vegetables wrapped in a delicious pastry, then boiled. I bring them back to my apartment and rest them on top of the heater, pouring some hot water from my thermos into the bowl. A large stack of marking waits for me on my desk. There are two letters to reply to, three magazines sent on by my mother to read, and an unread three-day old issue of *China Daily*. I dip my chopsticks into the bowl of now lukewarm *jiaozi*, savour the melt of juices in my mouth, pray that no one comes to my door tonight. It's too late for that anyway. Already the ping-pong players above have packed it in.

I don't know why I choose the *China Daily*. The marking should be done for tomorrow; the magazines have more direct news of home; I have a yearning to write a good letter. But I choose the newspaper and her note falls out immediately, nearly drowning in the *jiaozi* bowl before I fish it out. It is folded and taped, with my name, *Rudy*, written on the front in her small, compressed, mature hand. Gently I take out my pocket knife and cut it open. *I will knock on your window tonight. If you do not want to see me, do nothing. Li Ming.*

I sit up late marking, then read the magazines till my eyes turn red and drowsy and cannot focus any more on the small print and tire even of looking at the pictures. Finally I turn off the light and heater and sit still on the sofa, looking out the window at the grey night, remembering Madeleine's advice and my promise. But maybe this has nothing to do with what I might feel. Maybe I'm fooling myself.

There are bars in the windows. I don't know why it has taken so long for me to notice them. Bars. As if I were living in New York City. In the darkness, the sound of water dripping somewhere. A slight wind, rattling something across the compound. The door. Rattling the door of my dining room. I can just make it out, as my eyes adjust.

It occurs to me that, like that character in Henry James's story "The Beast in the Jungle," I've spent most of my life waiting for something to happen, waiting for whatever it is that is finally going to happen. Now I'm on the other side of the world, all alone in the dark, tired, still waiting. But something *is* going to happen. Finally.

In my mind I go through the movements of the *liu he ba fa*. The opening, standing still, then easing my weight over to the right foot and sinking down, the left foot sliding over, and the hands coming up and turning, then waving right and left, and the left hand sliding under the right and both hands pulling back, winding in a huge circle . . .

Her knock is gentle, timid, but when I hear it my eyes jerk open as if an alarm has gone off. Her shadow in the doorway. I get up clumsily, make too much noise opening the door, her eyes find mine, startled. "Li Ming!" I whisper and she slides in. She is cloaked, hidden, small. I take her arm and guide her the two steps across the dark room to the sofa, and she sits down and her hand brushes mine and feels cold.

"Here, I'll turn on the heater," I whisper.

"No," she says. "It will make a light."

"I'll close the drapes." I get up, pull them closed, feel disoriented in the total blackness. Somehow I fumble back to the other side, find the switch. In a few seconds the coils reluctantly awaken, first a faint glow, and then stronger, bright orange. Li Ming holds out her hands, her face magical in the soft light.

"I almost did not come," she says.

I sit beside her, and we both look into the glow which makes the surrounding darkness even deeper.

"What's happened, Li Ming?"

"I cannot go to the conference," she says, her voice flat, her eyes still locked on the coils.

"It's been decided?"

"The leaders told me this afternoon." Her voice is thin, unemotional. She pulls back her hands a bit from the heat.

"I'm very sorry to hear that."

"It also means," she says, "that I will not be able to study in America next year."

"What?"

She nods her head, still not looking at me.

"I didn't know you were going to study in the States."

"I got a letter from Columbia University just last week. I have a fellowship to study for my PhD. Almost $20,000. But if I cannot go to a conference, it will be impossible to go abroad."

"You got a fellowship to Columbia? My God, Li Ming. Don't give up!"

"I have got to give up!" she says. "There is no way I can win. That is what the leaders have been telling me. I must accept it. If I fight hard again and lose, I will crack."

I don't know what to say. We fall into silence. I feel the moment spinning out beyond me.

"Columbia University is one of the best in the States," I say. "It would be a great honour for the college if you got your PhD from there."

She sits a long time, staring into the heat, warming her hands, not saying anything. It occurs to me that she is very close now to "cracking," as she says. Outwardly she looks the same as always, and there are no tears, the waters seem calm. But one more breath of wind will knock her over.

"Nothing in my life will work," she says.

About a thousand things occur to me to say, about being strong, about pride and dignity and all those noble qualities that are so easy to have when it is not you who is face down in the mud. But who am I to lecture this woman who has been through so much and always kept a straight back, a controlled face, a steady heart?

So I stay quiet and instead put my arm around her and we lean back together on the sofa, her face buried now in my chest, her legs curled up like a cat's. As softly as I can I run my hand along her hair and the side of her cheek. Her eyes close, she relaxes against me in either exhaustion or resignation, or perhaps both. It is our first physical contact, but there is nothing nervous, nothing strained about it, and it says a great deal more than any words I can think of.

In just a few minutes she is asleep, and in the same few minutes I become more fully awake, feeling her soft breath on my arm, and the heat of her against me, the occasional, sudden shudder that runs through her like a gust of wind rippling a calm bay. In the warm glow of the heater I study her beautiful, still face, with the strong, dark brows and the small nose and the high cheekbones, framed by the black of her hair.

I try to fill my senses with the moment, feeling at once as if everything has changed and yet it's all so familiar, too. Comforting. Outside the world is cold and cruel, but here, inside, there is just . . . the smell of her, the slight scent of jasmine, the same smell that greeted me so deliciously in a Hong Kong taxi the night I arrived so long ago in the rain and storm. A hundred dollar smell. For some reason it seems overwhelming. I want to laugh and have to still myself to keep from waking her up.

She sleeps against me, as still and lovely as any baby, and I stroke her hair and drift between dreams, awake and asleep, until I notice in a chink between the drapes the first timid approach of dawn, and then gently I nudge her awake. She curls even more against me, and then opens her eyes, a little startled at first, then slowly remembering.

"You should be going, Li Ming," I whisper.

She nods, looks down, I slide my arm away and shake it, slowly, reviving the circulation. There is a moment of embarrassment, as if we are both afraid the other is going to say something. She sits up, wipes her eyes, runs a hand through her hair.

"Will you meet me this afternoon?" I ask. "On top of that big hill where we went before. At four o'clock?"

She nods silently, getting up a little dazed. I walk her to the door, out of the heater's orange penumbra of heat and into the cold air of the rest of the world.

"Be careful, Li Ming," I say as she slips out the door, half turning back, but not looking me in the eye.

15

AFTER CHRISTMAS THE TRAIN BACK TO BELLSBRIDGE WAS INTERminably slow. For a while Rudy didn't think it was ever going to arrive; he was convinced that they would continue indefinitely creeping along at ten or fifteen kilometres an hour and then stopping for up to three-quarters of an hour in some deserted spot of blizzard while everyone looked at their watches and wondered why they hadn't taken the bus.

But for Rudy this train ride had begun as soon as he had stepped off the train in Ottawa the week before. His parents had been there at the station to pick him up, both unsuitably tanned for late December since they had come back from a conference in Jamaica just the week before. There had been hugs and hellos and quick, lively banter in the car, and then somewhere on Alta Vista Drive his mother had turned back to him from the front seat and said, "Did you get that letter from China that I sent on?" and Rudy's heart boomed in his chest like a series of underwater explosions that don't show on the surface but send shock waves racing underneath.

"No," he said casually. "When did it come?"

"Just the other day," she said. "I suppose you wouldn't have got it yet. I should have just held on to it. But it will be waiting for you when you go back."

"Probably just a Christmas card from one of my students," he said, and then the whole of Christmas week he could think of nothing else. He thought of phoning his landlady and having her just check to see if it had arrived; or maybe she could read it to him over the phone. But then again, if it were from Li Ming he didn't want anyone else reading it. It would wait. He could wait. Somehow.

But now that the wait was nearly over the train was slowing with every mile and he wasn't sure he *could* wait. For some reason the air got worse; there was a spillover from the smoking section that made him feel as if he was in China again. After three more unscheduled stops the snow outside intensified. When the train finally got in at ten o'clock, three hours late, there were no taxis at the station, so Rudy hiked in through the driving snow. It didn't matter. There was only one thing that he wanted and he would have walked through rock to get it. He leaned into the wind on Bridge Street, squinting his eyes, and fought his way over the bridge, and then with the turn it wasn't so bad, and in a few minutes he was there, pushing open the front door of the apartment building and shaking the snow off his clothes and pack.

In a few seconds my life is going to change, he told himself as he slowly, calmly now, fished through his pockets for his mailbox key. If she really loves me, for myself, then I'll know from this letter. If she doesn't, if I was just a way out of a box, then I'll know that too. One way or the other, I'll know in just a moment.

The mail slot was jammed with Christmas advertisements but it didn't matter because he saw her letter almost immediately, the bluish air mail envelope with the red and blue stripes around the edges and the Par Avion in the corner, the Chinese characters on top. And there was his name and Ottawa address, in her clean, precise handwriting, just as neatly stroked out by his mother and replaced with the Bellsbridge address.

The return address on the back surprised him. Beijing Agricultural and Technical Institute. She had not bothered to write her own name. But why had she gone to Beijing? He had thought perhaps she had been sent to a school in the countryside. But didn't she mention once that she had an uncle in Beijing?

The letter, no doubt, would explain everything. Suddenly he felt no hurry at all, now that he had her letter in his hand. He carried it down the stairs, opened the door and walked into his dark apartment, placing the letter on the kitchen table while he set down his pack and took off his overcoat and boots. He was excited but a little fearful, too. There were so many things she could say. It was beyond his control. He would just have to open it.

After something hot. He put on the water for tea and looked through the cupboards for the last of some old crackers and biscuits. It was really a light envelope. The Chinese paper was so thin. He picked it up and for the first time noticed a tiny cut that had been made in the top right-hand corner, beside the stamps with the classical Guilin paintings on them. Green towers of rock. He put his thumb in the slit but stopped and went to the kettle, which had started boiling. Before he got back to the letter the phone rang.

Waiting for Li Ming

It was Lou, whose sparkling voice was full of news that Rudy could not quite concentrate on. She started telling him a story about a horrible birth that had been described to her during the holidays by a well-meaning relative who usually is a very sweet person. Rudy didn't quite follow it, something about a forty-seven hour labour and then an episiotomy that required nineteen stitches and still got infected afterwards. He had picked up the envelope again and was just looking at it, her neat lettering, a tiny packet of heartbeats from the other side of the world.

"What's an episiotomy?" he asked. She told him. "Oh fuck!" he said.

"I know. Isn't it gross?"

"I don't fucking believe it!" he said.

"Well, that's just one of the things we are going to be learning about in our birthing classes . . . "

"*Those goddamn fucking bastards!*"

"Rudy?"

"Listen . . . oh, I don't believe this!" he said.

"It's actually pretty routine," Lou said.

"There's nothing in the envelope!" Rudy cried.

"What envelope?"

"There's a letter here from Li Ming. It's the first and only one I've got, but there's nothing in it. It's empty. Christ!"

"She sent you an empty envelope?"

"It's the fucking Public Security Bureau! They put a slit in the corner of the envelope and somehow took the letter out."

"But why would they send on an empty envelope?"

"Because they're fucking bureaucrats!"

"But what does this mean?"

"It means they're reading her mail. Shit! I have to go, all right?"

Rudy sat staring for a long time at the empty envelope. He took out her last note and read it over again. *I am being sent away. I have to go tonight. I have your address. Wait for me!* He remembered that night at the train station, the anger, how frantic he was and helpless in a foreign country. They could just make her disappear.

But maybe not. At least now he had her address, and there was something he could do. The next day, Rudy went to the University Centre as soon as it opened and made twenty photocopies of the application for graduate studies, and twenty copies of a short, impersonal letter he had written Li Ming for the authorities to read when they opened her mail. Then he made twenty separate packages so that every second or third day for the next few months he could send one of them off to the Beijing Agriculture and Technical Institute. In the note he asked her to write or phone collect if she had any questions. The postmark on her envelope was December third, 1988; probably she had sent several letters before that and they had been intercepted. Maybe it was just luck that the envelope had slipped through. So maybe one of his packages to her would slip through as well.

He thought of getting on the phone and trying to scare up a number for the Agriculture and Technical Institute, but he realized it would be hopeless. But he did send one of the packages to the Canadian Embassy in Beijing, asking the High Commissioner if he could have the package delivered to Li Ming.

And he thought of going himself, of flying in and finding her and doing whatever it took to marry her and bring her home. But all he had to do was remember that horrible night in the Laozhou train station when she had gone and all he had was a note and his anger and no language. China is not a place you take by storm. So he knew that mainly what he had to do was wait, and trust that time and love and whatever else was on their side would see them through.

Meanwhile, the first childbirth education class was held in the library of a public school over a mile from the university. Rudy suggested that they take a taxi but Lou insisted that they walk. It was bitterly cold and icy, and after forty-five minutes at a brisk pace it became clear that Rudy had gotten them lost on the darkened back streets.

"I thought you looked at the map?" Lou said.

"I did."

"Well, let's look again!"

He would have certainly taken another look if he had brought the map; instead he emphasized that the school must be just up ahead, perhaps in the next block. They walked another quarter hour before Lou spoke up again.

"We should have hit it by now, don't you think?"

"I'm sure it's just up here," Rudy said.

"You've been sure for a long time. Maybe we should ask somebody."

Rudy kept walking and looking at the street signs. The school was at the corner of Melbourne and Northampton. They were currently walking along something called Briarpath.

"Why don't you ask somebody?" Lou asked again, in an overly reasonable tone of voice.

"I would if there was somebody to ask."

"You're thinking that this is all my fault, aren't you?"

"Not at all," Rudy said in his own too-reasonable voice.

"If we had called a taxi we would have been there already."

"I'm not thinking that."

"Yes you are. Admit it!"

"*You* are the one who is thinking it, not me! *You* brought it up."

"Well, I thought it would be nice to get a bit of air and some exercise," she said.

"I know."

They were stopped now at some corner; the street sign was frozen over and illegible.

"I thought I should take the opportunity to exercise while I still can."

"I know. It's a perfectly reasonable idea," Rudy said.

"But you think it's really stupid. You think we should have taken a taxi! But if you had read the stupid map right . . . and now you won't even ask anybody for directions . . . !"

She was crying. Rudy could hardly believe it. He didn't know what to do.

" . . . and you think it's all my fault, but it isn't! It's *your* fault! And now we're going to be so late!"

"I'm sorry," Rudy said, holding her. It was so cold some of the tears were starting to freeze against her cheeks. He rubbed her back with his heavy mitts and turned so that he was shielding her from the wind. "It's okay. I'm sorry. It's okay."

They were twenty minutes late. Rudy knocked on a door and got directions from a stern-looking man holding a pipe who kept gazing over Rudy's shoulder and down the walk at Lou, who was still sniffling. When they finally found the right spot, and a door that would open, and then barged into the little library where the class was being held, fifteen other couples turned to look at them. Rudy took Lou's arm anxiously but she seemed fine by then, confident, winning. The instructor, a bright, solid mother of three in her mid-thirties, accepted the late-comers graciously, finding extra chairs, passing out the papers they had missed, making an easing comment about the difficulties of the weather.

Rudy helped Lou off with her coat and into her chair, then took off his own coat and settled himself as quickly as he could. The instructor went on with what she was saying, but Rudy missed several sentences as he took in the surroundings. He felt a tremendous sense of déjà vu looking at the tiny tables and chairs, the stacks of children's books, the audio-visual corner, and especially the long narrow panels of green poster running along one wall, up high near the juncture with the ceiling, with the familiar stylish, curling handwritten letters running from A to Z in lower and upper cases. He remembered sitting at one of those little desks, staring up at exactly that set of letters, the thick pencil clumsy between his fingers, as he tried to copy them *and* stay between the lines *and* avoid the wood chunks lodged like stumps in the rough paper of his notebook.

Rudy turned his attention to the other couples, whose curiosity about the late arrivals had gradually subsided. They all seemed older, the men with thinning hair and married-looking middles, the women almost all appearing to be around Lou's age. Only a few of them were obviously pregnant, but most were wearing maternity clothes — loose, motherly blouses which were not to be tucked in, long waistless dresses in delicate, old-fashioned prints, warm leggings under loose skirts instead of pants. They all looked married, too. He glanced over at Lou, who looked back at him and squeezed his hand briefly. It was a married sort of gesture.

"The thing I want to emphasize," the instructor was saying, "not only in this class but throughout the course, is that childbirth is a natural process. You are not sick. You are healthy, you are participating in one of the most magnificent natural events of a lifetime. So don't let your doctor or the hospital treat you as though you are ill. You don't *have* to have Caesarean sections; you don't *have* to have episiotomies; you don't even *have* to have epidurals if you don't want them."

Rudy leaned over to Lou. "What's an epidural?" he whispered.

"Do you have a question?" the instructor asked him. She was flushed from her speech, in full rhetorical stride, but smiling openly, as if trying to encourage participation.

"Just that last thing that you mentioned," Rudy said. "I'm not sure what an epidural is."

"Very good! Thank you for asking!" she said, a little too enthusiastically. "Perhaps some of the other husbands are not familiar with the terminology. An epidural is . . . "

"He's not my husband," Lou said, in a funny sort of voice, as if she were trying not to speak the thought, but was too late.

"Oh," the instructor said, on verbal tiptoes, as the rest of the room leaned in once again to look at Rudy and Lou. Rudy felt himself flushing, once again washed in the terrible, silent embarrassment of grade school.

"I mean, he's not the father either!" Lou blurted, and then hid her face with her hands while Rudy gaped at her and felt his skin roasting under the curiosity of the others.

"That's quite all right!" the instructor said cheerily, rummaging through her bag to pull out a needle the length of Rudy's forearm. "This is an epidural!" she said gaily, while the women in the room gasped and Lou turned to Rudy and said, "Oh, I'm *so* sorry!"

"It doesn't matter!" he whispered, taking her hand again and holding it, the way his father would take his mother's, sometimes, when something had gone wrong.

In the break Rudy retreated to the boys' washroom and took a long pee, towering over the urinal, then combed his tangled hair while leaning over a tiny sink and peering into a battered old mirror which seemed to make him look like a little boy again. He needed a haircut. He should have had one before Christmas but had forgotten, more than anything else, and had returned home the wild-looking artist to his family of lawyers, his curls crowding the top of his collar. In China his hair had been kept very short and conservative by monthly haircuts at the local barbershop, where he was a celebrity, his picture hanging in the window after his very first visit.

Out in the hall Lou was talking with another woman, both of them unconsciously rubbing their stomachs and swaying, very slightly, as they stood.

"I feel so much better now that I've started getting morning sickness," Lou was saying. "Before, you know, I just didn't believe I was pregnant!"

The other woman, with long black hair tied back and her

face flushed and healthy, laughed and said, "I think the romance of it wears off!"

Lou introduced them. Her name was Yolanda and she too was there with a friend instead of the father-to-be. "My husband Ron is a geologist," she said. "He's sitting on a drill project right now somewhere up around Ear Falls."

"Is he going to be here for the birth?" Rudy asked.

"God knows. He feels he has to go wherever they send him. He's only been with the company for a year and a half and he's terrified of being laid off. It's such an up-and-down industry. And with this kid coming, God, he's just getting hyper!"

"What do you mean?" Rudy asked.

"Let's just say he has a heightened sense of his own RESPONSIBILITY," Yolanda said, verbally capitalizing the word. "I don't know if it's just him or if it happens to all men, but Ron has this feeling that he has to suddenly turn into his father and shoulder the whole world all by himself. It's kind of frightening how seriously he takes it."

"I wouldn't mind a little bit of that," Lou said, smiling ironically. "If I told Gary about this little one I'd never hear from him again. He'd change continents, I'm sure."

"You haven't told him yet?" Yolanda said.

"I will. Of course I will. But it has to be the right time."

Rudy noticed then the other couples in the hallway, most engaged in animated conversation with people they had just met. One woman was explaining her family's tendency towards high blood pressure, and how her sister had given birth seven weeks prematurely to a two-pound infant who thrived in the incubator and is now getting straight As in school. Another woman was talking about her leg cramps coming on so painfully at night she would wake up kicking her husband and screaming. Another said she was constantly farting now, especially at her mother-in-law's house; the woman she was talking to just laughed, said she had the same problem, but at least she wasn't getting her headaches any more.

When the instructor called them in to begin again, it seemed as if the group had changed its character, had gone from an assembly of strangers to a collection of sudden friends. Rudy thought of a story his parents often told about a trans-Atlantic flight in which a couple of the passengers had started singing as they roared along the runway, *Off we go, into the wild blue yonder*, and then everyone joined in. They were still singing songs upon touchdown hours later, and the plane's entire liquor stock was wiped out en route.

He told the story to Lou as they were riding home in the taxi, the ghostly snowbanks sliding past them effortlessly, white mounds in the dark, and as she was laughing he thought suddenly, and with shock, of Li Ming. When he was writing she was all he thought of; his life was complete. And yet a few hours spent with Lou and that other side of his life seemed just that, another side, a chapter in someone else's book. How could his mind work that way? He looked over guiltily at Lou, then gazed out the window into the darkness, worried.

16

THE DAY IS COLD AND GREY AND INTERMINABLE. I AM SUPPOSED TO meet Li Ming up on the hill at four o'clock, which seems to be decades away. I teach a writing class in the morning, experimenting with little ten-minute exercises which the students endure, humouring me because their exam is coming up. They are sitting crouched together in their winter coats, hats and mitts, miserable vapour clouds rising with every breath. Teaching them now, here, today, is like trying to pour ice. But we all have to be here, although the window does *not* have to be open. I stare at it a moment, know exactly what my students will say if I close it. "The leaders want us to have cold air in the classroom — very healthy!"

I take out a black and white magazine picture showing troops marching in the darkness across a chasm on a rope bridge, their backs slumped forward, packs and rifles in silhouette. I give my students ten minutes to write a paragraph describing the picture. Then, at the end, when I have them read me the results, almost every one begins, "The Long March was the most glorious struggle in the history of the founding of our China."

We do better on a picture of an extremely fat man sitting at a desk, surrounded by papers. "I want a *description*," I say. "Give me an *image*. What does this man *remind* you of?"

"A mountain of glutinous rice, wearing a suit," writes one. "He is very sad," writes another, "because his arms are too short to reach the papers on his desk, and he will soon be up for self-criticism!" A third writes, "He is a fat pork woman, wondering when is lunch?"

Lunch is an eternity away, but finally the hour arrives and I leave in a cloud of chalk dust, my head light from the fatigue of not sleeping the night before. The electricity off, lunch is cold, a plate of sugared apple pieces, another of sliced lotus root, and a bowl of limp, greasy soup. Touchingly, my cook has left a bottle of cold beer for me as well. He has a coal stove as well as the electric one they gave him to cook on for the foreigner. He could very easily heat me up a proper meal. But I am too tired to complain. I eat what I can, shivering in my dismal dining room, then head back to my cold little apartment.

Nothing heats me up, not the down blankets on my bed, not the rubber bottle I fill with lukewarm thermos water, not all the clothes I can put on my body. Though tired, I run around, bounce up and down. I go out to my little courtyard to try some *wushu*, and make it through half the *liu he ba fa* before the cold wind drives me inside again. "It's unbearable," I say to myself, and then again out loud to the concrete walls. "The cold is unbearable. It's unbearable."

Unbearable. I keep saying the word over and over as I pace in my little room. Unbearable. Unbearable. It becomes my mantra. Unbearable, unbearable. Unbearable!

I go to the bathroom and catch a glimpse of myself in the darkened mirror. My eyes are sunken, my skin is very white, pasty, sickly-looking. My hair is plastered to my head, the curls exhausted. I look too gaunt, too thin, my skin stretched too tightly around the bones of my face. Unbearable! I cannot bear it.

The thought echoes through me for the rest of the day, through the afternoon nap, which I cannot take because the bedroom is too cold, through the history class in which I lecture about the relative *unimportance* of the English Peasant Revolt of 1381 despite its extensive coverage in their thin Marxist-Leninist textbook of English and American history. My class just looks up at me, dull-eyed, wondering what the foreigner is saying; wondering even more what he is writing on the board in his deteriorating scrawl. At the end of the hour I leave that class, too, in another cloud of chalk dust, my voice sore and thin from lecturing in a refrigerator with so few lights turned on.

Three o'clock. Just half an hour before I leave and one more hour before I see Li Ming. The electricity still off. No mail. It has been days since Fang came by. I know I'm getting mail, he's just too busy to bring it. All the little things adding up. It's unbearable. Unbearable! Weight after weight, discomfort after discomfort. And the way they make you feel guilty by implying that *you* are a foreigner, at least *you* get an electric heater and a fine apartment and a cook to make your meals!

I sit down with my journal and a blanket and try to relax, think warm thoughts. I haven't written about last night. About Li Ming. I pause, thinking of her face in the glow of the heater. How warm it was, sitting with her snuggled against me. It felt as if I never needed to sleep again. My feet, even my feet were warm! They have been ice chunks all day long. I've given up on them. They'll never thaw.

It occurs to me then that I should not write anything. My journal could be evidence; someone could easily come in during the day — God knows there seem to be enough keys around — and find it and there would be Li Ming's name. I should not keep a journal at all. Wouldn't that be obvious to a Chinese anyway — don't write anything down?

I sit, sickened, looking at my pen suspended over the page. I can't afford to write anything down. It's as simple as that.

A knock comes at the door. I look up and there's Fang, finally, with the mail. Quickly I rise, snapping the book shut, and then see that it isn't just Fang, it is Dean Chun as well and one of the other officials, a man whose name I always forget. As I am opening the door I look at my watch. Three-fifteen. I told Li Ming I'd meet her at four.

"Ah! Ah! Seaborn, not busy now?" says Fang, nodding and smiling. "You have time for discuss with leaders?"

"Of course, yes," I say, ushering them in, shaking hands with all three men.

The dean asks something in Chinese. "Why so cold?" translates Fang. "Heater still work, yes?"

I tell him that the electricity is off and after the translation the dean shakes his head, of course! "Very poor country!" Fang says. "Very poor!"

We sit down and I offer them lukewarm tea, which they refuse once and I leave it at that.

"So, Seaborn!" Fang says, translating the dean's torrent of Chinese. "How is everything?"

It is a how-is-everything sort of discussion, friendly, aimless, interminable. The dean, round-faced and prosperous as ever, shoots out the questions and comments like effortless artillery barrages, while Fang gropes with the English, along the way saying far more in Chinese to the other two than is eventually said to me in English. I tell him some of my reservations about the food, and Fang makes an earnest note that he must have a talk with my cook. Then we talk about how cold it is, which gets us on to Canada, and how cold it is at home, except that *indoors* it is much warmer than here, which all three men find very funny, once it filters through the shaky wiring of our communications.

We spend a long time laughing over how little Chinese I have learned. The dean insists that I tell him something in Chinese, so I trail out my pitiful vocabulary and my few faulty phrases. Because I still can't recognize the Chinese tones, whatever I say is probably not what I mean to say, and before too long the three men are practically rattling their teeth over my incompetence. So I tell them the story about buying yogurt that time, how the crowds had gathered around and no one could figure out what I was saying and even though I'd passed around a note no one could read it because it was in pinyin. I keep the story as short as I can so that Fang can translate it before the sun completely disappears.

I look at my watch several times but the hint is not taken; the men stay on, smoking now, discussing with me travel plans for the Spring Festival break. They have mapped out a prodigious trip for me through the south, through Xiamen and Guangzhou and Guilin, and then up to Chongqing and on the famous tour through the Yangste River gorges to Wuhan, then back to Nanjing and Shanghai.

"How much will it cost?" I ask. The three men confer at great length. Four o'clock approaches, passes; there is nothing to do but wait.

"Perhaps it will not be so expensive," Fang says at last. "For a foreigner."

"Can you arrange the tickets for me?"

Again, another long consultation. The dean himself speaks at great length to me and I nod my head as if I'm following. Finally we both turn to Fang for the translation.

"If you like," he says, "our college may use some of his . . .

contacts, is that right? Sister schools may, uh . . . give you hospitality. And perhaps, uh . . . buy for you tickets you will need."

"You can't set up the tickets from here?"

"Impossible!" Fang says, without translating. "Must to be at city to buy tickets!"

I thank the dean as effusively as I can and tell him that I must think about my plans.

"The dean says . . . if you will to go on trip . . . then I will accompany you." Fang says it gravely, humbly.

"You would come with me?" I say. "As translator?"

"Yes!" he says, nodding, smiling now. "As translator!"

I nod at Dean Chun, thanking him, thinking of how fabulous it would be to go not with Fang but with Li Ming. But clearly that is not a choice. I look at my watch again. A quarter after. They have been here an hour.

"You will to consider?" Fang says, translating, and I nod my head, ready for them to leave, but no, we go on talking, about the exam schedule now. That takes twenty minutes, and then we have another long discussion about the Yangste River trip. Dean Chun, who is from Hangzhou, says that I must visit that city as well, since it is so close to Shanghai. "There is saying," Fang translates. "Above there is heaven, below there is . . . Hangzhou."

Then, it turns out, if I am going to Shanghai and Hangzhou, I really must go to Suzhou as well, the Venice of the East. At the dean's insistence, Fang amends the famous saying: "Above there is heaven, and below there is . . . Hangzhou and Suzhou!"

The geography lesson continues until the names of the cities and places are not only swimming in my head, they are sinking and drowning as well. But again and again we come back to the issue of the Spring Festival trip they want to plan for me. The dean keeps saying I must think it over, I must consider carefully, I must let them know . . . but finally I realize that they want the answer *now*, this afternoon, and it must be the right answer as well. I must agree to go with Fang.

149

We're at an impasse. It becomes dark outside, five o'clock, I'm hopelessly late. Li Ming will be waiting there, wondering what has happened. We sit in the gloom, talking now about the good universities in Canada. I can hardly believe it. Chun is telling me about his program of sending junior staff abroad to upgrade their training. He asks me which are the best Canadian universities?

"You really want to send your young teachers to Canada?"

"Yes! Yes!" Fang translates. "Important for young man study abroad."

"A young *man*?" I say.

"Yes! Yes!" Everyone nods as Fang translates.

"Why not the young women too?"

The question catches them off balance, but only for a moment. Fang takes a long time translating for Chun, far too long to just be getting across the sense of the question. I can't know what he's saying, of course, but I imagine him explaining to the dean what he should say to humour the foreigner.

"Women too, yes!" Fang says, smiling, and then he ruins it by adding, "but not so diligent as men in study."

"No?"

"Because they must to ... look after the children," he explains.

"But I thought Chairman Mao declared that 'women hold up half the sky'?"

I have to say it several times before Fang finds the right phrase in Chinese and then repeats it for the other two, who laugh and smile and nod their heads, repeating the phrase over and over, as if I have just clinched their argument for them.

They leave, finally, at twenty after five, with no answer from me about my Spring Festival plans.

Waiting for Li Ming

It is dark now but it doesn't matter. If I hurry, if I ride my bike, perhaps I can get there fast enough, before she leaves, if she hasn't left already. I cross the compound and enter the little building with the kitchen and my dining room, hoping the cook, Xiao Zhang, isn't there. Of course he is, sullen now that Fang has talked to him. My bike is in a small storage room outside the kitchen. I can't get to it without disturbing him.

"*Ni hao,*" I say, nodding, my hand going up in greeting. He says something in Chinese, pointing to his watch. We've been through this before. He's trying to tell me that dinner isn't until six o'clock.

"*Hao, hao! Xie xie!*" I say, pretending that I have somehow forgotten. I start to pull out my bike. "*Zai jian!*" But it is not good-bye, because my back tire is flat.

"Oh shit!" I say, feeling as limp as the tire.

Xiao Zhang comes over, wiping his hands on a rag. "It's okay," I try to tell him. "It doesn't matter! I'm too late anyway." But of course he doesn't understand, and I don't understand what he is saying to me, except that he leads me with the bike out the door. I guess we are going to find a pump.

Out of my courtyard, around the corner. Wait here, he motions to me, and disappears into the dark front doors of the Foreign Languages Department. I am not alone for long. One of my students, a second-year whose name I think is Xia, or perhaps it's Qing, I'm not quite sure, gives me a big smile and comes over. She is dressed in a fine white cloth jacket that looks warm around her, and is wearing a yellow plastic barrette holding her hair back over one ear.

"Hello Mr. Seaborn!" she says. "Where are you going?"

"Nowhere right now," I say. "I've got a flat tire."

We stand around discussing the tire, and several times she asks if she can help, but I tell her that Xiao Zhang has gone in for a pump. We're still talking when Xiao Zhang returns, empty-handed. So he and my student have a lengthy conversation, with Xiao Zhang pointing back into the Foreign Languages

Department and my student pointing somewhere else and the bike resting forlornly between us.

"He says that there is a pump in the Foreign Languages Department, but Mr. Gua, who keeps it, has gone home."

"Ah," I say. "Your English is getting better, did you know that?"

Xia or Qing blushes, her eyes childlike and bright.

"I guess I might as well wait until tomorrow. It doesn't matter, it's too dark anyway." I turn to Xiao Zhang, nodding my head and thanking him.

"But I know where is another one!" my student says. "I will take you there now!"

"No, no, that's okay," I say. "I think it's already pretty dark . . . "

"It is no trouble," she insists. "Not very far from here. And I will have a chance for . . . free conversation!"

We go, of course. At this point I am too tired and cold and hungry to put up any sort of fight. We walk, teacher and student, my bicycle hobbling in between. Along the way I confess and learn that her name is neither Xia nor Qing, but Hua. "In English it is 'flower,'" she says.

Hua, flower, with the yellow barrette and the quick smile and the easy way she nurtures the conversation, even in a foreign language. We talk about bicycles, in China and in Canada, and then she turns us out the gates and we are talking about families. In one of my writing exercises I had her class describe family members, and now Hua remembers the little piece I read out about mine. "In my family," I wrote, "my older sister is the horse, and I am the turtle." Hua asks me why I would say that.

"Because I am!" I say. "Here I am in China, walking my bicycle, and my sister drives a sports car and zooms ahead in her career and looks very beautiful while she is doing it. I am the turtle and she is the horse. But I feel very lucky being the turtle. I think it is much harder to be the horse, and when you are running that fast you miss so much."

"In my family, I am the intellectual," Hua says.

"What does your father do?"

"My father works in Number Seven Lightbulb Factory, and my mother works in Number Three Toilet Paper factory. I have two sisters, and they work in two other factories: refrigerators and fans."

"What kind of animal would an intellectual be?" I ask.

"In China," she says, "an intellectual must to be a rabbit. Run very fast, eat very little, appear very soft and unharmful."

The man with the air pump, it turns out, is not as close to the college as she thinks. The walk turns out to be about twenty minutes, in fact, and the man is not even there on his street corner where he usually does business.

"You must to wait here!" Hua says. "I will go find him!"

"No, no, please," I say, nearly limp now with fatigue. "It's all right. Let's just go back. I'll get it done tomorrow."

"No! It is my fault. You have come too far, and I will find him. In just a few minutes! Wait here!"

I wait. The street is quiet, nearly everyone is in having their dinner now. But the lights are on, at least, meaning there's power. Heat. Maybe I will eat my dinner on the sofa in front of my heater. Poor Li Ming. I hope she has not waited. If only she could take me on this trip of Dean Chun's. I think of her sleeping so peacefully in my arms. Was that just last night? It seems as if years have passed since then.

Finally Hua returns with an old man in tow, tiny in a huge blue peasant jacket. Grey beard, sunken face, quick eyes. He brings with him the pump, too — black, heavy, battered, endlessly useful.

I nod and smile and greet him, and say to Hua, "I hope he wasn't having his dinner."

"Doesn't matter!" she says, and he kneels down to work on the tire.

"No, no, I can do that!" I say, kneeling down awkwardly beside him. But when I unscrew the valve I see that I can't do it — I'm unfamiliar with the Chinese mechanism, and have to back off.

"Please thank him very very much," I say to Hua. "I feel very embarrassed that he would come out just to help me."

"Doesn't matter!" she says again. "But I will tell him." When she does he looks up at me, grinning broadly. As he pumps he asks Hua questions about me — where I am from, how old I am, how long I have been here, whether or not I am married. She answers them briefly and when I press her she tells me what they are talking about.

"How old am I?" I ask her.

"Twenty-five!" she says.

"How do you know that? I've never told the class that."

"Everybody knows that," she says.

Then he is finished, and I spend several minutes trying to get him to take payment for his trouble. He refuses categorically, shaking his head, putting up his hand, waving no to my money.

"It is his pleasure," Hua says.

"But it's also his business!" I say. "I must pay him for it. I feel awful dragging him out of his home, probably away from his dinner. Please, he must take it."

There is no way. He is gravely serious in his refusal. He will not take money from a foreigner. I put it away.

"*Xie xie! Xie xie ni!*" I say, nodding, shaking his hand. His face is all smiles again. He walks off, back down the darkened road, dragging his pump behind him.

I see Li Ming the next morning. She is at her desk in the little corner room working on a paper, her face in shadows, her work in a bright shaft of sunlight. No one else is there.

"I'm sorry I didn't make it yesterday afternoon," I say in a soft voice. "I was about to leave and then —"

"You had a meeting with Dean Chun," she says, without turning.

"How did you know?"

"Everybody knows," she says, turning finally, smiling. "Are you all right?" she asks.

"Fine, yes," I say. "I didn't sleep very well."

 Waiting for Li Ming

"Are you going to go on the trip with Mr. Fang?"

"You know about that, too?"

She nods, a little shine in her eyes.

"I, uh . . . I guess . . . I don't know. I guess I'm expected . . . "

"You don't have to go," she says, and then someone else comes in the room. It is Jiang, his young face lit to see Li Ming, suddenly dark when he notices me as well. The two have a long conversation in Chinese while I put my hand on one of the books in the shelf beside me and look through the *Encyclopaedia Britannica* and read part of a very interesting article on ringworm. It becomes something of a contest — Jiang talking and talking, smiling, waiting me out, while I stand and read and pretend to be researching something. Finally, with quiet anger, he goes away.

"I will show you Shanghai," she says, looking at her notes. "Unless you want to go with Mr. Fang."

"No," I say. "I'd like to go with you."

"Then I will make the arrangements," Li Ming says.

17

MICHAEL ADAMS DIED ON THE FIRST DAY OF FEBRUARY. LOU HAD GONE to Toronto twice to visit him and each time he had looked worse. She told Rudy it was as if the knot in the balloon holding his life forces had been loosened just a bit and he was deflating before her eyes, becoming old, wrinkled, shrunken. He collapsed upon himself in an obscenely quickened old age, which was made all the more painful for its pace, and he was spared none of the indignities that come with the body's dissolution. For the last month or so he had no control over his bowels; his coughing sputtered through the day and increased at night, seemingly tearing the flesh of his lungs, chest and throat; his hair fell out and the compounding illnesses ate his body from the inside; and he suffered a cruel intensification of the migraine headaches he had lived with most of his life. In the end he did not rage, rage against the dying of the light; it came more as a merciful gift gratefully accepted.

The funeral was held in Orangeville, where his parents lived, but there was a gathering in Bellsbridge at Professor Rogers's home. The day was frighteningly cold, and Lou wore an ancient raccoon-skin coat which had been her great-aunt's, so large she called it her walrus-skin. Rudy and she and Amanda walked together, the non-pregnant friends helping Lou up the icy walk. She was showing, definitely, and at first she had not wanted to go, but Rudy had talked her into it.

It did not seem like a wake when they arrived. The gathering was spread over three rooms in the Rogerses' sprawling old house, and the noise indicated that people were talking about anything and everything except death. A great deal of alcohol was disappearing, and Rogers children of varying ages threaded through the groups with trays of new drinks and old glasses. As Rudy helped Lou off with her walrus-skin he noticed Amanda taking in the scene, her eyes darting among the clumps of people.

"Christopher is coming, isn't he?" Rudy asked.

"How would I know?" Amanda shot back.

Rudy took the three coats upstairs to pile them in a bedroom. On his way down he saw Lou, clutching her fruit punch, surrounded by women no doubt asking about her pregnancy. The flush of expectancy was on her face, the death of a lover notwithstanding. She had taken the news very calmly as far as Rudy could tell. Amanda had called him and he had called Lou, to see if she was all right — did she want to go for a walk, or have a back rub, or . . . But she said no, she was fine, it was a relief finally. She said she didn't think she was going to cry.

Rudy found Amanda and the department secretary, Elizabeth, whispering in a corner. Amanda asked him then about Li Ming, and he told her he had heard nothing since her mysterious envelope had arrived a month ago now. He wasn't sure his letters were getting through. The department had not received her application, as far as he knew.

"I suppose you've been following the news from Tibet?" Amanda said.

"What we get of it," Rudy said. There was rioting, there were rumours of deaths, but reports were sketchy. He had started to tell them about seeing the Potala from the bus on his own short journey there when Christopher approached, smartly dressed in a dark suit, a purple tie knotted tightly against his Adam's apple.

"Ah. The arrival of Casanova," Amanda said dryly, "I don't think I see the Hat Lady around anywhere."

"Who?" Christopher asked.

"Your doe-eyed co-ed."

"Karla?" he asked, raising his eyebrows. Everyone laughed.

"Is that her name?" Amanda said.

"Is that her name?" Christopher mimicked, turning his head slightly the way she did. "Your jealousy, my dear, is not a pretty sight."

"I was just thinking of pretty sights," she said, "and I was noticing that one of them was absent. That's all. I was merely inquiring."

"She seems to be ill," he said. "An interminable flu. She has left me to struggle alone in my garret."

The two continued to circle one another verbally for some minutes in feigned jest, as if with drawn swords even though they kept hold of their cocktail glasses. It was mesmerizing and then revolting as the pretence of humour evaporated and they sought to jab and wound in earnest over some event, long past and now unexplained but evidently still bitingly alive for them both.

"Oh come on, Amanda," Elizabeth finally said, pulling the tiny woman away to another room. Christopher was left holding his drink in suspended anger, half-turned to confront an adversary who was no longer there.

"She's like a dragon, that woman," he said to Rudy. "You should pay no attention to anything she says against you. That was strictly between the two of us."

"I think she loves you," Rudy said, and Christopher laughed so hard, a sudden loud honk, that he spilled his drink. "She doesn't know the meaning of the word," he said. "You can be as intimate with her as you can with a cactus. That I learned from experience. Thank heavens I'm out of it. I think you've found the perfect solution."

"What's that?"

"Have your love thousands of miles away, so she can prosper in your imagination."

Rudy said nothing, looked thoughtfully at nothing in particular. Then he saw Lou coming to them, her gait rolling a bit. "This is so depressing," she said to them. "I just . . . we were all talking about Michael, and I can't take it any more."

"I wish *we* had been talking about Michael," Christopher said. "I'd probably feel a lot better."

"What were you talking about?"

Nobody answered, but Rudy nodded to let her know that he would tell her later. It seemed to him that she really did look splendid, despite the sadness of the occasion. Her red hair had taken on an extra thickness and lustre; her body was so rounded, abundant with life; her face seemed to generate its own light.

"I hear Rogers is going to read from some of Michael's work," she said. "I'm not sure I can stay for that. I think it'll be really heavy."

"Whatever you feel like," Rudy said. "I'll walk you home if you want."

As it turned out she stayed for a little while and then suddenly had to leave, touching Rudy's arm as he stood with the others listening to Professor Rogers, whose voice seemed hesitant. Rudy slipped upstairs for their coats and they left together quietly, thankful for the cold air outside and the solitude. She took his arm when they approached an icy patch and they walked that way afterwards, not saying very much, her steps short, laboured. She had a pain in her hip, a price of the hormonal loosening of the joint, which made walking difficult, though she was still trying to do as much as she could to stay in shape.

Later on he would tell her about the conversation between Christopher and Amanda. What he was thinking about now was the one poem of Michael's they had heard before leaving. It was one of his last, painfully written in a shaky hand on the inside of one of his favourite books, a collection of Greek myths. The verse went —

> *Each day I feel the great bird's shadow*
> *before I hear the disturbance of its wings;*
> *know the pierce of its eyes on my entrails*
> *before its scream of delight.*
> *If only I had stolen fire,*
> *then every day my organs would reheal.*
> *But I have stolen no fire,*
> *made love, now bleed.*

18

GOD, YOU LOOK WIPED OUT!" MADELEINE, WHO DOESN'T LOOK SO fresh herself, makes her observation while pouring the water for tea. "Have you decided where to go for Spring Festival?"

"I'm staying here," I say, pulling off one of my sweaters, which used to be greyish white and now is blackish white from the weeks of collecting airborne coal dust since its last wash.

"Oh come off it — I thought you were sick of this place."

"Well, I am, of course," I say. "But I'm applying to a program back home and I have to get some writing done. They're asking for a portfolio."

"About the misery of human existence?"

"I'm not sure what I'm going to write about," I say, and then, because she knows there's more, I say, "Maybe I'll go to Shanghai for a couple of days."

"Didn't your college arrange a trip for you?"

"If I left it to them they'd have me retracing Marco Polo's expeditions. They want me to sail down the Yangste . . ."

"That's what I'm going to do! The Yangste River trip! Oh, it's going to be great. Why don't you come along?"

"I really . . . I don't think I have the money to do it," I say, not quite looking at her. "And it's going to be so exhausting. I was thinking, you know, if I'm going to go on a huge trip while I'm over here I should try to get to Tibet. Maybe I can save my money and do something really special."

"Tibet?"

"Yeah. In the summer. If it's open. Sometimes it isn't. I've

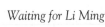

heard you have to go to Chengdu and then negotiate for your plane from there."

"Well, that would be all right then," she says, uncertainly.

We push onto other topics, discussing for awhile the plight of the Polish couple, the Volstovs, who have been given a crushing teaching load, much larger than that of the English teachers, and are also responsible for translating an engineering textbook in their "spare" time. And now that the woman, Mila, has fallen ill the authorities have complained about her missing classes.

"A couple of days ago some of the *waiban* officials came in and screamed at her for about an hour," Madeleine says. "It was unbelievable. They were saying she wasn't really sick, she wasn't pulling her weight, her teaching wasn't even any good, all kinds of crap. It was very upsetting. All the foreign teachers got together and met with the officials, and you know what they told us?"

"What?"

"That the Volstovs are from a socialist country, and therefore much more is expected from them."

"You mean that's an excuse for treating people like shit?"

"Exactly." And then Madeleine asks me about Li Ming, and I tell her that not only was her request to go to the conference stymied, she has a fellowship at Columbia that she must refuse as well. We talk about her case for a long time, and then she says, "I thought you weren't supposed to see her anymore. They got you another translator, didn't they?"

"I bump into her sometimes in the department," I say.

"That's all?"

"Yeah."

"Well, I'm glad you restrained yourself. You won't regret it later on," she says.

Rudy and Lou were either seeing one another or talking on the phone every day now, sometimes eating lunch at the university cafeteria, or meeting before a class, or slipping out for a late afternoon walk. She phoned him nearly every evening, and when she didn't phone he called her and they talked about the changes going on inside her, or about the new direction of her play, or the gossip from the department. There was an accumulating day-to-day awareness that they were becoming great friends; at the same time, whenever they were together, something else was happening that they did not talk about. Rudy had supposed that as she became more and more obviously pregnant the physical attraction he felt for her would decrease; on the contrary, he seemed to become more aware of it, and wondered if something was wrong with him. But she really was radiant, full of this new life, and she was not one to hide that sort of energy.

One evening as Rudy and Lou were walking home from another childbirth education class, Lou was worrying about whether or not she should have an epidural. On the one hand she was not very good with pain, and part of her wanted them to just knock her out completely and hand her a baby a little while later. But the woman at the class that evening had stressed the negative aspects of epidurals: how when they wear off it can be like being plunged headlong into the middle of labour; how if they give it at the wrong time the woman has no control over her muscles to push, and so there is a much higher tendency towards forceps deliveries and episiotomies.

"I just . . . I don't want them cutting me up," she said as they walked along, her arms folded across her chest. "I want to keep control over this. I don't want to be in someone else's hands."

Once home she was quite happy to have Rudy rub her feet again on the sofa. He had found some wood in the garbage and so they had the rare luxury of a fire, and Lou insisted that he tell her a story, so he talked about finding a book of tai chi sword movements in a little store just off Bridge Street and how he was working through them step by step, trying to put them together.

"You have a wonderful lecturing voice," she said, at some point, after he had gone on for quite a while. "It's very soothing. As soon as you start talking like that I begin to fall asleep."

"Thanks a lot," he said.

"Well, I wish my husband had had a voice like that. We probably would have gotten along a whole lot better. I wouldn't have cared so much what he was talking about."

By now he was working on her back, through the soft cotton of her dress. He leaned in to press his thumbs down the sides of her spine, feeling the slow bump of each vertebrae as he approached the small of her back. Then briefly he felt the fullness of her belly, and moved down to squeeze her thigh and calf.

He talked on, no longer sure what he was saying, happy to look at her and feel her warmth and listen to the soft noises she made when he rubbed the right spot. It wasn't too much later that she fell asleep, and he tickled gently down her sides, watched her muscles react from reflex while the rest of her stayed still.

"Huh?" she said in a bit, starting awake again.

"Nothing."

"You've stopped."

He started gently rubbing again.

"I must have dozed off."

"What did you dream about?" he asked.

"Oh, it was really weird."

"Yeah? Those are the best kind."

"Everybody thought we were having an affair," Lou said, laughing, her eyes still closed.

"Yeah?"

"It was ridiculous. I have never been this ugly in my whole life, and they thought I'd seduced you or something."

"You're not ugly."

"Oh right. I'm ravishingly beautiful."

"You are," he said.

She opened her eyes then and turned to give his shoulder a little shove. "I am so bloated I can hardly even fit into my aunt's walrus-skin!"

"And still, you're all the more beautiful," he said softly.

She sat up a bit, turning again to look at him. "Why are you so nice to me?" she asked.

"Why shouldn't I be?"

"Because I'm a real bitch sometimes. And I never rub your back, or cook you dinner at your place, or lecture you until you fall asleep."

"It feels good," he said. "Things work better when you're nice to people."

"There's got to be more to it than that."

"Why?"

"Because you are no fucking saint, that's why! I know you enough to know that!"

She would not let him change the topic. When he started rubbing the small of her back she squirmed around and wrestled with him, yelling out when he got the upper hand, "Don't! Don't! I'm a pregnant woman!" until he let go and she lunged at him again, laughing. Her hair flashed across his face and her eyes became black pools and then they slipped off the couch and she landed with a thud on her side, but rolled quickly onto her knees and pinned him and began tickling until he rolled her off and straddled her hips, holding down her hands, being careful not to put weight on her belly.

They paused, breathing, tense, watching, not quite laughing. The skirt of her dress was pulled up above her knees; their loins were together; it was a lovers' posture, though they were fully clothed. Her face was just a few inches from his.

There was no way she could not feel him harden. She looked directly in his eyes and the play part of the moment evaporated. She had her head tilted back, waiting.

"You see, the reason why I'm so nice to you," he said, almost whispering, "is because I like you, and because . . . then I get a chance to help somebody with her pregnancy, which is an experience I normally wouldn't get. And as a writer, I have to . . . to 'see life steady and see it whole,' if you know what I mean. I'm reading the Victorians these days. I have to know life, so that my insights are not . . . narrowly based."

The corners of Lou's eyes crinkled. "So this is grist for the mill, is it?"

He wasn't good at lying, but he did his best anyway. "I still have to learn how to write fiction. Maybe I don't have a good imagination that way. I'm reading Thomas Wolfe, too — maybe like him I have to live it in order to write about it."

"Maybe you should get off me," she said, trying to make a joke of it but having the words come out a little sour.

"Oh, I'm sorry. Was I hurting your legs?"

"It's okay. They were just a little stiff." She got up awkwardly, pulling down and straightening out her dress. "It's getting late, isn't it?"

"I should go," Rudy said, and she nodded, not looking at him. But at he door he hesitated. "I . . . I'm not sure what to say," he said.

"Just go home," she said, her arms crossed. "You need your beauty sleep."

He nodded his head and opened the door, then turned back.

"I thought these things would be simple," he said, not quite looking at her, trying hard to think of the right words. "I thought I would fall in love with someone and that would be it."

"And I thought we had this figured out," Lou said. "Listen, don't stand in the doorway. Either come in and close the door or go home. It's cold out."

Rudy came in and closed the door. Lou waited, her arms still crossed.

"I didn't count on meeting you. I thought that I would have

heard something from Li Ming by now, more than just an empty envelope. I . . . I didn't think that I could love two people at the same time."

"What are you saying, Rudy?"

"I don't know."

"That's what I figured. Listen, go home will you? I don't want you mixed up with me unless you really know what you're doing."

Rudy nodded his head, but didn't leave.

"You see," she said, "I can't compete with some mythical Chinese goddess that you're never going to see again. I'm here and now and flesh and blood and I'm pregnant and in a few months I'm going to be a single mother. I think that's a lot more than you're ready to deal with. Isn't it?"

Rudy didn't answer.

"Well, this is a great discussion," she said.

"I gave her my word, Lou," he said, looking finally into her eyes.

"Yes you did," she said. "And the world keeps turning, doesn't it?"

That was the problem. Just when you think you have things worked out, the world turns again. On the way home Rudy thought of Chaucer's *Troilus and Criseyde*, how the lovers are separated by political events when Criseyde is sent to the Greek side as a hostage, and how she promises to return to Troilus after ten days. But on the tenth day, just as she is slipping away, there is Diomede waiting for her outside her tent, asking for just a little time to state his case, and then convincing her that Troy is a lost cause, that the war will soon be over, and that he will be as gentle and will love her as much as any Trojan could. And Rudy thought of her pain and her decision and the way Chaucer did not blame her.

It had turned colder; some sort of new front was moving

through, the frost smarting on his cheeks, the wind chilling through his clothes. Maybe he was being a fool, trying so hard to believe in something that would not work. Maybe Criseyde was right; maybe life has its own plan and he was ignoring the signals, clinging to something in the past that was impossible now to continue. Maybe Li Ming realized that, and that was why there had been no word. Maybe he should call Lou as soon as he got in.

Rudy started jogging and that helped to warm him. The wind was not so bad. Maybe it was time he made a decision. Maybe that was what this was all about — his body was telling him what his mind hadn't figured out yet. He loved Lou. He wanted to be with her, help her, share the day-to-day. He wanted to laugh and feel good and not worry about keeping those feelings under control. You can't control them. He couldn't control them with Li Ming and he can't control them now with Lou. We can't be rigid; life makes us bend, and if we don't bend we break. He would call her as soon as he got in.

From the cold of the outside air to the warmth of his apartment. It's funny how you can be going along in a muddle for so long, and then suddenly it all becomes clear so quickly. He didn't take off his jacket. Maybe she would want him to come back over. He walked to the phone.

And it rang as he reached out his hand. Lou. Undoubtedly it was Lou. He thought of Arnold's line — the one where he watches the waves crash upon the shore the same way they did for Sophocles — *Ah love, let us be true to one another.* He wanted to read her that poem.

"Hi, listen," he said, picking up the phone. "I'm just going to go — "

It wasn't Lou. The line was scratchy, windblown, like a string stretched between opposite ends of the earth.

"Yes, yes of course, I'll accept the charges. Hello?"

"Hello, Rudy," came a very small voice, a whisper from the bottom of a well. "It's Li Ming."

19

*H*E COULDN'T BELIEVE IT FOR A MOMENT; THE PHONE NEARLY DROPPED out of his hand.

"Listen, Li Ming, you'll have to speak up — I can barely hear you!" He was yelling himself and pressing the receiver to his ear.

"Is that better?" she asked, her British accent filtering through the fog of the connection. "Can you hear me?"

"My God!" he said. "Where are you? Are you in Beijing?"

She said where, but he didn't catch it, the Chinese word slipping by too quickly.

"I'm sorry, where? In Beijing? How did you get to Beijing?"

"My uncle has helped me," she said. "I am now working at the Agriculture and Technical Institute."

"That's terrific, Li Ming. I was so scared when I didn't hear from you for so long. I didn't know what had happened to you. I've only got one letter so far and that didn't even have a letter in it! Did you receive my packages?"

"I received one," she said. "It was delivered to my room."

"Then they're stopping our mail. You must phone me from now on, using this number. Do you understand?"

She hadn't heard; the connection faltered. "Li Ming! Hello? Li Ming!"

Nothing. He held his breath, thought that he could hear every mile of ocean between them in the line. "Li Ming?"

"Yes. I can hear you," she said, a bare whisper.

"How are you?" he asked through tears. "Are you well? What's happened to you?"

"Yes, well," said the whisper, and then there was static again. "Hello? What's that? Hello?"

"I was ill for a time," she said, "but now I am better. My mother has died."

"Oh my," he said. "I'm so sorry to hear that." It was the last of her family. Now she was alone. "Li Ming," he said, feeling the line fade out again. "Listen, Li Ming — do you hear me? If you can fill out that application I think there will be a scholarship — " He paused for a moment. "Hello? Li Ming? Have you got a number there? Can I call you? Hello?"

Wind.

"Hello?"

He slumped to the floor, the phone still at his ear.

"Li Ming, I don't know if you can hear me, but I love you, and we are going to be together somehow, I know it. Okay?"

There was a terribly long pause, in which he desperately wanted her to say something, just one little thing before her voice got lost. She did say something at one point, but he wasn't sure what it was — the line was crackly; he couldn't quite hear. He waited for a long time after that and hung up only reluctantly when it became clear that they had lost the connection. Then he waited up for three more hours in case she called again, but the phone did not ring.

What he thought she might have said was, "I love you too."

The next days were a blur. Rudy ran their conversation through his head over and over. Somehow it didn't seem so bad now that they had been cut off; it was a miracle just to hear her voice after all those months without a word. She was in Beijing; she would be in a good position to come over after all. That was something to hold on to. And yet . . .

He saw Lou again in the writing class and somehow couldn't find the words to tell her that Li Ming had called. There was a moment when he might have mentioned it and then it passed and the class was beginning and it wasn't the right time. He sat through the long discussions of other people's work but was unable to concentrate, his mind a mass of tiny threads from which he was trying to extract a single line, the right direction. At the end of the class he was pulled along to Lee's Pepsi-Cola Restaurant with Lou and Amanda and Christopher, feeling uneasy, not quite sure what was going to happen or how he should handle it.

But a booth was waiting for them by the window even though the rest of the restaurant was full of a strange mixture of students and shift workers from the car plant. Maybe everything would be all right. Even Christopher and Amanda were being civil to one another. They talked about the class for quite a while, and then Amanda said, "Enough, let's talk babies!" grinning playfully and blowing smoke out of the side of her mouth away from Lou. She looked twelve years old, her fingers as slender as her cigarette. "Is she moving yet?"

"She's kicking so much I think she's going to be a Rockette when she grows up. God, especially when I lie down and relax."

"Do we know it's a she?" Christopher asked.

"Well it's obviously going to be a she," Lou said. "I wouldn't go through all this for a man, would I?" She gave Rudy a quick glance as she said it.

"Ooooohhhh," Amanda said, looking between the two.

"How is it you two are so buddy-buddy all of a sudden?" Lou asked, shifting the focus back to Amanda and Christopher.

"We're not buddy-buddy," Christopher said, mock-affronted. "We are sworn enemies who happened to get drunk together last night. That's all. The world seems much more reasonable in a haze."

"I wish I could have a cigarette," Lou said, running her hand roughly through her hair. Christopher started pulling his pack

 Waiting for Li Ming

out of his pocket when Amanda slapped his hand. "She didn't mean it!" she said.

"Ah hell," Lou said, slumping back in her seat. "It's really shitty being pregnant."

"She doesn't mean that, either," Amanda said.

"God dammit I don't! I don't think I can keep on with my job, you know. I have to work so late, and it's so smoky, and I'm just exhausted. And my back is sore, my hips are killing me, I walk home late at night and it feels like all my joints have rusted over. I don't know how I can keep going. I think . . . I just . . . I feel so old."

"Have you told Gary yet?" Amanda asked.

"Oh fuck, I know exactly what Gary would do. He would kick holes in the walls if I told him I was pregnant. I've spent too many years pinning my hopes on Gary. He's not that kind of guy. God."

"Maybe we can help," Christopher said. "Maybe this could sort of be a . . . departmental baby."

Lou looked at him, sourly at first, and then with some gentleness. "I'm sorry," she said. "That's a wonderful thing to say. But I got myself into this mess, and I made the decision to keep going, so . . . so I'll just have a find my way through it. People get through this. Lots of people do. I'll get through it. In fact, I was just talking to my mother this morning. After the birth I'm going to live with her for a while. Have a little help." She didn't look at Rudy as she said it, but the casual news was clearly meant for him, and he had a sudden feeling that he was in a card game, that all of them were holding things close to their vests, letting them out gradually, and disguising their reactions.

"Anyway," she said, "Rudy's been wonderful. I think . . . I think we make a good team. I'm going to be there turning the air blue, and he's going to be . . . Mr. Slow, just rubbing my back, giving me a lecture on the nature of world communications. You should hear him lecture — he puts me right to sleep!" They turned to look at him, and he sipped his beer thoughtfully.

Then another card fell which Rudy had been hoping wouldn't but there it was on the table. Amanda asked him what was new from Li Ming, and he paused before telling them, carefully, about the phone call. He was looking at Amanda, and Amanda was looking at Lou, and Lou was looking at her hands.

"So you think she might be coming to the department?" Amanda asked.

"Maybe. Yes," Rudy said.

"Well, won't that be interesting?" Amanda said, and nobody said anything.

"She phoned when? Tuesday night?" Lou asked finally.

"Yes," Rudy said, pulling at the skin under his neck. "Pretty late."

"She has remarkable timing," Lou said, looking finally into Rudy's eyes while Amanda exchanged glances with Christopher.

There was another silence. They all seemed to know they were in the middle of a private conversation that was happening mostly without words. Rudy took a long drink of his beer and tried to sort through a storm of thoughts but couldn't. He had no idea what he would say even if he were alone with Lou.

And then Lou gave a little sigh, just a slight noise that made them all look. She was frowning and smiling at the same time.

"The baby's awake," she said, stroking her belly.

Rudy lay awake several nights in a row, thinking about Li Ming, then thinking about Lou, waiting for another phone call, wondering who it would be . . . wondering who he wanted it to be.

He started several times to write about the Shanghai trip, but somehow whenever he got to the typewriter the words didn't come out the way they should have. So he lay awake remembering how he boarded the train at four in the morning, following the conductor, climbing up to the third level of bunks in the darkness over bodies slumbering in the shadows, the whole train car full of stale air. He remembered wondering what would happen if Li Ming did not take the later train; if he was not able to stay at the Peace Hotel, if she did not meet him there at nine the next morning. Here he was going to a strange city where he did not speak the language in order to spend some time away with a woman he was not supposed to love. Would the authorities be suspicious that she was going to Shanghai as well? Did the Dean suspect something strange when Rudy had refused the college's offer of sending Fang as translator? Did he buy the excuse that Rudy was thinking of going to Hong Kong afterwards, where Fang would not be able to go?

He remembered just getting to sleep on the train when the propaganda box burst into life at six o'clock, the squawkings continuing throughout the day. He did not realize it then, but in first class there was a knob for turning down the volume, just like in O'Brien's office in *Nineteen Eighty-Four*. He remembered lying alone on his bunk, staring at the ceiling only a few feet above him, trying to read but feeling his stomach beginning to turn with the motion, the thought of being sick in a Chinese washroom enough to focus his will and calm him. He remembered feeling mute, wishing himself invisible as he lay above an entire culture he could not communicate with except in the most rudimentary ways, the men and women sitting on their bunks talking, eating pumpkin seeds, spitting the shells on the floor, reaching for their thermoses to make tea. Later on, he got up and walked past them, smiling at the few who called out English words to him. He sat in more silence by the window on a tiny seat that folded out from the wall and watched as they crossed the Yangste over the famous bridge at Nanjing, just catching a glimpse of the huge statue of Mao as they rolled past. Where was it that Mao had made his swim? Nanjing? No, Wuhan, the centre of the country.

He remembered buying food in a styrofoam container, a sort

of Chinese McDonald's lunch, and then not knowing where to put the box when he was finished. There was no trash can. Everyone else just threw theirs on the floor and so he did the same, and later on a stocky woman in a blue apron came by, swept up all the containers, and, to his amazement, threw them out the window. Rudy watched them flutter and come to rest beside the thousands of others that lined the tracks at that spot.

He remembered arriving in Shanghai late in the afternoon and not knowing which way to go, trying to follow the crowd out of the station, the people branching in different directions almost from the beginning. Then down some stairs, along a tunnel, suddenly being part of another larger crowd, the bodies wedged together as the tunnel narrowed into stairs like water suddenly forced into a chute. The masses. Here was the origin of the term. They were everywhere, on the buses, on the sidewalks, spilling over onto the streets. In the taxi along the Nanjing Donglu, metal fences to keep the people off the road. What would a demonstration be like here? Take away the fences and the masses would overflow like lava spilling down from a burning mountain.

And then, at the Peace Hotel, he was no longer in China. The man behind the desk spoke perfect English. The carpets, the high ceilings, the restored elegance . . . it might have been the Chateau Laurier back home. White skin, expensive shopping, elevators, gleaming surfaces. *Time* for sale. A young couple with backpacks, maybe Australian or German or American, resting in the lobby. A busload of elderly tourists, speaking in southern accents, walking through the doors laden with goods from the Friendship Store, silk robes and woven peasant hats and carved jade lions and stuffed panda dolls for their grandchildren.

He was trying to remember how much it had cost to stay the night. Was it 200 yuan? He had written nothing in his journal about it. It was the last room available. He couldn't believe it, but he didn't know where else to go. He could afford it the once, though it would have been nice if the hot water tank hadn't been broken.

Dining alone, in the huge room with the chandeliers and the white linen and Qingdao beer five times as expensive as it was in Laozhou from the local store. If there were so few people in the restaurant, how could the hotel be so packed?

Going out for a walk in the evening along the famous Bund, looking at the ships with their lights on in the harbour. A Soviet steamer, an Arabian vessel, another ship flying the American flag. One or two junks bobbing incongruously among the waves of the twentieth century. And three men in ethnic costumes — Tibetan, they must have been Tibetan — pointing at the tall buildings and laughing, laughing! and going on in some strange language.

Waking in the morning to the unexpected joy of hot water, and breakfasting like a prince at a table by the window over-looking the harbour, with the sun pouring in and the steel leviathans slipping by soundlessly except for the occasional horn blast. It was like being in a Western comfort warp: on the street, down below, China; up here, in the sunshine with the white linen and the silverware, civilization as we know it: fried eggs done beautifully, freshly squeezed orange juice, Corn Flakes and milk.

And then down on the street at nine o'clock, with her bag across her shoulder and the harbour winds of her hometown in her hair, Li Ming, squeezing his hand briefly and then letting it go as they walked together, anonymous for once in the breath-less rush of the crowds.

20

IT FEELS NORMAL, AND THAT IS THE EXTRAORDINARY THING. WE ARE WALK-
ing in a park, somewhere in Shanghai — as usual with Li Ming
as my guide I have lost all sense of where I am — and it doesn't
feel as if we are breaking any laws or committing any sin by
being together. Unlike in conservative Laozhou, here we are
surrounded by young men and women walking with their arms
around one another. I do not take Li Ming's hand, but I feel as if
I could. The air too feels like spring; there is no snow; I am wearing only one sweater and the ground smells ready for new life.

For the moment we are talked out, though that has taken a
few hours. She has told me how nervous she was on the train,
sure that everyone could read her thoughts. "We still have to be
careful," she said. "There are many eyes here."

As we walk I notice a man standing very still, his face a bare
inch or two from a tree, his hands out by his side. It looks a little
like a tai chi stance but he isn't moving. I ask Li Ming.

"He is doing *chi gong*," she says. "Breathing exercises."

"But why is he staring at that tree?"

"To be with nature," she says.

Traffic is rushing by us, trucks and buses and ancient black
limousines, while tourists, Chinese and Western, cram the
walkway only feet from where he is standing.

"That is one of the things about living in Shanghai," she
says. "You must work very hard for your privacy."

She is staying with her mother in one of the industrial
suburbs, about two hours away by bus. I tell her I can't afford an-

other night at the Peace Hotel and she says a sister college of ours not too far away has a guest house where I can stay for much less, as long as I show my college identification and work cards.

"It feels terrific," I say, "just being able to walk together in the sunshine, out in the open. I feel like . . . you're the easiest person to be with in the world."

"When in fact I am the hardest person," she says.

"Politically, yes. Personally, no."

"We must find a good place to meet," she says.

I laugh, although I know she is being serious.

"What is it?"

"There's just a terribly corny line in English. It goes — 'Darling, we have to stop meeting like this.'"

She doesn't react. She is waiting for more.

"That's it. I'm sorry. It wouldn't mean anything to you. You're talking about Laozhou, right?"

She nods.

"Well, maybe . . . when the weather gets warmer . . . there is that spot I found on our mountain. We could just meet there to talk. That would be enough. It could be our place."

She nods again, not speaking or looking at me.

"Are you okay?"

"Yes," she says.

"You look sad all of a sudden."

She shakes her head, but still doesn't look at me.

"What is it?"

"I cannot help thinking," she said. "That's all. If I could just not think, then . . . "

"Thinking about what?"

"About what we are doing. We do not have much of a chance. Maybe you do not know that. You are a foreigner, but I am a Chinese and I know that."

"I would like to have you come to Canada, Li Ming. I would like to marry you. I would like us to spend the rest of our lives together."

The words have just come out; I haven't thought of them before, really. They startle me a bit. But they also have come straight from my heart and I mean every syllable.

She doesn't say anything. She doesn't even stop walking. Her shoulders still square, her eyes straight ahead, but with tears in them. We walk in silence, leaving the park and passing through several city blocks.

"I must show you some stores," she says eventually.

"Some stores?"

"Yes. Shanghai is China's supermarket. People come here from all over the country to buy things. What would you like to buy?"

"I don't know," I say.

"We will go anyway," she replies, and there is no other conversation for another few blocks until we are in front of the largest Friendship Store in China. It seems to be a meeting place for foreigners. Taxis line the driveway; I quickly count eight Westerners outside on the steps. A Chinese security guard challenges Li Ming as we approach the revolving doors.

She answers his bark equally abruptly, and he nods, letting her pass. "What was that about?" I ask her.

"Only foreigners and overseas Chinese are allowed in here," she says. "But I told him I'm your translator."

Inside it is the best of Western capitalism, floor upon floor of gleaming consumer goods. A section for silk rugs, for ivory carvings and jade pieces and lacquerwork and other art treasures. Another floor for Japanese radios and TVs and VCRs, for compact disk players and cassette decks and, surprisingly, home computers too. Matching ancient urns eight feet high guard one section, their price tags of 280,000 yuan proudly displayed; a huge silk rug hangs in the background, the great wall of China slinking its way along the hills of its design. Then row upon row of silks, bolts of fabric or finished blouses, shirts, dresses, gowns, in peacock colours, lead to the furniture section, strictly antiques, intricate carvings running down every leg and up every arm, scenes of battle, of court life, of harvests in the rice fields and episodes from Chinese mythology. It seems more a museum than a store, but it is a store still — like the Smithsonian working overtime to sell off its treasures.

"This is the first time I have been allowed in here," Li Ming says, subdued, her eyes wide but critical. "These things cannot be bought by Chinese."

We wander through floor after floor. I buy a silk dressing gown for my mother, some silk long underwear for myself, a silver chain for Li Ming which she refuses three times, saying it should be for my sister, and so I buy two, and then she accepts. The saleswoman keeps looking at Li Ming, knowing from her clothes and her manner and any number of other cultural indicators, I suppose, that she is not an overseas Chinese returned to grace the old country with her foreign currency. In the end Li Ming puts on the chain and looks back at the saleswoman proudly, unafraid. She has a daredevil streak to her, there is no doubt about it, the pride of a fast rabbit showing her head.

"In Canada," she says, as we are walking away, "will people think me strange if they see I am not married to a Chinese?"

She is looking at me now, her eyes reflecting the knowledge of the full force of what she has said.

"No," I say. "Not where we will live." And I think, is this how people make the decisions that change their lives? One minute everything is one way and then the next it is changed and we walk on, and nothing is the same after that.

In Shanghai I do not meet her family. I stay at the guest house of the Number Three Television University, which is spartan but clean, quiet but friendly. All communications are done in pantomime; at the end of three days I leave impressed by how little one actually has to say if one has money.

We have spent most of our time walking, down the endless streets, through the occasional park, along the harbour. We buy food from stalls or eat magnificent noodles or wonderful fish soups in tiny, congested restaurants buried in back alleys. Will I get hepatitis, I wonder. We walk again until our legs are weary, but it doesn't seem to matter — we are together, we feel free. She asks me what I think of her hometown.

"I can't get over how many people there are here," I say. "I'm not sure I could get used to such crowds. That line-up there," I say, pointing, "that looks like the biggest line-up for the most popular movie in Ottawa. But it's for a bus, and this isn't even rush hour!"

"There were not so many people when I was growing up."

"What does a real Chinese crowd look like?" I ask her. "Like during the student demonstrations last year, before Hu Yaobang was ousted. So many people are here, and if just a fraction of them got together at the same time . . . "

"When there are demonstrations," she says, "even the biggest streets become too small. People march together and wave banners with huge letters. You get packed so close it becomes hard to breathe!"

"Were you in the demonstrations last year?"

"Not here," she says.

"In Laozhou?"

She nods.

"Did many teachers get involved in the Laozhou demonstrations?"

"I was the only one," she says.

"The only teacher?"

Again a nod.

"What happened? What did the authorities say when it was all over?"

"They were not pleased."

"What does that mean?"

"I had to make self-criticism to Dean Chun. And then I had my thoughts cleared."

"You had your thoughts cleared?"

Again she nods, not wanting to explain.

"Is that why you've been having so many problems with the department?"

"They have called me a Western bourgeois liberal."

The conversation doesn't go easily. As I'm about to ask my next question, she says, "What are large crowds like in Canada? Are there demonstrations?"

"Sometimes," I say, and try to explain that in Canada students are expected to get together every so often and wave placards and shout slogans — it's pretty well part of their education, and nobody pays much attention. There's not the same fear that the whole country will collapse into anarchy that there is in China.

We talk for a long time more and it begins raining, very lightly and then stronger, and we walk together under my small black umbrella. The world becomes smudged, hidden, the colours washed together in an even grey that touches us, too, makes us anonymous. Who could care that we would stand together on a corner, the rain washing down now in wild drops that pound on our thin fabric roof and splatter our clothes as they splash up from the ground around us and soak our feet in sidewalk rivers? Who would mind if we shared our first kiss and then just stood so very close looking at one another, to see perhaps just who it is, the loved one inside the stranger from so far away?

We return to Laozhou together on the train, soft seat, not so much confident after our four days as drawn together, bodies orbiting in such a way that they can only come closer. I am terribly aware of the way her eyes look, of the warmth of her hand and the shape of her mouth and the smell of her, the slight jasmine that fills me with fine associations even as we sit facing one another for the twelve-hour ride. Her foot brushes my calf under the table. She pours me water for my tea and her hand runs slowly along the inside of my arm. When we get up during a stop to stretch our legs on the platform our bodies lean together and there is a thrill in that brief contact, a tension later on as we ride, looking well into one another's eyes, waiting for the hours to be over.

We leave separately. I file ahead, she stays behind and then joins the crowd streaming out from hard seat. It's cool, the air wet as it is after a rain. I take a motorcycle taxi home, catching a glimpse as we leave the station of her standing in the crowd at the bus stop, her bag over her shoulder. Her eyes shine across the expanse of parking lot.

Then it's back along the dreary streets of Laozhou, past the crumbling buildings, the mouldy factories, the high fences, the huddled beds of winter cabbage, the slummy apartments, the lonely intersections with the carts, people, bikes, trucks all threading through somehow, oblivious to the traffic light over-head. At the gates of the college I pay my driver ten *yuan*, an extravagant sum, then get out and walk into the gloom, past the basketball courts, around the corner, up the hill to my cold, wet, welcoming apartment. I'm not really expected back so soon, so there's no food except some instant oatmeal which I mix with some water I heat up in a new Shanghai electric kettle I have bought for myself. It isn't much of a meal, but I sit in front of my little heater and savour the lumps, the taste of winter mornings from my childhood.

That night Li Ming comes to my apartment. Half asleep, I turn at a sound, a slight bump and then the slow stretch of the door, which I have left unlocked, not because I expected her, but because I hoped for her. She enters shyly and I sit up and then she is in the shadows, peering through the bedroom doorway.

"You shouldn't have come," I say, half-heartedly. "It's too dangerous."

She stops, not speaking, unsure. And then she steps forward, taking off her coat.

"Do you know what you are doing, Li Ming?" I whisper. She shakes her head no, standing before me, her face lowered.

"Either do I," I say, and then I reach up and we fall together and there is this strange time when she is sobbing against me, her body trembling, tears wet against my chest. I clumsily pull the covers over her and hold her for what seems like a long time before the shaking stops. Then she pulls back slightly and watches me in the darkness, looks through the shadows at my body.

I unbutton the front of her shirt, and it falls open and she pulls back her shoulders in a tiny movement and then her shirt is off. I lean down and kiss, very gently, all around her breasts, but it is hard because my breathing is heavy in just a few moments, and then we are rolling on the bed, beneath the covers and then exposed to the cold and then beneath the covers again, and I'm not sure how the rest of her clothes come off, it's happening too quickly . . .

Too quickly and too much, too much to take in. The flash of teeth in her smile and the round of her breasts and the smooth heat of her skin, and how beautiful she is with her head back, eyes closed, and the raggedness of her breathing, and her hands grabbing at my back, squeezing, pulling, running up and down . . .

I hang on and try to relax with the motion, but we are bolting in some unknown direction. I want to go but I'm also afraid, and part of me wants to take a moment to ask, is this the right direction? But maybe this comes naturally and I can't help the way my body reacts, finds its own way, and maybe I can think about it later, maybe it's better right now to just do what our bodies have been yearning to do.

Maybe there is no choice. Maybe the wave just builds, maybe we are two waves building together and the channel has been narrowing for a long time and it's inevitable that when we hit the wall, together, we carry right on over into the free waters. The impact leaves me dazed; the draining makes everything seem softer, cloudier, less focused. What I remember most is the warmth I felt all over when she appeared at the door, so unexpected and so yearned for.

"I love you," I say, holding her, kissing the soft curve of her neck from behind, but she is already asleep and doesn't hear.

21

THERE SEEMS TO BE NO REAL SPRING HERE. IN THE SPACE OF A DAY OR two the bone-chilling cold of the concrete that surrounds us suddenly turns to inescapable white heat, and the layers of clothing we have wrapped ourselves in are suddenly too much to bear. In the course of my lecture I strip off sweater after sweater until I am sweating in my shirtsleeves, a thin layer of chalk dust caking my forearms. My robust, padded students become thin, bony ones before my eyes, their desks spread out now to avoid the huddled heat they coveted just yesterday. My voice is hoarse from trying to reach the outer edges of the room, I've so much marking I can barely carry it all, and I'm looking forward to a short nap before dinner. But there at the door of my apartment is Wang, as tiny, energetic and intense as ever, in his usual floppy blue pants and a loose military sort of green shirt, long-sleeved despite the heat. My teacher has kept his promise to return in the good weather.

There is no Li Ming, of course, to translate. I look around for a student to help us. But he shakes his head and points to me, starting the hand movements for the *liu he ba fa*. He wants me to do it for him right now.

I go inside, clumping down the pile of marking and changing into the light, baggy blue cotton pants I have bought mainly for *wushu*. Then I return and do some stretches, trying not to feel nervous. I have been practising, but still it's difficult with him looking on, his arms crossed, face hard. I know that I can sit lower now, that my back is straighter, my movements smoother, that when I kick the foot snakes up over my head now instead of barely above my waist like before. Even my breathing feels better, but still . . . to do it with him looking on. I must move like a spider, I think, as I begin. Calm and quick and deadly. Don't look at him. Just move.

Soft steps, slipping across the concrete like a shadow dancing. Eyes watching the hands whirl, turning, quiet feet, the way he moves, like water slipping over stones. Slower here, careful, pulling the hands apart as the breath slips out noiselessly. Don't think; just move, now turn, and low, and around . . .

It seems even longer than usual. I am conscious of the strings of movement slipping into each other like different parts of a piece of music, balancing one another, sliding together so seamlessly the piece seems to have been discovered rather than created. I get over the rough transition from the first half to the second, where, like a fumbling pianist, I usually have trouble, and then the second half, usually a little ragged, builds instead with an authority I haven't felt before. It's happening, my body is finding this rhythm and I'm letting it. The kick, high, a beautiful snap of my foot against my hands, and then around, into the next move, whirling circles upon circles. It's easy now, I have to keep myself from going too fast, just stay relaxed, enjoy the last few moves. Turning towards the end, I look for the little spot on the pavement where I started, aim my right toe to find it on the last step and then straighten up, my hands coming together in front of me in a gesture of prayer and completion.

When I finish I try to disguise my breathing so that it seems to have been easy, but break down finally and gulp the air. More practice. I know I need more practice. But the breathing will come.

Wang nods once, his face solemn. Then he walks over to me and shows me two corrections — on an early move he slaps my bum in so that when I sit my back is perfectly straight, not curved, and then near the end he shifts my right hand outside rather than inside the left. I go over the moves for him and he watches, nodding when I get them right.

Then he steps back and motions for me to do it again. So I go through it and then without rest he has me do it once more, and then the tai chi set he has taught me. As I go through the movements, concentrating, feeling something building inside that was not there before, a crowd gathers, of course, at the gates, and watches. But it feels different now, I'm like an actor drawing energy from the audience. When Wang performs in public it is perfect, and I am Wang's student, so I must be perfect as well. That is all. The grace, strength, agility, effortlessness of Wang's movement must become part of mine.

He never takes his eyes off me, never changes his expression. It's just master and student; nobody else counts. On his side are hundreds of years of strict obedience and unwavering tradition; on my side, simply the effort to realize and hold what he has taught. If I am unsuccessful, it is understood, he will not teach me any more; but if he likes what he sees, then I will always be his student.

In the end he simply nods his head, as usual, then waves to one of the students watching, who approaches to be our translator.

"In Chinese *wushu* . . . uh, that is, the martial arts . . . " the boy says, "you must to . . . uh, to remember the strength of . . . being gentle. Yes. When you to attack snake . . . there is no, resistance, yes? Because snake very flexible. Cannot punch snake. But already snake has turned to make his, uh . . . counterattack. Especially in *taiji*. Very soft, very gentle . . . not appear to harm anyone. But *taiji* fighters almost invincible, because they cannot be hit. They win by giving in, yes? You must to be . . . more gentle in your fighting.

"Master Wang also say . . . he will to come back again, and teach you more. How long you will to stay in Laozhou?"

"Perhaps another year," I say.

"Then he will make you great Chinese fighter!" my student says, translating and laughing as Wang laughs now too, an old, old laugh. I stand smiling and dripping with sweat, aware now that it is my body, and not so much my mind, that is full with what he has taught me.

Lou began craving oranges. Most days she could not eat them fast enough, and Rudy took to buying two bags at a time, and then bought a whole box, which was empty in three days. She would not eat the pulps, but would cut the oranges into quarters and then suck them dry, dropping the remains haphazardly while reaching for another section. Sometimes he would watch her from the doorway in her kitchen and she would look up like a guilty hyena, orange carcasses strewn around her, juice and stray pulp sticking to her lips and chin.

Her hip bothered her more and more, so she began taking out an old baby carriage when she went shopping, something to carry groceries and lean on, especially when the sidewalks were icy. Sometimes Rudy would escort her and it was easy then to imagine being a family. People would pass them on the streets, smile and peer in at what they thought would be a child.

She wasn't sleeping very well. There was really only one position, on her side, that was comfortable, and it was only on the coldest of nights and with the window open that she wasn't too hot. She had bad dreams as well, about her baby arriving with stunted arms or a huge head or, once, with scales and a ridged, dinosaur-like tail. She tried to imagine the face of her daughter but could not; tried to think of her as a living human being inside her, but despite the kicking, rolling and hiccuping, could not. Her body was bloating out of shape like a piece of modeling clay. Her belly, breasts and hips were swelling, her ribs stretching, joints loosening, digestion tightening, even with a daily horrid dose of bran and prune juice.

Strangely enough, for all her cravings, Rudy had to tell her when to eat. She seemed to have lost her reference points, was continually surprised by how much she needed to consume in order to fuel the revolutionary changes inside her. Several times she suddenly became furious with him, over small things usually, the newspaper he had left out on the table, the pulpy, dry oranges he had bought, a book he had said he would lend her and then forgot — and each time it turned out she had missed her last meal. "I ate so much at breakfast," she would say. "So I really didn't need to eat lunch."

She kept trying to do too much. If Rudy vacuumed the living room she would insist on doing a laundry, and if he did her shopping then he would come back to find her scrubbing the kitchen floor, or wiping down her cupboards, or giving Oswald a bath. He tried, once, to teach her some tai chi to help her relax, but she could not remember how one move became the next, and felt stupid and awkward. "I'm a cow trying to be a ballerina," she said, finally quitting because of her hip.

She started sleeping in the afternoons and then staying up endlessly at night, an insomniac, writing in her journal or pecking away at her play. Sometimes she would phone Rudy at three in the morning asking about a particular line of dialogue, or if he was worried about how the birth was going to go, or once just to find out how he was able to sleep when it was so hot.

She said she didn't know how anybody got through this alone. "I know I'm still a single woman and everything, but I've got a Rudy to call on. What do those other women do?"

Rudy and Lou approached the park by the river, Rudy feeling free in his shirtsleeves and light cotton pants, Lou leaning heavily on the baby carriage. It was early afternoon and winter's hard back had finally been broken: the river was full and high, flowing smoothly beside the wet playground grass, which looked dark and groggy, as if waking up after a long sleep.

"Do you remember that night in the winter when we walked by here?" Rudy asked. "When the moon was so bright, and it was so cold?"

"Was that here?" Lou said.

"It was this park. The snowbanks made everything look silvery, and in the woods the light was bluish."

"Yes, I remember it," Lou said. "But I don't think it was me."

"What do you mean?"

"That was the other me, *before* I was pregnant."

"No, you were pregnant," Rudy said.

"No I wasn't!" Lou said, and then, after thinking, "You are such a pedant sometimes! A very good friend, but a pedant. I was pregnant, yes. I just didn't know it."

"I remember you told me that story about cross-country skiing."

"What story?"

"Well, you were telling me about you and Gary cross-country skiing at midnight."

"We did that?"

"And then you stopped in at a lodge and started a fire."

Lou was nodding, but she said, "That's funny. I don't remember that."

"You pulled this picnic table up to the fire, because the floor was too splintery . . . "

"Oh stop it!" she said suddenly. "I told you that story?"

"Yes! And then you started to make love, but you thought you heard a sound, and arched your back . . . "

"Shit, you are terrible! I told you that story? I can't believe it!"

They jostled one another jokingly, then stopped to face the sun as it shone down on the river.

"Oh God, no wonder I scared you off!" she said. "I can't believe I told you that story. I must have been drunk!"

"You didn't scare me off," he said, his eyes playful but partly serious, too.

"I didn't?"

"I'm still here, aren't I?"

She didn't answer, but looked down. "I can't see my shoes," she said, straining to the left and right. "God I hope this thing comes early!"

"It'll probably be a month late," he said.

There was a lengthy pause as Lou tried again to see her feet. "Do you think she's going to come?" she asked then, looking up.

"Who?"

"Your Li Ming."

"I've written her, but I haven't heard anything more," he said. "If she's going to apply for grad school, her application isn't in yet. So I don't know. I hope so." He scratched his chin. "You're going to like her."

"You're just lucky I'm not like Amanda," she said, pushing the carriage again.

"What do you mean?" he asked, walking beside her.

"It's hard for me. That's all!"

He nodded.

"It's hard to be with you so much. I keep thinking that we're married. You're so much more relaxed than Gary was, and you do all these little things for me, and I just . . . I would feel so lonely . . . "

In a moment she was crying. Rudy put his hands in his pockets and then took them out and put his arm across her shoulder.

"You see, this is your fault," she said, snuffling. "You just . . . you shouldn't ask about these things."

They started walking again, Rudy's arm slipping back by his side. At the far edge of the playground they stopped once more.

"You see . . . she's going to come . . . and then I'm going to be all alone with this baby, and I am not . . . I am not a martyr, Rudy, I don't have the patience to be, like, this superwoman who can be a mother and then also work and raise a kid and . . . and not have somebody there, and just . . . I am so scared. I mean, what if we die?"

Rudy shook his head. "Die?"

"I just . . . I keep thinking of Michael. He was so healthy and beautiful and he had such a rich mind and then bam, he's gone! And it's like . . . what if there's this thing inside me, that was inside him? What if they missed it in the test? What if it lies dormant and then all of a sudden my little daughter dies because she came from me, and I die because I was with Michael? I feel like . . . it should have been me! Why wasn't it me, Rudy? Why are we having this conversation?"

Rudy shook his head and put both his arms around her. He could feel the great size of her belly against his own as they stood.

"This is so romantic," she said, finally disengaging herself and wiping her face with a tissue from her pocket. "You're not going to be grossed out when you see me wallowing on the hospital bed, are you?"

He smiled.

"I mean, you should have seen how beautiful I used to be before this happened to me. Now you're just going to think I'm a walrus. This is a strange situation, you know."

She was walking again; they were leaving the park.

"What do you mean?"

"Oh, you know. Everything about this is strange. Our *conversations* are strange. I can't believe I told you about cross-country skiing. I'm going to have to ask you for an equally personal story from your mysterious past. You're going to have to tell me something so scandalous . . . !"

Rudy shook his head.

"Yes! You must! You owe me! How can I trust you in the writhing agony of childbirth if you don't tell me something horribly naughty and scandalous about you? Come on! I'm waiting!"

Rudy shook his head again, but was laughing.

"What? You're thinking of something! Come on, don't clam up. If you're going to be my best friend you'd better talk, buster!"

"No, there's nothing really to compare to your skiing adventure," Rudy said, still smiling.

"Then what are you thinking about? There's *something* there!"

"It's just . . . a wonderfully sunny day," he said, jumping aside to avoid the swing of her arm and then breaking into a run as she chugged after him with the carriage.

"This is like God kissing your face," Li Ming says, turning hers to the sunlight. We're perched on our secret pillbox on a blanket I have brought and it is *shuxi*, nap time for the rest of the country. Down below, green rice fields stretch out along the plains of the ancient battlefield, surrounded by gently moulded hills and a sky that is as blue as it gets here. There's the permanent coal dust haze over the city, of course, but up above that it's clear, and that is where Li Ming has turned her face.

"I thought you didn't believe in God?" I say.

She keeps her eyes closed and her face tilted towards the sun, as if that is her answer.

"I love the smell of the cedar trees up here," I say. "In town I feel as if the coal dust makes everything smell the same."

She gives no sign that she has heard me, and there's a long pause while I try to think of what to say.

"Master Wang has been working me extremely hard these days. I've got all these moves whirling in my head, the different sets are kind of running into one another. I get the feeling he wants to teach me everything he has learned in his entire life, all in a couple of months!"

Again, silence. It's getting hot here, the concrete of the pill-box baking under the sun.

"As soon as I get home I'm going to have to put in another hour of practice before he shows up, so I can make sure I know what he taught me yesterday."

She doesn't say anything, but turns to me finally and strokes the inner part of my arm, very lightly, without looking in my eyes. It's her shy way of beginning, and I lean over to kiss the back of her neck, which is just slightly salty from the sun.

"I meant to ask you," I say, nervously interrupting.

"What?"

"Well — we should really be doing something about — "

"What?"

"Well, we don't want to have a child. I mean, accidentally."

"We will not."

"Oh," I say.

She turns to kiss my neck.

"How do you know?"

"Because . . . I have had an insertion."

"A what?"

She averts her eyes.

"You have a diaphragm in?"

She doesn't answer. "Please tell me, Li Ming."

"I do not know the word," she says, still looking away. "I had it done . . . in Shanghai."

"The insertion?"

"Yes." There is quite a long pause. "So," she says finally. "Nobody knows." When I still don't understand she says, "I cannot get such an insertion in Laozhou if I am unmarried."

An IUD, she must mean. The Chinese ones are notoriously faulty, according to Madeleine, whose students tell her everything, even that the doctors cut off the "tails" for fear that women will try to remove their IUDs to have a child.

We don't talk about it further. I just imagine her, deciding, doing it, not telling a soul. On our Shanghai trip. My Li Ming. What else don't I know?

We aren't patient lovers, not this afternoon, because she must return by 3:30 for a political meeting and because it has been days now since we have been together, and maybe too because we are in the open and feel exposed, literally naked before the world. But it's hard, the thin blanket over the concrete, and under this sun we are oiled in sweat with the salt stinging my eyes even when I close them. I have to reach for a piece of clothing, my tangled underwear, to wipe them.

"Not so hard," she says, beneath me, and so I slow down, and lift my body off her as much as I can and still stay in position. I maintain my half push-up for a time and then it is too much, I collapse upon her with a huge squelch of the sweat between our bellies, which, I can't help it, makes me laugh. When I resume the motion the squelching starts up with it, obnoxiously loud, like exaggerated farting.

Slow down. Concentrate. Get it back together. I close my eyes and think of her in the moonlight, the fine curve of her breast and the ivory shine of her smile as she arches her neck back, how smooth her face is and the beautiful taper of her legs . . .

Damn! Mosquitoes! I reach behind and slap my bum, but with no satisfying squish. "Sorry," I whisper to her and then it's the back of my shoulders getting bitten, right in the fleshy part between the blades. I slap again but miss and then it's buzzing around my ears with the same piercing whine as a dentist's drill.

Just ignore it, I say to myself. This is a price of passion. Go back to the moonlit room. The tilt of her neck. Her fine brown nipples, and the way that she tenses, just a bit, with pleasure when I kiss behind her ear. I bend close to do that, to kiss behind her ear, but I am bitten right on the cheek and I slap with my support hand and miss, then collapse upon her and she moans, not with passion but annoyance.

These Chinese mosquitoes. They're smaller, faster, meaner than the Canadian brand. I grab my shirt and wave it over my head, but she pulls me back down. "Don't worry about it," she says. "Keep going."

The mind can conquer anything. I go back to the moonlit room, ignoring the squelching of our sweaty bellies, the drilling of the mosquitoes, the intense glare of the sun which is reddening my poor white bum. We rise above these earthly things, the waves within us growing steadily until . . .

Until there is an odd flapping noise that I cannot ignore. It seems right above our heads and at first I think it's a bird and will go away and so I don't look. But it doesn't go away, it gets louder, and so I open my eyes and there, swooping down upon us is an immensely ugly red dragon with a long spiny body and golden pop-out eyes and a tail that snaps in the wind like a forked whip.

"Oh God, Li Ming!" I cry and roll off her, clutching my clothes, and of course I know it's just a kite, but somewhere down below at the end of the string there is a person, looking up at us.

"They cannot see us," she says, but her voice is a little panicky. It's true, I want very much to believe that it's true. When I look past the edge I see the string curving over the tops of the trees and disappearing. If he could see us, then we could see him. But we retreat to the woods anyway to put on our clothes, fighting a rearguard action with the mosquitoes all the way.

"I'm sorry," I say but she shakes her head, smiling, slapping her thigh as she pulls up her pants. "It doesn't matter," she says, buttoning her shirt. "I have to go anyway."

"You go ahead," I say and she nods. We arrive separately, we leave separately.

"I hope you have a good meeting."

"Don't be stupid," she says, poking me in the belly and then pulling me close for a kiss that reaches to the tips of my toenails and wipes away all clumsiness, all sweat and mosquitoes and intruding dragons.

22

"THIS DOESN'T COUNT," LOU SAID, PUTTING DOWN THE PAGES.

"Why not?" Rudy asked. They were sitting on the sofa in the late afternoon sun, Oswald asleep on the rug underneath the coffee table.

"Because you've written it out so that anybody can read it. What I told *you* is never to be repeated to anybody, ever, and certainly never to see *print*."

"You asked for something personal and scandalous," Rudy said, shifting now to squeeze the ball of her left foot. "That's as personal and scandalous as I can get."

Without thinking she slapped the chapter down on the coffee table and Oswald gave a sharp bark and went to the door, whining.

"Oh God. Oswald — shut up! Go back to sleep!"

Oswald whined louder and scratched at the doorframe until Rudy let him out, giving him a soft boot as he opened the door.

"I wonder if raising a kid will be the same as raising a puppy?" Lou asked, holding up her foot for Rudy to continue.

"You're certainly going to find out." Rudy settled back on the couch. They could hear Oswald yapping outside on the porch.

"I think he wants to be let back in," Rudy said.

"You're not going to show this to Li Ming, are you?" Lou asked, leaning to pick up the chapter again. "Just from what I've read so far I'd have to say she'll be furious with you for writing it."

Rudy looked out the window for a while, and listened to Oswald's continued barking.

"Rudy?"

"I guess . . . I decided that . . . I wasn't going to think about that," he said. "If I do then . . . everything stops, right? I've got nothing to write. So I'll write it all out, and if I have to change something, then I'll do that, or, if I just . . . can't have anybody read it . . . then I'll put it away. You see, this is . . . something I have to get out of my system first, and then maybe I can go on and make up stories, the way real writers do. This can stay in the drawer. I don't want it to hurt anybody. I think I'm mostly writing it for myself."

Oswald was getting louder and scratching now at the outside of the door in his effort to get back in.

"Could you get that?" Lou said, putting her hands behind her head. "I'm pregnant."

"A likely excuse!" Rudy said, standing up and opening the door for Oswald, who scampered in, trailing mud. Rudy had to chase him through the kitchen and upstairs before he finally caught up to him with an old towel and wiped off his shaggy legs and belly. "How could you get so muddy if you just stayed on the porch?" Rudy asked him, towelling off Oswald's slobbering face as well. "Eh? How could that happen?"

"Am I just fooling myself, or what do you think?" Rudy asked as he was coming down the stairs, Oswald running noisily ahead of him. But Lou was asleep on the couch, and he paused by the door to watch her, her head back and peaceful, and her hair so lustrous and tangled about her shoulders. He took a blanket from a nearby chair and laid it over her before quietly leaving, giving Oswald a *shhhhh* sign as he closed the door.

It wasn't often that Rudy cried, but he did then, walking along in the sunshine, thinking of Lou, and knowing now in that strange way the heart knows that he had settled on Li Ming.

Some days later Rudy was surprised to find Amanda sitting behind the secretary's desk in the department office. She looked tiny next to the monuments of paper casting shadows over different corners of the office, but she seemed to be seized too with a purpose that Rudy had not seen in her before. Her pale cheeks were flushed now, her eyes narrowed and intense, her thin shoulders braced as if carrying a new and important burden.

"I can't believe how disorganized things are around here," she said when he walked in. "That's not true. I can believe it. I just don't know what to do about it."

"Where's Elizabeth?"

"Vacation," Amanda said. "There's a package for you."

"For me?"

She got up and lifted a three-foot stack of paper, balancing it somehow as she shifted it to the far corner of the desk. "I'm going to have to take a weight training course," she said.

"What package?" Rudy asked.

The phone rang. Amanda fielded the call while sifting rapidly through another smaller stack that was in the middle of the desk. "Uh huh . . . yes . . . right," she said, cradling the phone in the hollow of her neck while two-thirds of the papers were being dealt like cards into the wastebasket. "I'm afraid it's too late. The deadline was in March."

She put down the phone. "Poor guy," she said, still flipping and discarding. "He got stuck in Robinson's second year Romantics and only now is he realizing what a fool he's been."

"What's wrong with Robinson?"

She told him the problem with Robinson in the offhanded way that she could probably tell him the problem with every professor in the department. While she was talking she took the papers she hadn't thrown out over to the file cabinet, and combed through the drawers with the speed of a worker ant.

The phone rang again. Without looking she stretched back her hand, snatched the receiver and rested it again in the hollow of her neck.

"Yes . . . right away . . . thank you." She put the phone down. "I didn't realize there was so much to do," she said, slamming the file drawers closed. "What was it you wanted?"

"You said there was a — "

"Oh right! Not for you, though. For Dr. Creighton. From China."

"Li Ming's application!"

"Yes!"

Rudy ran the two steps around the desk and hoisted her high in the air. "It's here! I can't believe it — it's here!"

"Careful!" she said. "Put me down — hey!" She pushed her way out of his arms. "I thought you might want to know," she said, allowing herself to smile.

"Oh God, it's not too late, is it?"

"No. Monday's the closing date. She couldn't have cut it much closer, though. Did you hear on the news about the demonstrations?"

"No," he said.

"Somebody died, and the students were having demonstrations in Beijing."

"Who?"

"Yes, that's it."

"What?"

"No, who."

"Sorry. What?"

Rudy caught on. "Oh, Hu Yao Bang! He died, did he?"

"Somebody did," Amanda said.

"He was the one who was ousted the year before I was there, during the last student demonstrations."

"Was he?" Amanda said.

"God, I can't believe that her application is finally here! I wish there was something more I could do. I feel like Lou now, waiting for her kid to pop."

"Her kid to pop?" Amanda said.

"Yes."

"That's a horrible way to put it."

"Well, you know what I mean."

"Yes," Amanda said, turning to pick up the phone even before the end of the first ring.

Outside, rain lashing down with a fury that reminds me of August thunderstorms rolling along the Ottawa Valley, exploding the late afternoon heat. There is no lightning yet, and with the power off it seems almost night as I sit on my vinyl sofa, trying to go over my notes for another lecture to the masses. But soon it's too dark and I have to get up to watch the rain fall in bombs upon my concrete courtyard, creating its own wind that rattles my flimsy shutters and shakes the pole of a loudspeaker that I wish would fall over, I'm so sick of hearing the same music at the same times day after day after day.

Today was supposed to be my day off, when Wang would not come and I would go to the mountain with Li Ming. But the rain washes away those hopes, and I can't hope either that she will come tonight because it's getting too dangerous.

I turn for a moment to the English-language *Beijing Review* and read through its reassuring lead article: Struggle Against Bourgeois Liberalization Deepens, which urges people to "seek truth from facts," "consolidate stability and unity," "counteract erroneous trends" and "maintain social bearings." It's the kind of language echoing through uncountable Wednesday afternoon political meetings, massaging the ears of every worker in every unit across the country. They don't have to pay attention, much less believe it; but they do have to be there, hour upon hour.

I check my watch for the fifth time, look out the window again, and reluctantly gather my notes. No use putting it off any longer. I dash with an umbrella around to the Foreign Language Department door, my trouser cuffs soaked in the seconds it takes to get there. On the stairs I pass one of the older English teachers, and he nods to me as I say "*Ni hao*," then his eyes find the floor as he squirts past. We've never had a conversation because he has so little confidence in his English. Like many of the older teachers, he originally did his language training in Russian in the 1950s, and then, as if he were a machine with changeable gears, he was ordered to switch when the two great communisms began their rift.

Up to the second floor. What am I doing today? "Shooting an Elephant." As I step up the stairs I imagine myself a young Orwell, in my white officer's uniform, carrying my gun as I follow the trail of destruction left by the elephant in heat, and the crowd growing behind me, pushing me on, until I'm just the figurehead, the man with the gun who, though nominally in charge, must use it, even though the elephant I finally find has passed her rage and is eating peacefully in a field. The crowd expects it. I am the imperial power. Having a gun means having less choice. The gun must go off, or else what does my power mean?

As I think of that scene I pass a doorway and, looking in purely through reflex, see Li Ming. She is sitting, straight-backed, with a book on her lap, and looks up just at the second I gaze in, the waves of some speech washing over the entire room. No one is listening — they are reading, like Li Ming, or knitting or talking or eating the candies, pumpkin seeds and oranges left out for them on little tables, spitting out the shells, turning to laugh at something someone has said a few seats over.

Only Li Ming sees me and it is as if the air has turned to glass. Then I'm past and walking into my own classroom, disoriented. What was it I was going to speak about? I wander to the podium at the front as they calm down, my talkative fourth year students who will be graduating soon into the harsh world of the middle school teacher. What was my topic? I look through my notes. A few students come up to hand in papers. "Thank you," I say, accepting them, waiting for my head to clear.

"We are going to read a story today written by a servant, and a critic, of what you call the 'sun-never-setting empire.' It's a personal story that gets to the rotten heart of imperialism, of the efforts of one people to rule another . . . which you know about, of course, from your history. Hong Li Mei, could you begin reading please? This is the handout I gave you last time." To my surprise the introduction falls out of my voicebox, apparently without first passing through my brain. Maybe this means I'm becoming a seasoned teacher, still functioning outwardly even though when Hong Li Mei stands up and reads haltingly through the first paragraph I'm clutched with the bizarre sense that I can no longer understand my native language. That the words are going past my brain but are not registering, as if they have been twisted through a wire that scrambles the sounds. But it isn't her reading that causes the problem; I am stuck, still, in that locked moment with Li Ming, in the wonder of catching the eye of someone I share love with, in seeing such naked feelings in the briefest, most spontaneous glance. But if we are so easy to read, who else saw our exchange? Who else knows?

"You should not have come," I say at night, stirring at the sound of the door in the other room, the muffled shaking of her umbrella, the heavy rustle as she peels off her wet jacket and leaves it hanging on the hook by the couch.

"I'll go then." But she moves, silently now, into the bedroom, her footsteps soft as light.

"No." I haven't really been sleeping. I've been lying here, hoping both that she would come and that she would stay away. Outside the rain washes against the walls of our fragile haven.

She turns her back as she takes off the rest of her clothes. In the darkness I can just make out the slimness of her hips, the gentle line of her buttocks, the fine taper of her legs. It must be very light inside that body, I think. She carries nothing extra in her steps.

"How was your meeting?" I ask as she slips between the sheets and slides against me, her body cold from the rain. I warm her as best I can, delighting in the softness of her skin and the perfect way we fit, one against the other. Does this get usual, I wonder — does the press of a mate's body ever become too ordinary to savour?

"It went on too long," she says.

"What were they talking about?"

"Nothing."

"They must have been talking about something."

"No."

We lie luxuriously dry and warm in our cotton sheets, listening to the rain.

"I should close the drapes," I say.

"No one is out in that," she says sleepily. "Leave them open." She rolls and pulls the pillow close to her head, then backs up against me.

"I cannot sleep any more unless I am with you," she says, and I snuggle my cheek against the thickness of her hair.

Sometime in the night a sound wakes me from a dream that evaporates before I open my eyes. But — silence. Did I hear a noise at all? Is that a light on outside the window? No, the moon. And no rain. It must have cleared. I reach to the table for my watch with the illuminated dial. Two-eighteen.

I'm sure I heard a noise. I almost wake Li Ming, asleep on her side, a blade of moonlight cleaving us.

Damn. What was it? Nothing? There isn't even any wind. It sounded, though, like footsteps. Like someone pulling himself up the bars on the window and looking in through the open drapes. Why didn't I close them?

Probably it's nothing. Maybe an animal. Do they have raccoons here? Quietly I slip from between the sheets and look out the window. Nothing. Just a narrow alley and then the wall of the college. Nobody would be back here. Except to spy on me.

I close the drapes, then through the new darkness feel my

way to the hook where I hang my robe. Stub my toe on the dresser leg. Shit! Where are my tongs? She's going to wake up. I find them under the bed, carry them to the other room, sit on the couch to put them on. Look out the door.

Nothing. Night-time. One light only in the centre of the campus; everything else in shadows. Moonlight gleaming off the puddles. Too wet. I won't be able to practise tomorrow in my courtyard. What a stupid thought to have! I sit back down on the couch in the shadows.

Maybe there was no one there. Maybe it was just a cat. Or a dream. Or there wasn't even a sound. Maybe there's nothing to do but go back to bed.

But what if it was someone? "Li Ming!" I say, getting up. It might not be too late. If we move quickly. "Li Ming!"

Shaking her. Stay calm. "Li Ming!"

"Hnnn?"

"You have to go. I think I heard someone at the window. Get up!"

She says something in Chinese, then is awake. "Someone saw us?"

"I think so! We shouldn't take the chance. You should go as fast as you can."

I don't turn on the light but collect her clothes for her and help her push them on. Why did I wait so long? Maybe it's too late already. Maybe the army boots are already on their way.

She swears in Chinese, struggling with the buttons on her shirt, then pulling her sweater lopsidedly over her head. There's no time to say anything. She runs to the door.

"I love you!" I whisper, but to her back as she runs across the puddles and then is swallowed by the shadows.

Silence. Is that it, then? Now what? I catch myself standing with my fists clenched, as if the soldiers will be here in a moment and I will try to fight my way out. Of what? Silence. The night is utterly still. There are no sirens, no lights, no barking dogs or jackboots.

But it's no use trying to sleep, because the moment I close my eyes fists will be on the door. Tiny, angry men in ill-fitting uniforms screaming long streams of tangled Chinese. Searching everything, turning over my desk, ripping off the sheets, scattering my books and letters.

How is it they execute people here? A bullet to the back of the head. You would not be arrested if you were not guilty. Of what? It doesn't matter. When you have a billion people, a man and a woman are meaningless.

I open my eyes. Silence, still. Deceptive.

I should write to my mother and father. What would I say? I could pedal straight to the Technical Institute. The other foreigners would protect me. How? I wouldn't even get past the gate. Fuck. Don't panic. Rudy. Calm. *Don't panic.*

If I don't do anything, then what proof will they have? I'll deny whatever they say. I'm a foreigner, they can't just push me around. But what about Li Ming? *She* would be the one who was punished. Probably they would send me home. But her . . .

Oh God. Madeleine, of course, was right. I should have just . . . if I'd only shown some . . . if only I wasn't so selfish! It's my fault.

It's my fault. The refrain runs through my mind, soothing as broken glass. It's my fault. I'm the one to blame. It's my fault, it's my fault, it's my fault . . .

We must marry. As soon as possible. Can we do it here? If only we had an hour to make plans! But she's probably already been hauled from her room. They're probably beating a confession from her right this moment. Who can I talk to? What can I do? There must be some way . . .

I pace, look out the window, double my fists and unclench them and say *shit!* out loud in the middle of the darkness. Maybe she should have stayed here. We could have talked then, made a plan. I would know what to do. But now there's nothing I can do, *nothing!* Except wait.

And wait. The night passes with the agony of a snail crawling along the edge of a razor blade. Standing by the window, all the scenarios running through my head like Grade B movies with prison cells, interrogation chairs, naked lightbulbs, truncheons. This is a country where those things exist and are used, and I'm looking through the bars of my window waiting for them to happen to me. The entire country is a prison. There's nowhere to run.

But maybe, with Li Ming here, we could do it. I have the money; she knows the country. If we left now maybe we could get to the train station in time to catch the southbound to Shanghai. Or somewhere. We could disappear. Even here. Melt into the crowds. If I stole some clothes. There are ways out of the country. There must be. Why did I send her away? Should I go now to her residence and get her up? I know the building, but not the room. No. Impossible. Too late. I have to wait.

I get my watch and look at the illuminated dial. Three-twelve. Is that all? If we left on bicycles, and rode at night. It's better not to let them catch us. Then you have no chance at all. If we run together maybe we could make it out. Why did we get into this? Why did Li Ming have to come here? It was stupid, foolhardy. Why didn't I just close the drapes? I should have been firmer. She's too much of a gambler. That's her problem. I'm the patient one. I can't trust her, she's too hotheaded. We could have made it if we'd been careful. In the long run. That's what this is about. Not one night's pleasure.

Shit. If only I could take back the time. Rewind the tape. Just close that curtain. This is too much to pay for such a small mistake. It can't be right. There must be another chance. Or something we can do. What?

Nothing. Don't look at the watch. No sleep. Nothing to do but wait.

And wait.

The night sky gradually lightens from the black of the abyss to the colour of an ugly bruise to, somehow, the innocent blue of a sparkling new morning. It seems impossible, a miracle, this morning, as bright as any dawn could be. No soldiers. There are no soldiers. The puddles on the world are dripping gold and jewels and there are no soldiers whatsoever. I pull on my clothes to step outside and listen to the slow wakening of bicycle bells and donkey carts. Someone walks by along the alley on the other side of the college wall carrying at least two bird cages. Probably he is an old man with a bent back wearing blue, and the cages are covered in an identical blue cloth and are hooked onto a pole that is stretched across his shoulders. It's all in my mind the instant I hear the tangled songs of the two birds.

There are no soldiers. It is morning and there are no soldiers and the air smells freshly made, the newest air in the universe. And when I see her, after breakfast, sitting in her seat in the tiny library working on another paper, she gives me a tired, safe, relieved smile. We're all right after all.

23

AS THE STUDENT PROTESTS GREW IN BEIJING, LOU ENDURED THE FINAL weeks of her pregnancy. The two swellings seemed somehow to be related, and Rudy watched both with a growing sense of awe and anticipation. He was sure the demonstrators in Tiananmen Square would soon be dispersed, as the student protestors had been at Christmas 1986, and yet day after day the government was mute. Western journalists and camera crews freely documented the occupation of the square, and the Chinese press grew increasingly bold. Rudy discussed the protests with Dr. Creighton as he waited for Li Ming's application to be processed, and while they viewed it from different angles they agreed that the government would soon put an end to the dissent, certainly before Gorbachev's visit to reopen relations between the two great enemies.

Meanwhile, Lou's baby turned itself the wrong way around. It had been in perfect birthing position, head down and engaged, and then just a week before the due date the doctor, after feeling Lou's belly, announced that the baby had slipped out of place and now had its feet pointed downwards. The customary procedure so late in the game was to sign her up for a Caesarean, but Lou found another doctor at the hospital who had trained with midwives in Newfoundland outports and could do external versions. The whole procedure took barely ten minutes, as the doctor dug his fingers under Lou's pelvic bone to pry the feet out, then slowly rotated them counterclockwise, to protect the cord. Lou gripped Rudy's forearm and did not speak; the doctor remained very calm, although the veins on his neck puffed out with effort. And on a little screen across from them the ultrasound showed the eerie black and white landscape of life within the womb.

The doctor stood back and wiped his face with a towel, then watched the screen as the nurse probed Lou's belly with the ultrasound.

"Is it not going around?" Lou asked.

"It's in, actually," he said. "The head is fully engaged."

"What?!" Lou said.

"Yes!"

"Already! You've done it?"

His smile was answer enough, and she howled ecstatically. "I don't believe it!" she said. "My God!"

But they still had to wait to see if the baby was responding normally. The nurse strapped on the fetal monitor and the room was filled with the chugging sounds of the baby's heart. A machine beside the ultrasound graphed out the rise and fall of the life pulse.

"I think she might be asleep," Lou said, feeling her belly. "She doesn't seem to be moving."

There was no rise in the heart rate, just a quick and steady thump-thump-thump-thump-thump. The doctor tried waking the baby with a tiny horn. They waited five minutes, tried again. Nothing. Fifteen more minutes, and then Lou was taken across the hall through a set of doors labelled, in immense red letters, HIGH RISK. "This is Nurse Meyers, she'll look after you," the doctor said. "I'll be back to check in a little while."

Nurse Meyers, heavy-set and abrupt, with a few loose grey hairs straying from under her cap, took the clipboard with the doctor's notes without looking at either Lou or Rudy. Then she led Lou to a table and hooked her up to another fetal monitor, pulling a screen beside the bed to give them some privacy.

"How long ago did the doctor turn the baby?"

"I think it's been . . . maybe twenty minutes," Lou said.

"*Twenty* minutes!" the nurse said, flipping on the machine. "Well, you aren't going to leave here until you have three proper movements, do you understand?" She then left the room.

Together Rudy and Lou watched the slow seismograph of the baby's heartbeat, spinning out so evenly that Lou could not believe it. "With parents like Gary and me this kid should be bouncing off the walls. Well, I guess she was before. God, what if she decides to turn around again? I couldn't go through this another time."

"She's going to be all right," Rudy said. "You should be happy. That doctor just performed a miracle!"

"But what if my baby has got brain damage?" she said, suddenly close to tears.

"Your baby does not have brain damage," Rudy said, taking her hand. "She's having a *shuxi*, an afternoon nap, that's all. Can I get you something to drink?"

"No."

Nurse Meyers came back and looked at the graph. Then she

left again, and they heard her tired but loud voice on the other side of the screen. "I'm off now, Marcie!" she said. "That woman in there had her baby turned *and there's been no reaction for half an hour!*"

Marcie's reply was muffled, but Lou's was immediate. "Oh God!" she said, pulling up her knees and clutching her belly. "My baby! What have I done to my baby?"

"It's okay," Rudy said, stroking her arm. "They're just being paranoid."

"I hope so," she said, turning to look at the monitor again. "What, is that something?"

It was nothing. The child was oblivious. Outside the window, Rudy could see the afternoon fading quickly, and in fact it was starting to rain, the wind whipping up a few dead leaves from the autumn past and whirling them down the darkening street.

"I will not forgive myself," Lou said, biting her lip. "If something has happened to my child . . . oh God, I will *never* forgive myself. Why didn't I just go in for the C-section?"

"It's going to be all right," Rudy repeated. "Listen. You must be hungry. Can I get you something?"

"Maybe a little orange juice," she said.

Rudy got up and moved past the screen, then asked the nurse if it was all right if he got some orange juice for Lou.

"Of course! Here, we have some right here!" she said, as if surprised he had to ask. He brought back the juice, which Lou downed in a few seconds, then he returned with a second cup.

"I can't believe what this kid is putting me through," Lou said, sad, angry and weary at the same time. "I don't know why somebody didn't warn me . . . "

"About what?"

"I don't know. This . . . parenthood is murder!"

"Maybe if people warned us we wouldn't be so eager about starting the next generation. Maybe there's a genetic amnesia that keeps us reproducing."

"They say that you forget the pain of childbirth at some point. I don't believe it. I will never . . . oh shit! What's that!" She jerked around suddenly, spilling the last of her orange juice on the sheet. "She's kicking! Oh God, Rudy, look, she's kicking! Look at that heartbeat! Isn't that the most wonderful thing! Christ, I don't believe it! Oh Rudy, here, take this, I love you, take it!" she said, thrusting the paper cup at him and then turning fully to watch her baby kick. "It's a miracle," she said, through tears. "Come on — give me a real boot! Oh yes. Oh God. It's a fucking miracle!"

24

HE'S NOT SUPPOSED TO COME, BUT HE'S HERE. JUST AS I AM GETTING on my bicycle to ride out to the hill to see Li Ming, Wang arrives, looking calm as usual and quiet, unperturbed. He motions for me to show him what we have been working on and I hesitate . . . but he's my teacher, and I can't say no. I go through it for him and the crowd that gathers is silent, almost sullen. No catcalls, no laughter, just angry, sulking looks, especially from Jiang, whose burning eyes have been following me for some days now.

It's not a long practice. Perhaps Wang realizes that I'm distracted. He just shows me the two new movements to finish off the section I am working on, and then he points for us to go inside my apartment. One of my students joins us as translator.

"Master Wang, he . . . tell you story," my student says, after Wang has refused tea, and sat down only on the edge of his chair, leaning forward, measuring his words. "In Great . . . Cultural Revolution was not . . . popular to play *wushu* . . . not allowed, you see, because . . . these things very old, very ancient practices and . . . all the old things, in Cultural Revolution . . . suddenly backward, uh, feudal . . . no good. People . . . not allowed play *wushu* . . . and other people . . . they hate you suddenly for that . . . yes?"

I nod my head, yes, I am following.

"So, *wushu* players . . . like Master Wang's teacher . . . some sent to prison because of it."

"Your teacher was sent to prison?"

Wang nods when he hears the translation of my question. "Master Wang's teacher . . . have refused to teach a . . . cadre . . . before, because he was not . . . good character. Bad man. A good teacher will not teach . . . a bad man. So now in Cultural Revolution . . . this cadre denounced Master Wang's teacher . . . sent to prison!"

Wang is looking at me very deeply as he speaks now. "Wind shifts here . . . very quickly. Everyone .must to . . . stay alert. Change when . . . wind changes. We did not . . . practise openly then. Middle of the night. All in secret. You understand?"

I nod my head, yes. I think.

"Other thing in *wushu* . . . " Wang says, through the translator. "Must always keep . . . steady heart." He pantomimes several hand movements, then pats his chest where his heart is. "Slow, steady heart. Always."

It is a strange meeting, over suddenly. "See you tomorrow," he says through the translator at the end, and grasps my hand warmly. And when I leave on my bicycle the crowd is still mostly there at the gate, still sullen and silent, looking in.

"You are late," she says, not turning when she hears me coming through the bush.

"I'm sorry." I step out of the shadows suddenly and see her from the back standing on our pillbox in her plain white blouse with her blue pants. She has tied a white ribbon in her hair. "Master Wang showed up unexpectedly. I had to do my *wushu* for him."

No smile, nor does she turn around. Instead her arms are crossed and she is gazing out at the haze over the valley.

"God, I was scared the other night. I'm so sorry about that. I wasn't sure, but I thought I'd heard something."

She turns, finally, to face me, and I see she's been crying. I step uncertainly beside her.

"What's wrong?" I ask, but she shakes her head. "You knew I was going to come. I was just detained. Master Wang showed up. These things happen. I'm sorry."

She doesn't say anything. As much to fill the void as anything else I say, "I wish we'd closed the drapes. We have to be careful."

She looks at her watch and sighs, the noise sounding like a knife being pulled from a sheath.

It's better to stay quiet, and so I do, but she is not about to speak either, and so we boil silently until I can't stand it anymore.

"You look beautiful," I say.

"Do I?"

"Yes, I like your bow. God, though, I was petrified the other night. I really was. For you and for me. We have to think about what we're doing."

"So you haven't thought about what we are doing?"

"Yes. Of course I have thought about it. But — "

"It doesn't matter. We have to keep cold heads," she says, and then, when she sees my smile, "What?"

"Nothing."

"What?"

"*Cool* heads. I'm sorry, that's the phrase."

"That's what I said!"

"No, actually, you said 'cold heads.' It doesn't matter. It's just — "

213

She hurls a volley of Chinese at me then we stand, staring at one another, furious.

"What?" I say. "I'm in your country and I don't understand your ways. I *thought* we were in a lot of danger. I was worried about what might happen to you. That's all."

"Do not worry," she says, in a tone that freezes me with fear. "*Nothing* will happen to you. You will go home and marry a blonde-haired girl, that is all! It is my life that is running away!"

Head down, she pushes past me. "Li Ming!" I say, grabbing her shoulders too hard and then letting go. "Wait!"

She slaps her way into the bush, her shoes scraping against rocks and underbrush. "Wait! Listen. Hey!" I say, going after her. "Wait a minute!"

She stops, but doesn't turn.

"Look at me!"

I have to walk to the other side of her to see her face.

I put my hands on her shoulders. "It's no good if we have a wonderful time and then can never see one another again. That's not what I'm here for. I'm here because you're the one I want to spend the rest of my life with. Is there any way . . . I was just wondering . . . can we get married here?"

Her eyes brittle, she shakes her head.

"All right," I say, taking a paper out of my pocket. "This is my parent's address. If anything should happen . . . if we get separated . . . you can always reach me through them. Anytime. I mean it. It might . . . we might be separated for years before we can work something out . . . "

She takes the paper but does not look at me.

"It *will* work out. We have to believe in that. Whatever happens, we will find a way . . . "

"I should go," she says, looking down.

"Please, Li Ming, you've got to know — I'm in this for the long run. I want us to have children. I want . . . "

"Yes," she says slipping out from under my hands.

"I want us to have a home and friends and to be able to — "

 Waiting for Li Ming

"You should wait until I am far away," she says.

"What?"

"So no one will see us together."

"Do you know what I'm saying?"

She is several paces away now, disappearing into the shadows.

"Do you?"

"When my father died," she says, "my mother . . . was never well. She has been made dry, like . . . someone with no *chi*, no spirit. I am the only one left to fight, and I do that, I fight . . . through everything I do. If I don't fight, then I will lose too, my *chi*. I cannot . . . if they make us afraid when we love . . . "

She turns and disappears behind a tree then appears again and then is gone, like a shaft of light playing in shadows, and all that is left to listen to is the buzzing of cicadas.

Over the next several days newspapers piled up in Rudy's apartment and the television was rarely off as he switched between channels for up-to-date coverage of the events in Beijing. With the arrival of Gorbachev the whole city seemed to rise in peaceful revolt against their government, safe in the knowledge that the world's eyes were watching. A million people flooded the centre of Beijing in support of student hunger strikers in Tiananmen Square. It was hard to zero in on what the students were asking for — the end of official corruption? Better food in the dorms? Open dialogue with the government? Complete democracy for the country overnight? Gorbachev's visit to the Beijing Opera and the Forbidden City were cancelled for security reasons, to keep him away from the square. Then his press conference, which was supposed to be at the Great Hall of the People, was switched at the last minute. Thousands of journalists had to somehow make their way across town with the streets in chaos, the buses and subway not working. The city was practically swamped in a general strike. The newspapers were full of the fact that the Soviets had trouble making copies of Gorbachev's speech because their copier broke and the men who were supposed to fix it refused to work.

What was Li Ming doing in all this? Rudy wondered. Hadn't she told him she had been the only teacher at Laozhou Teacher's College to participate in the last demonstrations? She wouldn't be able to stay out of something like this, Rudy knew full well. She was not one to keep her head down.

Then Gorbachev left Beijing and every commentator Rudy read expected the worst. Under the hot sun at Tiananmen, two to three thousand crowded students continued their hunger strike. Then at dawn of May nineteenth the two government rivals, Li Peng and Zhao Ziyang, went together to talk to the students. Li lectured them sternly and then left; Zhao praised their good intentions but pleaded with them to leave while it was still safe. Then Li met in the Great Hall of the People with Wu'er Kaixi, a twenty-one-year-old education major in a hospital gown and running shoes who was told that he was being impolite to the Prime Minister.

"Impolite?" the boy said. "You've got a million people on the streets and you're calling me impolite?" And then they yelled at one another until the boy collapsed and Li Peng went away and imposed martial law.

On that night, May twentieth — when the hunger strike became a sit-in and the residents of Beijing defied Li and protected the students, blocking access routes, surrounding military vehicles, slashing their tires and staring down the young soldiers who had been brought in from out of town — Rudy got a call from Lou.

"What channel are you on?" she asked breathlessly.

"CBC."

"Go to 10. Hurry!"

He flipped the channel on his set and there she was, suddenly, her skin too pink and her shirt too green but the accent definitely British, the face unmistakably hers.

"What we are seeing today is the rising up of the people to challenge Li Peng and Deng Xiaoping, who have lost the mandate of heaven," Li Ming said. "The people of Beijing will not submit to martial law."

She was not saying it stridently; she was, in her way, gently affirming the facts. The picture switched then to a reporter in shirtsleeves who was summing up the events of the day, and then the camera panned the square with its makeshift tents and garbage piles, its Red Cross stations and weary-looking students in ragged clothing huddled around loudspeakers.

"Was that her?" Lou asked when he got back to the phone.

"Christ!" Rudy said. "Did they say her name?"

"It was on the screen for about ten seconds in very clear print. That was her?"

"Damn!"

"She's really pretty."

"She's out of her goddamn mind. Excuse me! Jesus!" His heart was slamming against his chest. He hadn't seen her now for almost a year, and suddenly her picture was beamed around the world, right into his living room.

"They've imposed martial law," he said. "Why would she want to stick her neck out now? It's unbelievable! This whole thing . . . the whole country is upside down. I can't believe . . . "

Lou started to say something then but he was lost in thought. He looked back through the kitchen doorway at the television. Boys in army uniforms sat cross-legged, unarmed, staring back at throngs of ordinary people who seemed to have them surrounded. Just minutes ago her face had been there. He didn't even have a picture of her. His stupid films! Why hadn't they come yet? He'd already sent four or five reminders. They must be lost. And now the screen showed students wrapping gauze around their faces and preparing wet towels in case of tear gas, and three army helicopters swooshing over the square like black dragonflies.

"Rudy?" Lou was saying. "Are you there?"

"I don't think so," he said, still looking at the screen. "I'll talk to you later."

As usual, there is no warning for the banquet. Fang arrives as I am practising in the shadows of my courtyard. He nods his head approvingly. "You making great strides!" he says. "You teach all Canadians *taiji!*"

"Actually," I say, "there are quite a few teachers now in Canada."

He breaks out laughing, possibly because he has not understood what I have said.

"Dean Chun have you to banquet tonight, yes?"

"A banquet?" I say. I'm supposed to meet Li Ming at our spot this evening. We have a lot of patching up to do. "What time?"

"Six o'clock!"

"I wish you'd given me more notice," I say.

"Okay?"

"Yes. Sure. Okay!"

"A car pick up you six o'clock!" He shakes my hand, laughing as he retreats.

The car is one of the old black limousines, perhaps the same one that was waiting for me at the train station back in August, with the crinkly black crepe curtains and the rounded steel body and the whispering polish of privilege. I haven't seen Li Ming, am hoping she will know, somehow, that I have this dinner with the dean.

We roll out through the college gates, Fang talking up front with the driver, me sitting alone in the back. I watch the cyclists on the street, think once that I see Li Ming but it isn't her, it's someone else in a white summer dress with her hair cut like that, short and sculpted smartly along the base of her neck.

We are at the dean's house in about two minutes. It's just barely on the other side of the campus, but by now I don't question things like why they felt we had to take the car. Maybe this is an important occasion. Maybe they think I'm an important guest.

At the door, Dean Chun smiles, happy wrinkles creasing his forehead. That one silver tooth. He shakes my hand with both of his, beckons me in, introduces me to his wife, whose name slips by too quickly to grasp. A tiny woman in a white apron, eyes on the ground. Several other men are in the living room. They stand when we walk in and I shake their hands one by one. All in blue, all older, perhaps in their fifties. I sit on a big sofa chair with a cup of tea in my hands, very much the focus of the room, which is modest, with a few bookshelves, a radio, a black and white television, a view of a porch with laundry hanging up.

We must struggle, as usual, with Fang's translations.

"I tell Dean Chun you . . . making great strides in study *wushu!*" Fang says. "He say you must to practise hard!"

"Yes, I do. Every day!"

"Dean Chun say when he young, he studies *wushu* as you now. Now, every morning, play *taiji!*"

I ask what time he gets up and the dean proudly announces five a.m. for his *taiji* and *chi gong* practice. Then he asks what time Canadians like to get up in the morning and I tell him later than that, for most of us.

"More healthier early in morning!" Fang translates. "When you play *wushu* must to do same!"

The other men in the room do not converse with me, but look at me and talk amongst themselves and laugh at something I can't understand. Fang doesn't bother to translate. Dean Chun goes on to tell me what a famous teacher I have, how most people must petition a man like Master Wang for many years before he will teach them. "But, because you are foreigner, and interested in *wushu* . . . then you can to learn immediately!" The implication seems to be that Dean Chun himself asked Wang to teach me, since I had mentioned when I arrived that I wanted to play some tai chi. But I'm not really sure what the shades of meaning are. I thank him, over and over, to get through the conversation.

The talk turns to my trip to Shanghai, which they want to hear about in detail, even though it was months ago and I was only there a few days. Most of it I have to invent, and of course I leave out any mention of Li Ming. I go on and on about the Shanghai Museum, which I was in for all of twenty minutes, and the Bund, which I tell them is a very famous street, even in Canada, and the wonderful gifts I bought for my family. If I speak quickly enough I know Fang will not be able to translate very much, but he will also not ask me to repeat or explain anything either. I can't know, of course, what he is saying, but my hunch is that he is filling in a lot of the details for me. Again, the others laugh at odd times and look at me and I have no idea what they are saying.

"I was also happy to use the free time to do some writing," I say. "I have applied for a program in Canada and am waiting to hear if I have been accepted."

It's a tricky thing to bring up, since I know they would like me to stay and teach for another year, and while there is no shortage of people who would like to be foreign teachers, there is a shortage of foreign teachers they know well enough to hire. Fang turns back to me. "Dean Chun say we very pleased with your teaching. He invite you stay and teach again topics you have already taught. So less work next year!"

Fang laughs again and is echoed by the others, who can't have understood his English words. So I make as gracious a speech as I can, saying that it depends very much on whether I am accepted into my program or not. "Of course if I am not accepted I would be delighted to stay and teach another year," I say.

The dean's wife arrives and announces dinner, and the men snap to their feet agreeably. We move to another room where a special table for eight has been set up in the middle. Dean

Chun, the host, shows me to the seat of honour and I sit down, and then I watch as the others play a particularly Chinese game of "after you" in which everyone becomes so humble it's impossible to seat them, and the eldest and highest in rank especially have to be coerced into their chairs before the others. The longer it goes on the more embarrassed I feel, seated and decidedly the most junior in the room, until finally I stand up and then they all turn on me, forcing me to sit again and watch.

Another endless feast. We focus on another game: "better to receive!" Dean Chun is a master, flicking his chopsticks into the centre and hauling out huge morsels destined for the plates of others. He is feeding us all, but me mainly, and the best defence is a good passing motion of my own. And so I pile up his plate, and Fang's, and the others, taking small bites for myself now and again. It's harder to avoid the liquor, which comes with every course and must be downed to the bottom of the shot glass, but the Chinese beer is weak and I use it to wash down every fiery gulp. And I talk, too, telling long stories too quickly for Fang to translate properly, but if I'm talking I can't be eating, and the courses pass just the same.

But the dean is a dangerous opponent. He bides his time, waits until we are into the carp soup, and then begins talking, slowly, with long pauses for Fang to translate, so that I must eat, and proposes several toasts along the way, all in my honour, so I must drink. He compliments me lavishly, says I have made immeasurable contributions to the college with my expert knowledge of foreign cultures and teaching techniques, that I have set a wonderful example of hard work and diligence for my students, have given up the luxuries and wealth of my homeland to live in poverty here in a needy country, contributing immensely to the rapid progress of the Four Modernizations . . . Says so much that here, too, Fang breaks down, until finally all I get is a kind of point form. "Very pleased . . . much progress . . . enrichment of entire department . . . extreme gratitude . . . forever by your debt . . . "

I do my best with a reply, talking about the great generosity of the college and the people of the People's Republic, as evidenced by this magnificent meal, etc. I propose a toast to the cook, and the dean, delighted, calls for his wife to come in and sit for a moment and taste some of her food. She peeks around the corner, wiping her hands, and sits briefly, looking embarrassed and miserable. Then I begin talking about the many things I have learned from my time at the college and the wonderful people I have met and what a fine and open country this is. I warm up as I go along and it seems natural to leap into a brief mention of the international misunderstandings of the past, and how important it is to have open exchanges so that people of the world can get together and find out they are not so very different after all, that we love fine food and good wine and friendly conversation, that even with a language barrier we can understand one another and be friends. It becomes a stirring speech, one I almost begin to believe as I pick up momentum and the liquor takes effect.

A few more courses, many more toasts, and then the presents come out. I am surprised, touched, beside myself. There is a jade incense burner with a fitted top and several rings intricately carved right into the side and top; there are jade lions, too, a pair shiny and strong, and a magnificent dragon teapot that sticks out its tongue when I pour it. And then, finally, when I am sure that is the end, Dean Chun brings out the real present, a ceremonial tai chi sword in gleaming brass and steel, with a red tassel and a carved sheath. It's too beautiful — I protest, shaking my head, no, I can't take it.

But I can't refuse it either; they won't hear of it. I stand and pull out the blade, and make a few introductory movements, to which they applaud thunderously. My own tai chi sword! It's a gift that shakes me all the way to my feet, makes me feel at the same time giddy with delight and sick with unworthiness.

Suddenly the party is over, like the closing of a door, my hosts all looking at their watches at the same time and announcing, "Time to go," and in a matter of seconds they are gone. Fang and the driver take me home in the limousine. If my hands were not full of gifts I would embrace them both. Fang helps me with my key, I bid him good-night, nearly drop my presents as I bend down to pick up something that is stuck in the door. He leans over my shoulder to try to see what it is.

"Just a late student paper," I say, smiling, laughing, waving good night.

And then I am alone and the room is spinning as I read the words on the note: *I am being sent away. I have to go tonight. I have your address. Wait for me! Li Ming.*

25

THE PHONE RANG SOMETIME BETWEEN EARLY MORNING AND DAWN, and Rudy flipped off his mat in a quick scramble and knocked the telephone off the table. "Shit! Oh, hello! Li Ming, is that you? Li Ming?"

There was a long silence at the other end and the fog in his head cleared rapidly, like a lost cloud under the desert sun. "Hello, Li Ming?"

"Hello," came a man's voice, evidently drunk. "Is Jennifer home?"

"No. No, it's the wrong number," Rudy said, gently easing the phone down.

He was utterly awake, the adrenaline sprinting through him. What time was it? He turned on the ugly overhead light in the kitchen. Ten after three in the morning. In China it would be . . . afternoon already. He tied his robe around him and went into the living room, turned on the twenty-four-hour news channel, and sat through a rehash of the budget leak, the election campaign in Poland . . .

"In Beijing today," the announcer said, "the mood was one of jubilation and triumph, as for the second straight day the government was unable to enforce the martial law decree issued by Li Peng on Saturday. In a scene reminiscent of the tide of people power which swept Ferdinand Marcos from the Philippines in 1986, millions of Beijing residents took to the streets repeatedly throughout the evening to thwart a huge military operation aimed at restoring government control in the capital. We have several stories we're working on at the moment . . . "

The pictures flickered from one scene to the next. A squadron of motorcycles fanning over the city, the drivers yelling through megaphones to call out the people. Buses turned sideways and abandoned, blocking the streets along with concrete cylinders, dumpsters, concrete blocks, timbers. Angry crowds yelling at the soldiers, pressing against the trucks with their bodies. Old women lecturing the young recruits, passing them bottles of beer, cups of tea, bowls of rice and noodles. Boys in oversized uniforms, looking on with wide, frightened eyes.

Rudy watched and napped, napped and watched until the sun came up, and then he bathed, changed and ate and had to force himself outside for his first bit of exercise in a week. But he could not concentrate and was back again soon to watch a parade of a thousand Chinese journalists, scientists and writers marching up and down the main boulevard crossing Tiananmen Square, chanting slogans against Li Peng and Deng Xiaoping. Unbelievable. Here were the former propagandists from the *People's Daily* suddenly on the vanguard of free speech and democracy. "Li Peng," one of them was saying, "was expressing deep concern for the health of hunger strikers, but at same time sending troops to Beijing!"

He stole some time to buy a newspaper and read about the seven top generals who had come out against sending troops to

Tiananmen, and about the military helicopters dropping "Firmly Support Comrade Li Peng's Important Speech" leaflets onto the students, who proceeded to make a huge banner saying Firmly Support the Fascist Dictatorship of Li Peng. He spent some time at his writing and then, at lunch, sat frozen over an article about Wei Jingsheng, the Democracy Wall protester who was arrested in 1979 and now, still in prison, had had his health broken. The article said that in 1987 Deng Xiaoping had brought up the case of Wei Jingsheng when convincing Party members that they should crack down on student demonstrations even though the rest of the world was watching. "We put Wei Jingsheng behind bars, didn't we?" he had said. "Did that damage China's reputation?"

He phoned one of the airlines and asked the price of a return ticket to Beijing. The woman punched in the information. "When would you like to go?" she asked.

"I'm not sure."

"If you give two weeks notice . . . "

"No. It would be sooner than that."

She punched some more keys. "It's difficult to give you precise information," the woman said. Then, "A return flight would cost about $2200, depending on when you would like to go. Would you like to book that?"

"I'll have to get back to you," Rudy said.

He had the money in his account. There wasn't much more in it, but he could go. And then what? If only he could see her, talk to her. Maybe they could get married. He had to tell his parents about this. He would need more money. He wasn't making any decisions. But, just in case, he wrote a quick letter to the Chinese consulate in Toronto, enclosing his passport, requesting a visa.

❦

The first thing I think is why did I fucking drink so much? Why did I do that? If I hadn't done that, if I had kept my cool, then I wouldn't just be standing here wondering is this real?

And then I think, Dean Chun! The bastard! On the same night, he has a banquet for me and he sends Li Ming away. On the same fucking night! I don't believe it. I can't fucking believe it. I don't . . . I won't . . . And all of them laughing — that's what they were laughing at. They all knew. Everyone knew. Except for me.

And then — the train station. Maybe it isn't too late. Maybe she hasn't left yet. Where would she go? Home? The train for Shanghai won't come through until early in the morning, three-thirty. There. I can make it. I'll just go. I'll just . . . fumble with the door and trip on the goddamn stairs and steady myself now, on my knees on the concrete, catch my breath, I must, I just have to get, to get up, fuck it's cold, why is it so cold? It wasn't cold before. The cold was . . . in the winter, and that was . . . now where's my bicycle? Where? Over here, in the dark, if I just talk my way through it, up now, to the door, shhhhhhhhhh . . . I just . . . careful, yes. Through the door. We are going *through the door*. Yes. Yes. Fuck.

Forget quiet. It's too late for quiet. I'm too drunk for quiet! Fuck them! Fuck fuck fuck fuck fuck them. On my bike. Cold air. Bloody dark. Stones. Wobble. God, air, give me air. Down the lane. Corner, too fast, no, go! Past the basketball courts. Calm. Look calm. I just have to . . . gates coming up. Get off the bike. Careful. Oh shit, my leg! Doesn't matter. Just look straight ahead. What time is it? Act normal.

Midnight. And the gate is locked. And no one is here. To get through I have to . . . oh shit. Wake up the gatekeeper. He won't let me through. I can't . . .

Damn! Think! Think! What to do? What to do? God, Dean Chun, I can't believe . . . I'd like to . . . if I just took my sword . . .

No time to think. I pick up my bike. Heave. As hard as I can. Don't think, just up, just *uunhhhh!*

Subtle as a garbage can getting run over by a truck. Freeze. Shhhh! Just for a second. Night swallows that sound and gives back . . . nothing. Don't get stuck. Do something. Keep doing something. Hand on the iron bar. Up! Other hand. Up! Kick, squirm, where's the foot, get the foot, oh! Shit, my hands, the iron is ripping the skin. Christ. Top, pointed, don't think, just get over! Falling, shit! Right on top of the bike. Rolling in the street. Still. Dazed. I must have broken something. I must have. Noises. Gatehouse. Lights. Someone. Up! Doesn't matter. Bike. Doesn't matter. Up! Roll, wheels, go! Yes! Long March, indestructible. On the seat, pedalling, what's he calling? Chinese. Doesn't matter. Away!

Lights, darkness, more lights. Brooding buildings. Shadows on bicycles. The air cold on my fingers. I have no money. What am I going to do if I find her? When. *When* I find her. Don't worry about that. Just pedal faster. Breathe. Breathe! Just go.

And then I'm retching, turning my head but pedalling still with the spasms, everything, the whole banquet coming up putridly on the side of my bike, on my pants, clawing the inside of my throat. I keep going. She's going to be there. Wipe my face on my sleeve.

Lose track of time. Is this the right road? How long have I been going? Lights on the corners, then long stretches of darkness. Have to watch to not hit the other cyclists. Who are these people, why are they out? Where's the train station? It's this way, I'm pretty sure. I just have to keep going. I just . . .

Something coming up ahead. Big rumble, must be a truck. But no lights. Is there a corner? Where's the edge of the road? Try to stay close, eyes low. Two bursts of white light, sudden high beams, *whhooosh!* it's past, a troop truck. A dozen sleepy young soldiers standing in the back. Lights go off as soon as the truck is past. Back to darkness. I could get killed. I could have just been killed.

Ocean bottom black. Must be along here. But if there are signs I can't read them. If there's anybody to ask, I can't speak or understand. What's the word for train? No idea. Complete blank. Why didn't I learn more? I've been led around like a little baby and now that I need to do something on my own I can't.

It should be at the far end of the street. That's the way I see it in my mind. At the far end, the street just ends, and then . . . and then, if there's a God, the station will be . . . maybe it's farther along. Maybe, since I've never been out here on my bike . . .

Maybe I'm going in the wrong direction and will end up riding all night, completely lost. Maybe I will never see her again.

"When it happens," Lou said, pushing the baby carriage, "I mean, when it really starts to happen, I want everything to be calm. Let's not panic."

Rudy nodded his head. She was overdue more than a week. Things had not been relaxed for a long time.

"I know it's taking forever and I'm practically ready to rip this kid out with my own hands, but . . . when it happens, let's just be calm. That's my goal. For once in my life I want to be calm when something major is happening."

"Okay."

"I know *you're* going to be calm. I want to be calm too. It's my baby!"

"We'll be calm."

"Good." She stopped for a moment to catch her breath. "I wonder—"

"Lou?" Rudy said, interrupting.

"Yes?"

"There's something I have to talk to you about."

"What?"

"Well, I phoned up . . . I mean, I called one of the airlines. About going to Beijing. I was just asking, you know — "

"Rudy — "

"And, it turns out, if I wanted, I *could* afford to go. I mean I could put it on my credit card . . . "

"Rudy — "

"What I'm saying is . . . of course I'll wait until you have your baby. I wouldn't miss that for anything. And it'll be any day, so . . . anyway, I have to wait for my visa to come through from the Chinese consulate."

"They're on the edge of a civil war there, Rudy!"

"I know." They stopped. It was brilliantly sunny and for a moment everything looked clear, and then tears were running down his face. "Whenever I watch the news now," he said, wiping his eyes with his fingers, "this happens. I . . . I think I have to go, Lou."

"Oh shit." She said it softly, watching him.

"I care for her . . . more than anything. I mean I'm just finding out how much . . . I keep thinking . . . I keep waking up in the night, thinking she's going to phone. I figure if I could just, if I could talk to her . . . "

He started walking again, taking her arm. "She's kind of like you," he said. "She's fiery, with a lot of heart . . . but she needs someone to ground her."

"And you're the one with solid, rational judgement?" Lou said. "Superman flying into the middle of a hurricane to save Lois Lane?"

"It's not that."

"Oh no, I'm sure it's not. I haven't seen you leap very many tall buildings lately, much less outrun speeding bullets. There's nothing you can do, Rudy. You have to wait. It's too late. There is absolutely nothing — "

Her anger startled him more than anything. Her whole body seemed to be balled into a fist, desperately wanting to strike.

"I'm sorry," he said, as if that would explain, or even help matters.

"You're sorry!" she said, pushing the empty carriage and moving on.

There it is! Oh God, thank you. The train station. An opening at the end of the dark, a ghostly glow, and not too soon. I was ready to change directions, to try something else. But here it is, the parking lot where I sat that time. In air-conditioned splendour while the officials looked for luggage that was already in the car.

It seems like eight years ago. Li Ming was there. I remember. The first time I met her. In the heat and everyone staring.

Now the station is cast in shadows like a film noir. What lights there are only seem to accentuate the gloom.

The same crowds. It's after midnight and yet there are still hundreds of people here. In the murky light I am not such an obvious *waiguoren*. I leave my bike on one of the stands and run up the concrete stairs, two at a time, and push through the ill-fitting wooden doors and into the cavernous main hall. Then I'm just standing, catching my breath, trying to see her. But it's not only dark here, it's smoky, too, the room full of men huddled by their bags, their cigarette tips sullen, piercing.

There she is! Standing alone just as I had imagined, her bag resting on the ground beside her. Huddled, shivering, deep in thought. I walk as fast as I can, without calling attention to myself, over to the corner where she is, but on the way she becomes someone old, with a face carved by wind and brown teeth bent sideways.

And so I stop, in the middle now, scanning the edges of the room. What if she isn't here? What if she's already gone through the doors at the far side and is by the tracks now, waiting for the train? I'll have to get past the man at the door. But I have no ticket, no money. And now people are starting to notice. "*Waiguoren*," someone says behind me. "*Waiguoren!*"

I spin, trying to decide what to do. Where is she? I was sure she would be here. Now what? "*Waiguoren! Waiguoren!*"

"I help you?" It is a security man in a green military shirt with a peaked cap and the blank, blunt face of an official.

"I hope so, thank you!" I say. "It's so wonderful to find someone who speaks English! I'm looking for someone. I thought she might be here."

"Where you going?" he asks, but at the same time recoiling when he sees the stain on my pantleg, smells the residue of vomit.

"I'm not going anywhere. I am *looking* for someone who is perhaps going to Shanghai. I thought she would be in the lobby here?"

"Ticker and passbore?" he says.

"I'm sorry?"

"Ticker and passbore?"

"Oh, oh!" I say. "No, you're confused. I'm not going anywhere myself. I am *looking* for someone . . . "

"You come!" he says, taking my elbow firmly and pulling me while still keeping his face averted.

"I *think* she's going to Shanghai!" I say. "So if you could just take me to the Shanghai platform, that would be wonderful. What time does the next train leave for Shanghai, anyway?"

He does not say another word to me, but pulls me through a door into another waiting room, much smaller, with old stuffed couches and plastic flowers in glass vases and dusty watercolours of bamboo forests on the walls. The foreigners' waiting room. Then he sits me down in one of the stuffed chairs and silently hands me a mug of green tea and motions for me to wait, he will return. But he isn't gone more than a second before I get up, leave the tea cup on the oversized arm of the chair and slip through another door that leads to the train yards.

Where is she? She must be on one of these platforms. I know the train hasn't left yet; it comes through from Beijing at about three or four a.m. Now which was the platform for Shanghai? It was along here, I remember, even in the dark something in my body remembers. Down the stairs, right, we go underneath and

. . . and here are all these people, yes, huddling together in the tunnel. Who are they? Are they beggars? Are they homeless? Or are they just waiting for the train? I don't know. I can't ask. As I walk by, the whispers, "*Waiguoren. Waiguoren.*"

Left here, yes, up the stairs, two at a time, the stars greeting me at the top. Where am I? Is this the Shanghai platform? I can't read the characters on the sign. But it's empty anyway. Just wind. I go down the stairs, along the tunnel, to the next platform. Running this time. She's got to be here.

"Li Ming!"

Heads turn in the darkness. As I rush by, silent eyes looking, following. Not her. No. Not her. No. No. No.

Running. Down the stairs. Into someone. "Sorry! *Meiguanxi!* Sorry!" Up the next platform. The next. The next.

"Li Ming!"

"Li Ming!"

To the last platform. Legs trembling. Tripping now, shit, my knee! Cold concrete. Cold wind. She *can't* just disappear! I know she's here. Somewhere. A person can't just somehow be gone.

"Harro!"

Another security guard. Wearing sunglasses in the middle of the night.

"I'm looking for someone. I don't have a ticket. I'm looking for a friend."

He says something in Chinese.

"I'm just looking for someone. I'm sure she's here. If you'll just . . ."

More Chinese. "Shanghai?" I say, pointing to the platform and shrugging my shoulders in a question. But his hand is on my elbow and his strong fingers press my nerve and I'm up on my toes in pain. Then skipping, half-running to keep up with him. He's just barely holding me with his left hand, but I'm completely in his grasp.

Back down the stairs, into the dark. Concrete tomb. Intense

whispers now, like the wind through fall leaves as we blow by. God. Li Ming.

Then we climb the stairs again and see the stars and the dull glow of the station, and a collection of green-shirted men with dull faces and peaked caps stand with their hands on their hips, waiting for me. And it strikes me suddenly that I'm alone here, completely alone, as far from my home as I can be, in a land where people disappear like rocks slipping beneath the water.

The twenty-fourth was a day of rumours, that the government had electrified the metal grates over the subway, that Deng Xiaoping had resigned, that he had died, that paratroopers were going to drop into Tiananmen Square, that troops were being brought in from remote regions and kept ignorant of what was happening in the capital. Another million people came out to march and protect the students, whose ranks were swelling with new arrivals. Rudy spent hour after hour scanning the channels looking for any sign of Li Ming, but of course it was hopeless, the scenes of crowds flickering too quickly to pick out individuals. At least she did not seem to be giving any more interviews. But just that one was enough, he knew, to ruin her life.

The papers were full of more rumours about the backstage power struggles in the politburo. Li Peng and the hardliners were seen to be on the retreat, Zhao Ziyang on the rise, as it became more and more obvious that the military would not fire against the Beijing residents who were coming out at night in astonishing numbers. They seemed to be on the verge of anarchy. Some students had thrown red paint at the nine-metre-high portrait of Mao which stood in the square and now student leaders were urging people not to photograph it since it might turn the rest of the country against them. As night started to fall the protesters huddled again in the square, writing out their wills, waiting for the attack.

Which didn't come. The city remained braced. Things were happening behind the scenes. Then after six days of unenforced martial law, when no senior Chinese leader had been seen publicly, suddenly Li Peng was on television meeting with third-world ambassadors. Rudy sat through interview after interview with Western China experts who all seemed to agree that Li Peng and the hardliners were now firmly in command. Factory workers who had been at the demonstrations were having their pay cut. The editor of the *People's Daily* was fired and replaced by a conservative. Journalists from the Communist Party were being required to pledge allegiance to Li Peng, who was blaming the West for plotting to fill students' minds with corrupt notions.

And the protesters in the square were getting tired, although their organization and discipline were remarkable. They had set up a system of ID cards and passes in the square to protect their leaders and keep out the police, a public relations centre to handle Western journalists, an accounting department to keep track of the donations coming in from around the country. They had an elaborate polling mechanism to count votes on major issues, a loudspeaker system wired to broadcast all decisions, and mimeograph machines to distribute their own newspapers.

Rudy phoned the consulate in Toronto daily to ask about his visa, but everything took time. And Lou's baby was taking forever. He put off calling his parents. Everything was on hold. Through the weekend the numbers of protesters started to drop. They were all tired. It was time to go home. Maybe he should wait, he thought. Maybe it would be all right.

And then on the Monday Li Ming's scholarship came through. Amanda phoned him immediately and told him they were sending off the package special delivery. Rudy ached to be able to take it himself, but he didn't have his visa yet, Lou still hadn't given birth. She was a swollen rain cloud too laden to be able to go much further, and yet still intact. No rumblings. Almost two weeks overdue. Unbearable.

And then on the thirtieth, the day his visa arrived, the students erected a ten-metre-high statue of styrofoam, plaster of Paris and concrete called the Goddess of Democracy, and Rudy was on the telephone, asking about departure times.

26

I'M TAKEN BACK TO THE FOREIGNERS' WAITING ROOM, WHERE MY untouched tea is still waiting for me on the arm of the overstuffed chair. As I sit down again I'm painfully aware of how shabby I look, of the dried vomit on my pantleg, of the pain in my knee where I landed on my bike after jumping off the top of the gate and then again later tripped and fell on the platform, of how late it is and hopeless, and that it's not over yet.

"Where you going?" asks the one security man who can speak a little English.

"Nowhere," I say. "I'm not going anywhere. I just wanted to see a friend who I think is going to Shanghai."

"Where you going?" he asks again.

"I just told you. Look, if it's okay, I'll just . . . "

"Ticker? Passbore?"

"No. I don't have either. I don't even have any money with me. It's stupid, I know."

He takes out his red work badge with his ID photo and waves it at me questioningly.

I shake my head, no. It's at home. Locked up.

"Where you going? Ticker? Passbore?" And then a long stream of Chinese.

"*Wo shi Jianadaren.*" I haul out the old phrase, but all it does is bring on an avalanche of Chinese. "*Wo bu dong!*" I say — I don't understand!

We have to play it several more times, then I stumble out the name of my school, and finally they back off. Several of the security men leave, but three of them stay on in the room, standing by the doors, watching in silence as I sit in silence. I take the lid off my neglected tea. Cold. The green leaves have all sunk to the bottom.

I just want to go home. That's all. I just want to go home and go to sleep, and then pack my bags and leave.

For a long time nothing happens. The men stand still and expressionless. I sit, listless, exhausted. A train comes in with a night-shaking blast of its antiquated steam engine, waits for several minutes and then moves on. Maybe that was her train, I think. Slowly, my anger starts to build as I think of Dean Chun, his face wrinkled with smiles, toasting me into defeat. And who told him? It must have been Jiang. Jealous. If he could not have Li Ming, then he would ruin her life. It's hard to imagine living with such thoughts, but Jiang and Chun are sleeping soundly tonight while I sit here stinking and aching, slowly boiling about what I'll say when I get the chance.

If I get the chance.

I can't sleep. But I do, my head nodding forward as I slump in the chair. And there is Li Ming in her white blouse as she moves through the woods like shadows and then sunlight. And then I'm fighting something, turning, kicking, but I can't quite see what it is. It's nothing I can hit, but all around me, fog, blinding, pressing me lightly, irresistibly, soaking through my skin, slipping inside, a gentle invader, nothing you can push against or repel, sucking out from inside me . . . nothing, nothing much. Leaving me intact. Just the same. Almost.

Li Ming turns to me, a sudden shaft of sunlight. "You've given it to them," she says. "Without even a fight. You've let them take it."

"What? What is it? What do they have?"

"Your *chi*," she says, turning now into shadows.

"Goddammit, why don't they make these things so ordinary people can open them?" Lou was wrestling with the top of a jar in her kitchen and Rudy, who had been watching the news, came in to help.

"I'll do it," he said.

"No, I don't fucking want you to do it!" she said, and then slammed her fist down on the counter so hard that a cupboard opened and a glass fell on the floor and shattered.

She swore again, her face was swollen with anger.

"Hey, listen, whoa!" Rudy said. "Hey!"

"Would you open this fucking jar?"

"Okay." He took it from her gently. Oswald trotted into the kitchen and started nosing around the broken glass.

"Oh no, Ozzie, no! Oh, God! Could you . . . "

He handed the opened jar to her and scooped up Oswald in the same motion. "Why don't you go up and have a bath?" he said.

"I don't want to have a fucking bath!"

"Okay, you don't have to have a fucking bath," he said softly.

"And you don't have to fucking swear!"

"Then I won't fucking swear. I'll clean up the glass."

"But I can fucking swear if I want to!"

"Of course you can."

"Because this goddamn kid is driving me crazy already and she hasn't even arrived yet!"

"Of course. You have every right." Rudy had the broom out and was sweeping up the glass, still with Oswald tucked under his arm. Lou stood there watching him. When he was finished sweeping she knelt down and held the dustpan for him, and then had to reach for his arm in order to get up again.

"Ow!" she said. "That hurts!"

"What?"

"My hand!"

He laughed, which was risky, but her fit seemed to have passed.

"You haven't said anything more about going," she said, hugging Oswald, pulling his ears, not looking at Rudy.

"I've . . . I've bought my ticket."

"You just put it on your credit card?"

"I got some money from my parents," he said.

"You're *parents* are sending you to Beijing?"

"I didn't tell them what the money was for."

She nodded her head, restraining herself. "Maybe you could get some for me," she said sardonically. "When are you going?"

"Monday."

"Early Monday, or late Monday?"

"Late."

She nodded, still not looking at him.

"You hear that, boy?" she said, talking to her belly. "Looks like we've got a deadline."

I wake up stiff and disoriented, opening my eyes to the fullness of a clear sunrise flooding through the window, gleaming almost painfully off the rails of the train lines outside. My neck is sore. I need a shave. I'm hungry. And my guards are still standing by the doors.

Of course. My guards.

"Listen," I say, getting up and stretching. "My bike is just outside. I'll just leave, if that's all right. I really . . . I thought I was going to meet a friend . . . "

They are shaking their heads, no. Of course they don't understand.

"Can I have something to eat?" I make a bowl-and-chopstick motion. "I'm really starving."

One of them leaves, nodding his head. Another one approaches to explain something in Chinese. "*Wo bu dong!*" I say just as he is getting started, and he smiles, shaking his head at the difficulty of the situation. It is the first sign of humour from any of them.

He takes me by the arm and we walk out the door into the main lobby again, which is brighter, of course, in the morning, but not a lot, and there seem to be the same number of people as last night. God, why haven't I learned any Chinese while I've been here? What an idiot I am! I can't even ask this man where we're going, or tell him that I need badly to take a pee.

And have a shower. And change my clothes.

We cross the lobby and then he leads me to another door which he points me to, standing back. Is this where I meet his superior? The characters over the door are familiar; I've seen them before. On the train? Maybe. It's so hard to tell. I push through the door, smell the air, and then laugh. Of course. A toilet.

I stand over the long v-trench and watch my pee and try not to breathe, just get out as quickly as possible. But then as I'm zipping myself up I notice a window on the other side of the row of holes used for shitting. It's small but open, with no bars, and there's a ledge right there that I could easily put my foot on.

It's stupid. I'm already in enough trouble. Li Ming has gone; there's nothing more I can do. Why even think of it? They would just follow me and then I'd have even more to explain. I turn back towards the door.

And yet . . . the window is there. And it's open. And they don't know anything about me. If I just . . .

Except they know I'm Canadian. I told them that. And the name of my school. They could pick me up any time.

But . . . but what? To hell with it. There's no more time to think. I pull myself up and stick my head out. It's a back alley of some sort, but there, to the right, is the parking lot where I came in. Just a few yards away. But it's not too late to turn back . . .

Of course it is. I've thought of it, I have to do it. I can't just sit back any more. So I squirm, pull myself through, dangle for a held breath with my head hanging down and my hips caught, but there's a pipe here to hang onto, and I pull, and then I am sinking slowly, clumsily to the ground.

Up. On my feet. Around the corner. Quickly. White, dusty day. Past a row of lean, hairy young men lounging by their motorized tricycles. Two of them spring up to offer me a ride, but I shake my head. "*Bu yao!*" I walk past them, and past three other men in green uniforms exactly like the security men from last night, but they don't even look up. My bike is beside a long row of others, the only one not locked. I calmly kick the stand back and mount and ride off, not looking back, sure there will be sirens any second.

But nothing happens. That's the bizarre thing. It's daylight; the plane trees shade the road with their dust-covered leaves; the traffic is the usual mix of bikes and green trucks and hand-drawn carts stacked high with piles of cement, garbage, hay, iron rods. Everything is normal. Maybe the guard is just now looking in the washroom to see what happened to me.

I pedal fast, keep my head low, mix in. Maybe I just imagined what happened. Maybe Li Ming has not been sent away. Maybe I'm just out on an average morning riding my bike several miles from home.

But as the streets become more familiar, as the cool morning air wakes my lungs, as I remember more and more of the Dean's flattering, poisonous words, the bile rises to my throat. When I reach the college I do not dismount but ride through the open gates, and when I reach the department I do not stand my bicycle, much less take the time to shave or change my clothes or think. I march into the drab, slouching building, then up the stairs and along the hall towards the office of Dean Chun.

27

WHEN THE PHONE RANG RUDY WAS PACKING HIS BAG IN THE LIVING room, trying to figure out what to take while watching the television while glancing at the newspaper he had spread out on the floor. The paper was saying it was very hot in Beijing now. He should take light clothes, he was thinking.

"Hi Lou," he said. "Listen, did you catch the news this morning? It's miraculous what's — "

"No I didn't," she said, a little sharply.

"Well you should go out and pick up a paper. The troops — " He stopped in mid-sentence. "Oh my God!" he said. "Is this — ?"

"Yes, Rudy," she said, very calmly. "I've called the taxi."

"I'm on my way!" he yelled, running out the door.

He could get there in under three minutes, and he did, his legs over-striding, as if it were the last lap of the Olympics. But he was breathless when he arrived, light-headed, and his legs were not solid. But there was Lou sitting cross-legged on the rug, rubbing Oswald behind the ears. "Amanda is going to look after him," she said when he burst in.

The taxi was there in a few minutes. Rudy tried to get her in the back seat as quickly as possible but she made him stand with her for a moment.

"What are you doing?" he asked. "Did you forget something?"

"Can't you smell that?"

· "What?"

"The air. It's spring. I told you, I want to be calm for this."

Well, it was spring, and the air was soaked with the smell of new blossoms and the feel of possible rain, the kind that does not fall so much as seep out and is not cold, but not sickly hot either. They tasted several deep breaths before she finally settled, gently, into the back seat.

The taxi driver was not so calm. A young man in ripped blue jeans, he drove with his foot to the floor and his eyes on the rearview mirror, sure that Lou was going to have the child right there. But when Rudy asked him to slow down he did. "I got a daughter at home," he said, jerking his head back to look at them. "Three and a half months. I know what you're going through."

It was quiet at the hospital, and Lou's unusual serenity seemed to enable her to rise above mere administrative details. It helped that she had had the forms filled out for three weeks now. All she had to do was mark in the date. She didn't let Rudy help her to the elevator. She carried her own bag. She was fine. There would be plenty of time to help her later on. She didn't want to get into bed immediately but wandered around the small rectangle that was hers, pulling aside the drapes to look out the window. To the far right they could see the river snake under the bridge. She played with the bed, cranking it up and lowering it, but then stopped and stood still, feeling her belly and closing her eyes.

"I thought this was supposed to hurt," she said after the contraction, nonchalantly shaking her hair as she slid off her jacket.

"It doesn't hurt?"

"It's not too bad."

A thick nurse wrapped in white took several quick steps into the room, which was empty of people except for Rudy and Lou, but which had two other beds in it. She introduced herself, snapped the bed down to a flat position, showed Lou the bedpan, the wastebasket, the alarm bell and the bathroom. "I want you to get straight into your hospital gown," she said, marking something on a clipboard. "We have to get you on the monitor."

"Actually," Lou said, "everything is fine. I don't think you're going to need the . . ."

"It's policy," the nurse said, as if waving a blunt instrument, and pulled the curtains around the bed. "I'll be back in a few minutes."

"They warned us about this in the class," Lou said when they were alone again. "God, why do they have to make you feel like there's this emergency happening? It's only childbirth. It's the most natural . . ."

"Maybe we should go along with them," Rudy said.

"But what do they need a monitor for? Everything's fine!"

"So, they'll hook it up, see that everything's fine, and then take it off again. It's nothing. Just stay relaxed."

"Don't tell me to stay relaxed. All right!"

"All right," he said. She closed her eyes again, was leaning against the bed, breathing deeply.

"That's not so bad," she said, opening her eyes. "It's funny."

"What?"

"Well, this is it. The day I've been concentrating on for so long now. And it's happening, but . . . on the other hand, it's just another day, too. Everything's normal. The river's still out there. And I'm in here and . . . it's not so bad."

"Well, maybe — "

"Listen, Rudy, could you go get me some water? I'm going to get changed here. All right?"

"Yeah, sure."

When Rudy got back with the water the nurse had already returned and strapped Lou on to the monitor, and the squiggly line was mapping out the rise and fall of the contractions.

"Have you been timing these?" the nurse snapped at him, not taking her eyes off the graph.

"Uh, no," he said, handing Lou the water. "I was just — "

"What are you waiting for?" she barked, and then left, clamping a pencil to her clipboard as she walked away. This time it was Rudy whose neck turned red and Lou who said to relax.

"Let's just . . . let's just get this kid born," she said, closing her eyes again.

"From the beginning of one to the beginning of the next, right?" Rudy asked, glancing at his watch, but Lou didn't seem to hear him this time. A single bead of sweat sauntered from her hairline past her temple and then down her cheek, gathering momentum as it fell.

"Breathe!" he said. "That's it. Good. How was that?"

"Unnggh," she said, wiping her cheek with the back of her hand, looking up with eyes slightly dimmer, slightly more shielded than just a few moments ago. "Not so bad. I thought it was going to be worse."

Rudy leaned against the edge of the bed and asked her if there was anything that needed rubbing, but she shook her head. For a long time they silently watched the slow, scratchy progress of the graph on the monitor, the long valleys of rest and the more or less gentle climb to the plateaus of the contractions. Lou had Rudy put his hand on her belly to feel how hard it became, from a water balloon to a watermelon and then back to a balloon.

"Did you bring the list of phone numbers?" she asked.

He had it in his wallet. "I should have brought some music," she said. "Somehow I thought . . . this was going to be over really quickly."

"I could read to you."

"Did you bring anything good?"

"There's the paper."

"Oh."

"No, listen. Big things are happening." He took the newspaper out of his bag and flipped it open to the first page. "This is Jan Wong from the *Globe and Mail* —"

"Rudy," she said, before he began to read.

"What?"

"I don't want to listen to the newspaper."

"Oh," he said, putting it down. Then, "Of course. Maybe . . . I'm not sure what else . . . "

The monitor jumped then and Lou closed her eyes and Rudy said, "Okay now, that's it, just breathe easy, yes, good. Good! You're doing terrific. Oh yeah, that's a big one. Look on the graph!"

"Fuck the graph," Lou said when she got her breath back. "Would you tell her to unhook me from this monitor the next time she comes? Power to the fucking people. Excuse my language."

That's okay," Rudy said, putting aside the paper.

It was quite a while before the nurse made another appearance. The contractions continued at five minute intervals and Lou became very quiet, closing her eyes for the difficult parts and looking down, seemingly inside herself, for the rest. There was nothing she wanted rubbed, she had enough water, she didn't feel like conversation or distraction of any kind. So Rudy sat at the edge of the bed and waited with her as the monitor continued its abstract portrait.

When the nurse finally did return Lou asked immediately if she could take off the monitor. At first the nurse continued marking on her clipboard, pretending she hadn't heard the question. Then when Lou asked again she said, "We keep the monitor on as much as possible during older pregnancies."

"I'm *not* an older pregnancy," Lou said icily. "Check your records. I'm thirty-four. You have to be thirty-five to be an *older* pregnancy."

Again the nurse did not let on that she had heard her.

"I'd like to walk around," Lou said. "While I still can. My legs are getting . . . "

"Do you want to endanger your baby?" the nurse asked, finally deigning to look up.

"Well, I don't think — "

But she had already turned on her heel. "What a bitch!" Lou said, loud enough so that she could be heard in the hallway.

"Can I rub your legs?"

"No, shit. Why didn't you say anything to her?"

"I didn't — "

"Why do they have to strap me up like this? God, did you hear what she said? 'Do you want to endanger your baby?' Who the hell does she think — "

Rudy was rubbing her legs through the sheet.

"No, don't do that!" she snapped. "It's my back. My back is — "

She stopped as another contraction came on her. Rudy checked his watch. Still five minutes. Holding steady. "Breathe!" he said. "Nice and deep." Her eyes were closed, she was clenching her jaw and forcing the air out through flared nostrils. "Wonderful! You're doing great! Oh, that's terrific!"

Slowly she opened her eyes.

"That's great! Maybe if you just leaned forward I could rub your back. Do you want me to crank the bed up a bit? How about some more water? Or some juice — there's some juice here. Can I get you — "

"Rudy?"

"Yes?"

"Just be quiet. For a minute."

"Okay. Sure. Anything."

"And get the nurse."

"What? You want the bitch to come back?"

"My water just broke."

Up the stairs. Classes have already begun. What day is this? Tuesday. I have a writing class. What time is it? Fuck it. It doesn't matter. It doesn't matter any more.

Second floor. Around the corner. One of my students staring. I don't look at her. This is between me and Dean Chun.

Past the classroom. They're all looking now. Good. They all probably know. They've all probably known for days and days. I hope they all hear what I have to say.

To Dean Chun's office. And the door is closed. And I stand there, staring at it, like an idiot.

What if he's not here? I'll go downstairs and the authorities will be waiting. Damn. It's not supposed to work this way.

So I pound on the flimsy door — Slam! Slam! — and it rattles on its hinges, the ancient brown paint cracking and falling under my open palm. I can't help it. I want to hit somebody. I want so much to —

"*Shi ma?*" Dean Chun opens the door, stands before me, looking up. "Ah! Ah! Seaborn — ah! Ni hao!"

And he bows and wrinkles his forehead and gestures me in like an old friend, streams of Chinese spilling out like smoke. Behind my back he gestures to my student, Hua, the shy girl, to come in and translate.

No. I don't want this. I want someone . . .

"Please to sit down!" Hua says, and both she and Dean Chun point to the Dean's own chair behind his desk. I wave it off but he shakes his head, insisting. I shouldn't. I should just stand and say . . .

He is looking at the stains on my clothes. Discretely. Not saying anything. "Please!" Hua says. "The dean insists that you have a seat."

I have a seat. It's a mistake. "Listen," I say. "I am really angry. Please tell him that. I just spent the whole night . . . "

"Would you like some tea?" Hua says.

"No."

"Please," she says. "Dean Chun would like very much to serve you . . . "

"No!"

"It is the custom . . . "

"I know it is the bloody custom but to tell you the truth I don't want any tea right now, thank you!"

I'm ready to take a man in my hands and throttle him and these people are offering me —

Dean Chun says something rapidly to Hua and she leaves. Fuck. That's it. No translator.

Chun gingerly takes a seat a few feet away on a rickety metal chair normally reserved for guests to the office. He folds his hands on his lap and looks across at me patiently. Then he starts to say something and stops, laughing. Of course. We can't communicate. I don't know Chinese.

As if he had forgotten.

Students peer in at the door. He waves them away. I just have to sit here and smoulder.

I don't have a chance. I know it already. I stink and I'm tired and hungry and out of my league. And now he has me sitting here, waiting. I shouldn't put up with it. I should walk out. I should . . .

Finally Hua comes back with one covered mug of tea, which she places on the desk in front of me. Despite my anger I say thank you. There. Those are the niceties. "What I am so angry about — " I start to say, but Dean Chun says something in Chinese to Hua, as if he could not hear that I was talking already.

"Uh . . . Dean Chun says that . . . the banquet last night was most graced by the guest of honour," she says, blushing horribly. "He says you must to . . . excuse the poor quality of food and drink. We are . . . just a humble school . . . "

"Tell him that he can go to hell."

She isn't quite sure what I mean. I wave it off. Damn. Why do I get the feeling . . .

"Dean Chun says that he hopes you are . . . pleased with the . . . gifts . . . he has bought for you. They are very poor gifts but . . . "

Waiting for Li Ming

"Tell the dean that I am not going to keep the gifts," I say in an angrily polite tone, "and could you ask him for me what he did with Li Ming?"

Hua starts to say something to Chun, looks back to me, looks at her feet, while Chun tilts his head in a concerned way, waiting.

"The teacher, Li Ming!" I say, exasperated. "What did he do with her? She's gone!"

"Ah, ah! Li Ming!" Hua says, as if finally understanding who I'm talking about.

Chun looks most avuncularly concerned as he listens to her translation. His answer takes about two seconds.

"She has been transferred," Hua says.

"Where? Why? What's going on here?"

Hua looks at me, frightened, too startled for a moment. "Ask him!" I shout at her. "Why did he send her away?"

Hua bursts into tears, but Chun is not affected at all, still looking at me in his patient, gentle way, as if waiting for the translation of some quaint Canadian joke.

"Li Ming!" I yell at him directly, and then stumble over the Chinese. Why didn't I fucking learn more of the language? I wouldn't be so crippled . . .

"Dean Chun asks to you," Hua says, regaining control, "why you are so . . . concerned with . . . Li Ming?"

"Because she is a friend, and she has disappeared!"

Chun nods his head as he listens to the translation. He turns his eyes to me as if embarrassed for the whole conversation.

"Li Ming is on . . . ordinary assignment," Hua translates. "You should not be concerned for . . . your friend."

"Why didn't you let her take her scholarship to the United States?"

There is another crowd at the door. Dean Chun snaps his hand at them, waves them off, and then methodically gets up to close the door.

"These are things you do not understand," he says through Hua.

"You're damn right I don't understand them! But I want an answer. I'm not leaving until I get an answer."

Chun turns pleasantly to Hua to hear what I've said. She doesn't seem quite sure how to phrase things. I'm past caring about her discomfort.

His answer is a shrug of the shoulders. I wait for more. He smiles ingenuously.

"Tell him that I would like an answer! I want to know why Li Ming was not allowed to take her scholarship, and why she has been sent away."

"Dean Chun says . . . perhaps if you so concerned . . . Li Ming not only . . . is she a friend."

"What does that mean? What does he mean by that?"

But the old man doesn't answer. He looks out the window as if he has more time than he knows what to do with, and nothing in particular to do.

"I categorically deny . . . Li Ming and I are just . . . "

He doesn't look. Hua doesn't bother translating. The words stop in my throat.

"Tell Dean Chun . . . that if he does not bring Li Ming back . . . immediately . . . then I will not finish teaching the rest of the term."

No reaction. Still looking out the window. He delivers his answer as if he is thinking of something else.

"Dean Chun say . . . no need for you continue teaching. Term is . . . over for your classes. No exams."

I get up, and then have to hold the desk because of the dizzy spell that comes over me. Suddenly I am exhausted, famished, dispirited. I have to wait several moments while my head clears.

"Dean Chun would like to . . . thank you for your . . . great contributions . . . to the cause of socialism and . . . our People's Republic. We will never to . . . forget what . . . you have done," Hua says as I am walking out the door.

28

As AFTERNOON CREPT INTO EVENING LOU'S CONTRACTIONS IN-
creased slowly until they were piling on top of one another like
box cars after some horrible circuiting error. Her eyes were
closed most of the time now and she didn't seem to notice or
care who came into the room. When Rudy asked her once how
she was doing, she said she felt as if her backbone had barbed
wire twisted around it. She couldn't change her position because of the monitor, but when the nurse suggested forcefully
that she have an epidural she replied through taut lips, "I don't
want an epidural. I want to be off this fucking machine."

Rudy held her hand, stroked her hair, brought her water and
warm towels and once a little bit of food which she could not
eat. Her face was white, her hair soaked halfway through with
sweat. When the nurse left that time Rudy undid the monitor
and quietly turned off the machine. Lou immediately knelt with
her legs apart and her head down, and through whispers told
Rudy to rub the small of her back and cover it with warm towels, which helped a little. It seemed like an entire half hour of
contractions passed then, with no pauses in between, just one
slamming into the other. Where was the doctor? He was supposed to be here by now.

He had expected Lou to be vocal, to scream and moan and
swear and gasp with everything that happened. But instead she
retreated into herself and became as silent as one could be with
such storms happening inside, marking the contractions only by

the occasional low moan that never lasted more than a moment, an escaped sigh.

"You don't have to go through this pain," Rudy said, rubbing her back, feeling her stiffen. "You can have an epidural. Any time you want."

"I don't . . . want . . . " Another contraction came on and Lou braced herself while Rudy gently rubbed — it was too painful if he touched her heavily — and rocked, a little bit, with what seemed to be the rhythm of the inner movement. "Take control of this," he whispered to her. "Push along with it. Don't let it knock you over."

There was a respite. Lou continued crouching, her head hidden, as if she were waiting to be kicked. But she was saying something.

"What is it, Lou? What is it you want?"

"I want . . . to have a shower," she said.

"You want a shower?"

"Yes."

"Are you . . . are you sure?"

Another contraction, constricting her whole body. Rudy rubbed her from behind and looked around for the nurse. He was sure she was going to come back any moment and give them a hard time about unhooking the monitor. Where were the showers? Nobody had shown them. They weren't in the bathroom in the room. They must be down the hall. But maybe this wasn't the best time.

"Rudy?"

"Yes, Lou — would you like some water?"

"I'd like . . . a . . . shower. Please."

"I'm going to have to ask the nurse, all right, Lou? I'm just going to be gone for . . . "

As an answer her fingers gripped his arm like steel pliers and he didn't go anywhere. They waited while she endured another contraction.

When he looked up at the clock again twenty minutes had gone by. Outside it was getting dark. He hadn't eaten anything since a sandwich a little before noon. Why hadn't he brought some food for himself? This was going to be a long night. There was no doubt about it. Then there was another series of contractions and a new nurse came by this time, young and very slim with black hair and kind, well-rested eyes.

"Hi, I'm Debbie. I'm going to be your nurse until seven o'clock tomorrow morning, by which time I hope we have our baby here. Hello Dad. And you must be Louise."

Lou did not look up. Rudy stepped aside while Debbie examined her. "You're dilated about two centimetres," she said. "That's excellent. Now I'm just going to strap you onto the monitor for a minute and then we'll take it right off, okay?" She and Rudy leaned Lou back and they turned on the machine again to verify the continuing mathematical equation of life.

"Good. Now the pain is mainly in your back, is that right? Yes. Has the doctor looked at you yet? No? He was contacted this afternoon so I expect he'll be in some time fairly soon. Let's just lean you forward again like you were. You seemed to be doing really well. Encourage her, Dad. She's doing a great job. That's it, Louise, wonderful!"

Her enthusiasm was catching. Rudy struck up a hopeful patter, feeling a bit like a catcher urging on his pitcher in the late innings of a tight game. He didn't mind so much being called Dad.

"Excuse me, Debbie, before you — Lou would like to have a shower. I think maybe the hot water on her back — "

"Could we wait until the doctor gets here?"

Rudy looked at Lou, who didn't seem to be listening. "Lou," he said. "We'll go have a shower after — "

"I want one now," she hissed.

"Just a short one," Rudy said to the nurse, and started helping Lou up. "Where did you say that shower is?"

"I really think it would be better — " Debbie started to say, but he was already helping Lou get a foot on the floor and there was nothing she could do but support her other side.

"We really do expect the doctor to be in shortly," Debbie said. They were walking now, though, Lou's feet in slippers on the cold floor, and then out along the hall.

Slowly. Another contraction came on but Lou kept going, breathing deeply, closing her eyes. Rudy felt like telling her again that she could have an epidural but concentrated instead on making sure they didn't slip on anything wet on the floor of the shower room.

They sat her down on a chair outside the shower and Rudy turned on the water. "I want it hot," said Lou.

"Maybe we can put this stool in," Debbie said, and Rudy took the wooden stool and placed it directly under the steaming stream. Then he helped Lou off with her gown and sat her down with the water running warmly off her back. "Thanks, Dad," she said, managing a brief smile.

"Are you all right?" Debbie asked. "Is that warm enough?"

Lou nodded her head without looking. Another contraction. She leaned up against the tiled wall so that the water fell directly onto the small of her back. Rudy sat on the chair just outside the stall, ready to catch her if she fainted. The water ran down every part of her full body, some splashing over the edge of the stall and soaking his shoes.

"Is that better? How does it feel? You're doing great!"

"Hotter," Lou said, and Rudy reached in to adjust the taps. When he had it hot enough she sighed heavily and melted a little against the tiles.

It didn't take long for the shower room to fill with steam. Lou kept asking for hotter water until finally it was on maximum and the skin on her back was bright red, but that seemed to soothe her. She could relax. The pain wasn't so bad. She could take the contractions one by one, as they came.

Rudy lost track of the time. The water fell, Lou leaned against the tiles, Rudy sat within arm's length talking to her, soothing, watching. Every so often Debbie would check in with some apple juice for between contractions, and twice they took Lou out, towelled her off, and hooked her up to the portable monitor to check the baby. Inside the shower room it didn't seem to be day or night; the steam built, the water drained, the pain in Lou's back was numbed with heat and the shower's gentle massage.

"Any sign of the doctor yet?" Rudy asked.

"No," Debbie said, handing in another plastic cup of apple juice. "I think we might as well stay here until he comes. Does it feel all right?"

Lou nodded, her eyes closed.

It was like a meditation. The dripping of the water on the walls, the steady noise of the shower, the fullness of her body, the way her hair clung to the sides of her back. Everything gentle now as steam. Even the contractions seemed to have been lessened; it was hard to tell just from looking when they came on, because Lou was more relaxed, yet concentrating so hard at the same time. Rudy wondered if the hospital was going to run out of hot water. But there was no sign of it, no need to hurry away.

Debbie came back more and more frequently. At one point Rudy asked her how long Lou had been in the shower and she said three hours, which seemed preposterous — they had only put her in perhaps forty minutes ago at the most! She sent him off to take a break but he refused, sure that Lou needed him every second. But when he looked at her he realized she was in her own world and so he took a moment, leaving Debbie to look after Lou.

It *was* late, after all. The lights in the rooms were dimmed and the half-lit halls were empty. As soon as he started walking, he realized he needed a bathroom painfully, and in the few minutes he took to find one he felt his bladder would erupt.

When he was finished he splashed water on his face, was happy to feel the roughness of his whiskers. He already looked as if he had been up all night. He dried himself off, then strolled for a bit down the hall, swinging his arms like a windmill, stretching his legs, kicking high above his head once with each leg and then bending low, his chin to his knees.

What was happening, this day, he would remember for the rest of his life. It wasn't even his child, but he would remember it.

He walked to the end of the hall and looked out the window at the blue-black sky. Where were the clouds from this afternoon? He looked west beyond the far edge of the town where a few lights shone, bare candles against the black of the universe. He felt a strange sense of the tilt of the planet. Soon he would be on the other side of it, flying into a city that was upside down.

"Wait a minute. Sit down," Madeleine says, calm and angry at the same time. "You told me that nothing was happening between you and Li Ming."

I just look at her.

"You *promised* me that nothing was going to happen. That you were going to stay out of this — "

"I know."

She waits for me to say more. There isn't anything more.

"Oh for Christ's sake, Rudy!"

I stand up again. "I have to . . . I have to go."

"And what about Li Ming? Where is she? What's going to happen to her?"

"I . . . I'm not sure." Now she is shaking her head, almost crying. "It's going to work out, Madeleine. You see, she has my parent's address in Ontario. She'll get in touch with me as soon as she can. And then I'm going to work to get her out. I know . . . I know it seems bad, but . . . but we have time. A whole lot of it. And we love each other."

"Oh Rudy."

I hold her and feel the crinkles in her hair against my face. It seems too sudden to be saying goodbye. But my classes are cancelled, Li Ming is gone, and there is nothing now to stay on for. I'm leaving in the morning for Tibet, and then home.

"We'll keep in touch," I say.

"Oh Rudy."

"What?"

"I'm sorry, yes, we'll keep in touch."

She doesn't say anything for a long time. "What?" I say. "What are you thinking?"

"Nothing."

"Yes you are! There's something you're just dying to say. So say it!"

"All right," she says slowly. "What I was thinking . . . is that you are so young . . . and so sure . . . so white and so male . . . and so screwed up."

"Oh."

"Just think, will you? Think real hard next time."

"Li Ming and I are going to get married."

"Of course," she says, shaking her head, looking hard into my eyes.

The doctor arrived after midnight. They had taken Lou out of the shower by then and she was back in bed, crouching on her knees with her long hair wrapped behind her in a towel. Debbie explained to them that in back labour the child was turned around so that his back was pressing against the mother's spine, and the narrow part of the head was not flexing as it should through the birth canal. "It's really common for first pregnancies," she said a little too cheerfully. But Rudy was not sure that Lou was in a state to follow any of it; she seemed to have retreated to a small part inside her, far away from anything that might be happening beyond the present pain.

"Sorry I didn't get here earlier," the doctor said, smiling

wearily through a thick black beard. "How are we doing? All right? Louise?"

Lou just barely managed to lift her head.

"I'm just going to examine you here and we'll see what's what." It only took a few minutes. "You're pretty tired, are you?" he asked. Lou did not respond. She was going into another contraction, and Rudy quickly put another hot towel on her back and pressed gently.

"That's good! That's wonderful! That's very good breathing!" the doctor said, through a yawn.

"How . . . how much?" Lou asked, when the contraction had subsided.

"You're only dilated four centimetres."

"*Four!*" Rudy said. "She's been in hard labour since the afternoon!"

"Well, I'll tell you what's happened. The baby is keeping his neck rigid, instead of relaxing and tilting back through the passage. And your cervix is swelling because his forehead is slamming into it. So that's why you've only come four centimetres . . . "

Lou was listening with her eyes closed and her head down almost between her knees.

"That's it," she said.

"Lou," Rudy said, "would you like —"

She was nodding her head.

"I think she wants an epidural. Do you want an epidural?"

"Yes," she whispered.

"Okay," the doctor said. "That's a good decision. An epidural will relax you right up. I think that's the way to go." He straightened up and marked something on his clipboard, and then talked with the nurse in the corner for a minute.

"So we're going to book you in," he said, returning to the bedside. "There's just a little bit of a problem in that you'll have to wait awhile. There's been a traffic accident and a number of people are in Emergency right now, so the anesthetist is tied up for a while. You're going to have to hold tight, Louise. All right?"

"How long?" Rudy asked.

"Well, I don't think it's going to be any more than . . . two or three hours," the doctor said.

Lou moaned as if she had been hit.

"It won't be so bad. You've come through the worst of it," the doctor said. He left shortly after that, and Rudy and Debbie set up a production line of hot towels. They turned off the lights in the room and swathed Lou with heat as she rocked with the contractions. She moaned now and burrowed down into the sheets like an injured animal, and sobbed between the contractions as she tried to get her breath back. Rudy wanted to try her again in the shower but she was too weak to move anymore. She would not drink now, seemed to be just gritting it out until the medication. But the clock had stopped; it did not want to go past one, although the sweep was definitely moving. Every time Rudy looked up the hour hand was in the same place.

"Just relax. You're doing great. You're doing a terrific job. This is going to be such a great kid! God, you're not going to believe how beautiful this kid is going to be. That's it, breathe, yes, if you can, relax your shoulders, that's it, just ride through this contraction, that's all you have to get through, this one contraction and then have a rest, yes, beautiful, that's it, keep moving. Control it, get control of it, yes, that's magnificent!"

"I can't!" she sobbed, her first words in a long time.

"Oh yes you can! You are! You've been doing it all night! Just one at a time, get through one at a time. Here's another hot towel, here, how's that, does that feel better? It won't be long now. It won't be long. Things are just fine . . . "

They weren't fine. Her fists were twisting the bedsheets into hard knots and her jaw was welded shut and she was sobbing continuously now, shivering with the strain. Rudy thought suddenly of that boy in the accident all those years ago, with the pool of blood and the bright white of the bone showing. Was he in this much pain? Where was the doctor now? Why couldn't they get something for her? Why couldn't they do anything?

"I just checked down at Emergency," Debbie said, coming in. "You have to hold out for a little while longer. Here, here's another hot towel. They sure don't say it's going to be like this in the brochures, now do they?"

And then three hours passed which Rudy could not account for. Lou got very quiet again and he felt his legs getting extremely stiff as he kneeled on the bed behind her, so he could rock her back. When all was still he took a moment to stretch, finding that his neck was suddenly rusted in place and his shoulder muscles were wood. He could not move his head more than a few inches to either side without pain. He looked over at Debbie who was wiping Lou's brow with a warm hand towel.

"How do you do this as your job?" he asked her. "I mean — how do you last?"

"I take lots of breaks," she said. "You should too. In fact, you should get some sleep."

"I'll just take a walk," he said, and creaked down the half-lit hall, feeling his body slowly coming back to life.

It was four o'clock in the morning, an odd time to be awake. By the window at the end of the hall he watched what seemed to be the first, faintest sign of light on the horizon. It looked like a mistake, surrounded by the black all around it. Maybe the lights of an all-night gas station just over the hill. Then he walked into the washroom again and, feeling the change in his pockets as he did up his pants, went quickly downstairs and bought himself a coffee from the machine, knowing he wasn't going to enjoy it, but drinking it down nonetheless, as if it were medicine. When he got back to Lou's room nothing had changed.

"That's wonderful! That's great! You're doing terrific. Yes! Magnificent!" he said, feeling the coffee suddenly hitting his system. "What's that?"

He had to lean close to hear her.

Waiting for Li Ming

"Shut up," she said.

From four o'clock through to four-thirty, very slowly, and then to four thirty-five, and then . . . the clock stopped again. Rudy looked up three times, on the last two waiting purposely for a decent amount of time to pass, but each time it was four thirty-five. If they just got through until five o'clock. He was sure the anesthetist would be ready by five. How long could he be needed for those other operations? Not all night. He couldn't be needed all night. Traffic accidents are not that big around here.

A quarter to five. She was just huddling there, tortured. It wouldn't be long. Just fifteen minutes. Anybody can make it through another fifteen minutes.

"That's super," he whispered to her. It was hard to tell now what were the contractions. She didn't seem to be reacting anymore. But she wasn't asleep, either. She was in another state. "I'm so proud of you," he whispered, offering her some juice, which she took this time.

Five minutes. Five more minutes. And then it would be five o'clock and the anesthetist would be here. It was going to be all right. Just another few minutes. That's all.

An hour passed. The faint glow in the east turned into the sun and it blazed between the trees as the moon looked on overhead, pale and fading. The river shone, briefly, like mica, and the new light showed Lou's face pale and worn and aged, startlingly, as if that one night had counted a decade.

If Rudy hadn't been so tired he would have been furious about the anesthetist. How could it happen that an entire night could pass like that and nothing would be done to ease her pain? But he felt numb, sluggish, his brain circuits dulled. He and Lou together were in a mode of getting through time. That's all that counted; that's what their job was. Getting the baby out was someone else's concern. Theirs was a battle with time.

And then Debbie had Lou lie back one more time to put on

the monitor and Lou screamed, she shrieked with the pain and Debbie said, "Oh!" just like that, it was a sound he would always remember, "Oh!" high-pitched with surprise, like a noise from a cartoon. Because there was the very top of the baby's head, a mass of sticky hair, and then they were wheeling the bed out and about eight things happened which he didn't remember, but somehow he was dressed in greens and they were in the delivery room and the doctor was there smiling, refreshed after several hours of sleep, and he had no time to say anything because Lou was pushing now, really pushing, she had grabbed Rudy's arm and was yelling like a shotputter with every thrust — *Unngghh! Ughnnggh! Ughnnghg!* — and the baby was fighting his way out, the head and then a shoulder and then slippery like a fish and aloft and suddenly all red and purple and alive on her breast while she cried tears that she should not have had left.

"Look at that placenta!" the doctor said, holding it aloft like a huge liver. "Double-lobed — have you ever seen anything so healthy?" It seemed enormous, bigger than the child, radiating energy.

"Here, Dad! You can cut the cord," he said, clamping off the ends and handing him the surgical scissors.

"I'm not . . . I'm afraid I'm not . . . " he began to say, but they were looking at him, the doctor and Debbie and Lou, with the baby up against her, and so he snipped the surprisingly tough, rubbery cord while the baby sniffled, his eyes open, everything a storm of sensation.

"Six-eighteen a.m.," Debbie said, a dazzling smile for the mother and baby.

At seven o'clock they were in the recovery room. The baby had been washed, weighed, tested, poked and swaddled, and now was happy to keep his eyes closed and suck at Lou's breast. His hair, like his mother's, was a wild mass of red; his eyes were brilliant blue; his face was pushed-in and solemn, like a tiny, shrivelled, hundred-year-old man's. And he had a voice, which he showed off from time to time, his screams more proud than frantic, as if he somehow knew the significance of the passage he had just taken.

"I wish you had let me bring my camera," Rudy said.

"I would shoot you if you took a picture of me now!"

Everything was green — the curtains around the bed, the bedspread itself, the clothes he was still wearing. But hospital green, timeless institutional green that has nothing to do with life. He wished there was a window right there, where they could look out at the river. But then he looked at Lou and realized it wouldn't matter where they were. She had her baby and all was well with the world.

"Have you thought of a name?" Debbie asked, coming in with a carton of juice.

"Michael," Lou said, without hesitation.

At eight o'clock he was at the telephones. He really should have some breakfast, he knew, but somehow he wasn't hungry and he wasn't tired. He had seen the battle of the beginning of life, and for a time it seemed to step him outside those mundane human requirements. He should write something down, he knew — anything, just to describe, preserve the way that he felt.

"Hello? Hi — Amanda? I didn't get you up, did I? Good. Listen, I just wanted to tell you it was a hell of a night, I mean, it was really long and crazy and Lou is so strong I can't believe it, but she had a boy, eight pounds six ounces . . . yeah, pretty big . . . doing fine, doing great . . . oh yeah, on top of the world . . . absolutely . . . but she's wiped too . . . Yes, Michael. That's what she's calling him . . . No, I don't know the middle name. Maybe there isn't a middle name yet . . . Oh yes, she was just terrific."

What Amanda said then didn't register immediately. The

words seemed familiar, but the connections weren't working properly. And then, when the meaning started to filter through, he didn't believe it. It didn't seem possible. It was as if someone had shot him with a cannon through the telephone line.

"I guess you didn't get a chance to listen to the news," she said. "The Chinese army just killed thousands of people in Beijing."

29

AT FIRST HE COULDN'T WATCH, COULDN'T LISTEN, COULDN'T READ about it. While the whole world saw that man standing alone in front of the line of tanks, moving left when the tanks moved left, right when they moved right, halting them just long enough for humanity to see before his friends pulled him to short-lived safety, Rudy was on the telephone to External Affairs, asking if Li Ming was on any of their lists of the dead. "Are you a relative?" they asked him.

"Yes. Yes I am," he said.

But she was not on any list, not on the Monday, not on the Tuesday, not on the Wednesday or the Friday or the next Monday or the Monday after that. But the massacre was the kind for which records were not going to be very helpful. Even as the evening news was showing the tanks and armoured personnel carriers mowing over the barricades and the tents, even as it documented the fall of the ghostly Goddess of Democracy, even as bullets sprayed and people fled screaming, falling, bleeding, over and over again on the world's television sets, the Chinese government seemed to know only how many soldiers had been injured by the "handful of extremists" who were involved in the uprising.

Very quickly it all seemed sickeningly familiar, the obvious progression from the purges and the denials to the new rhetoric, and the hollow outrage of governments most upset, behind the posturing, by the setback in trade with the world's largest untapped market. Rudy knew if he dwelt on it it would sicken him, but he couldn't help it, not when day after day passed and there was no word, there were no calls and no mail arrived. He ran up an enormous telephone bill jamming the number Beijing residents were supposed to use to turn in friends and neighbours who had been involved in the demonstrations. And a good portion of the money he got when he exchanged his ticket he spent faxing article after article about the massacre to any number in any part of China.

And then, as that Tiananmen spring turned into a summer of miracles elsewhere, he watched with the rest of the world as government after government fell in eastern Europe, as the dead shell of Communism cracked finally and began to fall away from the living body of new countries. Poland, Czechoslovakia, Hungary, East Germany all turned from the horror of a government so old, so cynical, so bent on self-preservation that it would mow down its own people in the heart of its own capital and then deny it. It seemed unbearable to Rudy that the people in so many other countries could ride the winds of such swift change, while the Chinese once again sank into silence, sitting through their political meetings, bowing their heads in self-criticism, waiting, with that strange mixture of fear and patience, for the old men to die.

Waiting. That great Chinese pastime. Surely the shock of June the fourth would freeze the whole world the way it froze Rudy, flattening him into a fossil while everything inside him focused on one thing — waiting for Li Ming.

On waiting, as he had been all year, as he had been, it seemed, for his whole life. How could life go on if he did not know what had happened, where she was . . . *if* she was anymore? Surely he would remain frozen until he knew.

And yet, even through glaciers, water still runs. Relentlessly, perversely, new days kept presenting themselves. Lou moved to Calgary. She tried living with her mother and it lasted nearly a month, and then Gary got word from a friend and came to see his child. Lou could not explain, really, what happened then, except that there are some people who just know your combination. When they come around, you fall open, and sometimes it's love and sometimes it's a disease. Gary had his own construction firm now; he wasn't drinking so much; he was crazy about Michael.

Rudy got sick. He had not been sleeping well, had been eating poorly, had not found the spirit to do his martial arts at all. His apartment was littered with newspapers, with dust and pizza boxes and clothes he did not bother tidying, and when the fever hit him he had not spoken to another person in several days. He didn't call anyone. He felt as if he was falling in a vacuum where there wasn't even air rushing past his face, there was just heat, a constant burning sun baking him into clay, scorching even the insides of his eyelids scratchy and dry. He thought of taking a cold bath but did not do it for a long time, lying instead on his hard mat in the darkness behind closed curtains, as if he did not deserve relief. It was his fault. If only he had gone when he wanted to. If only he had listened to the voices inside.

If only he could have talked to her.

He got in the bath, finally, when something inside told him this was getting dangerous, when he couldn't walk very well and the apartment was wavy and his fingers were burning from inside. He turned on the cold water and instantly his teeth clattered and his body was thrown from fifth gear into reverse with no brakes, no warning, and the room was so cold his fingernails suddenly were blue, in the middle of a heat wave, blue, and his hands shook as he turned the taps the other way, hot this time, hot, God, give me hot!

And so it went through the afternoon and into the night, from one extreme to the other, and he didn't think of calling Amanda, it didn't occur to him that he deserved help. Then in the morning, when his fever had broken, he went into the clinic and found out his temperature was 103°.

He returned to Ottawa a few days later, leaving his apartment in a mess, his manuscript in a box, his new answering machine on. It still seemed possible to him that Li Ming might be alive, that she might phone sometime in the middle of the night. Some of the leaders of the movement had gotten away, were collecting in Paris, although the papers were dwelling on stories of the young radicals, children almost, who were being shot on Chinese television to teach the country a lesson. He called in for his messages nearly every day but there never was anything except for one time, when a man's voice came on asking Rudy to get back to him as soon as possible so he could qualify for an enormous discount on quality factory broadloom.

On the train to Ottawa he had thought he saw that girl again, what was her name? The one he kept running into every few years. Janine. Yes. He remembered her name. But it wasn't her, it was somebody with the same colour hair but the face, the smile, the eyes were wrong.

He tried to think about things rationally. Nobody knew exactly how many people had been killed on June fourth. The Chinese government admitted only to twenty-three student deaths. Even the Western governments were scaling down their estimates. But maybe it was a thousand. How many residents of Beijing were there? About eight million. Now one thousand over eight million, that was . . . he worked it out . . . only .0125 percent. Those were very good odds. But still, there were the purges now going on, people being executed. Like that newscaster who stammered purposely when announcing Li Peng's martial law. A bullet in the back of the head.

Li Ming had been on Western television. The security police would not forget that. Maybe she wouldn't be executed. But she would surely be sent to prison, or to the countryside.

But the more he thought about it the more he realized that she would have been one of the ones to stay in the square. It was in her nature to do that. The picture that haunted him most was the one of the young couple huddled together on the last night, not moving, ready to die. Li Ming was stubborn like that. She would have seen this as the battle for her country. People were convinced by then that the soldiers would not fire on them. They had been stopped so many times before. No, she would have stayed too late, until the tanks were on top of her, and if she wasn't killed then she would have been arrested.

For a long time that summer Rudy felt a chilling wind blow through him. He went with his parents to the cottage and got sick again, this time a bad cold that he couldn't shake, and it turned into pneumonia. Three weeks. His mother cared for him and he read magazines, forgetting what the articles were about almost as soon as he put them down. He lost weight. He forgot the moves of the *liu he ba fa*. His joints ached when he tried to do anything.

"We've got to beef you up, son," his father told him, tracking sand into his bedroom on bare, tanned feet. "Thank God you've come to your senses finally, but you're going to have to gather your resources. First year is the hardest."

He was talking about law school. His father had pulled strings to get him in.

"You haven't been yourself since you started this writing business," his father said. "I knew it wasn't a good idea."

"It's nothing, Dad. I'm just sick."

"Well, you deserve a break. Take it easy for a while. You've been working too hard."

"I don't think that's the problem, Dad."

"No?"

Rudy shook his head. "No."

 Waiting for Li Ming

Something inside him wanted to not recover, to slide into apathy. But there was a conspiracy against him — the sunshine, his mother's cooking, some other part of himself that wouldn't listen to instructions. He couldn't even do a proper job of remaining ill. Gradually his strength began to return. He had to think what to do next.

He got a letter from Lou. She spent four pages describing young Michael, how alert he was right from the beginning, how hard he kicks his legs, how loud he yells at night, how solemn he is, never smiling, like some brooding poet trying to work out a difficult image. She was up all hours of the day and night rocking him, feeding him, singing to him, soothing him. They had put hooks up all over the house so they could string a hammock, the only place he would be sure to fall asleep. "I don't know what we're going to do when he starts to roll over," she wrote.

"I never imagined I could be this continually tired, Rudy. Why are people so enthusiastic about having these little things? They're absolutely exhausting, they need constant attention, they don't give anything back. I really don't know why there are so many people in the world. And that birth. Thank God you were there. I thought I was going to die."

In the four pages she only mentioned Gary once, and then not quite by name. "I'm not sure what I was thinking when I decided I could raise a child by myself without any help. Now, I can't imagine how anyone does it. Even *with* help this is the most difficult thing I've ever done in my life."

Slowly, a feeling built in Rudy that he had to do something to get Li Ming out, or, at the very least, to discover the truth about what had happened to her, whatever that truth might be. He returned to his parents' home in Ottawa and dug out his old Chinese tapes and textbooks and began again to try to learn the language, which somehow was understandable on a tape, spoken slowly, with the written text beside it and a translation at the back.

He began again to practise his martial arts, to make his body strong again. He had a fantasy, a bizarre twist of Boxer Rebellion thinking in which he, a foreigner, would use martial arts to battle the dynamite and steel of the modern Chinese army. Of course it hadn't worked for the Chinese Boxers against the cannons and rifles of the foreign devils, and it didn't work in his imagination this time either. The armoured personnel carriers still broke through the barriers, still ran over the people, whose blood still soaked the dust-choked streets.

And then, one hot afternoon, as he stumbled over his meagre Chinese phrases, a package arrived at the door which, when he opened it, momentarily froze the breath in his body. It was his photographs, his long-lost photographs from the developing company in Hong Kong. They came in a battered box with so many postmarks on it he could barely decipher where it had travelled. He looked at it a long time, reluctant to open the package. From what he could tell it had been sent at least twice to some address in Ontario, California, before finally arriving at the right house in Ottawa, Ontario.

Slowly he took out his penknife and cut the remaining string and tape, and then opened the flaps of the box. There was no covering letter, just fifteen envelopes of pictures he did not want to see anymore. It was too much of a sign. Somehow it was quite clear to him while the photographs were lost that she was still alive. And now here they were.

He took out one of the envelopes at random and opened it. Laozhou. In the fall. He remembered immediately. It was that day he had gone through the back streets. There was Jiang shooting the basketball. His stomach nearly turned to see him and he flipped it over quickly, remembering the whole scene with Jiang talking on and on, trying to impress Li Ming. *If I can't have her, no one will.* He had to get up and take a deep breath. This was not such a good idea, looking through these pictures. He stood by the window, though, until his mind cleared, then picked up the envelope again.

Was it that grey, that dusty? The man pulling the cart with

the concrete pillars on the back, then four men pulling one of those carts up a hill. Black and white would have been better. And there was another thing he had forgotten about, the way the bricks in the little buildings seemed to be just piled loosely, hardly any mortar holding them together. The wind would blow right through. No wonder earthquakes level towns like that.

A little boy on his stool wearing an army uniform. Rudy wondered, does he wear it now, after what the People's Liberation Army did? Maybe the people in Laozhou don't know. Maybe they believe the newscasts.

An old man, his face dark and wrinkled, bundled in a thick cotton jacket, asleep on a stool. A rooster tied by the leg, looking right at the camera. Wonderful shot. The old woman and the boy, neither one smiling. He should have sent them a copy. Impossible now.

The picture of Li Ming. Rudy couldn't quite breathe when he saw it, was suddenly full of tears. Her confident, striking face, the way she held her shoulders back and the curve of her dark eyes. He put it away immediately, packed up the box, stuffed it in his closet behind old notes from college. Another time. He would have to look at them another time.

It was then he knew that she was not going to come, that she had not survived the morning of June fourth and was probably buried in some secret hole beside uncounted others who were not important, who could disappear without a whisper, and about whom no one would dare ask. At least not now, while the old men were still alive. The realization made a cold, hollow place inside him; he carried it with him day after day.

Rudy returned to Bellsbridge in the middle of August. It was steaming hot like the inside of a dry-cleaner's and he sweated through his shirt walking from the train station. It reminded him of Hong Kong, although of course there weren't the crowds to make even the air seem closer, more confined. His apartment had not been aired in many weeks. He felt revolted. It would be too difficult, he should just walk out and not come back. But he started by opening the windows, and that made it a little better, and then he cleared up some of the debris, and his hand seemed to fall naturally onto the broom. It wasn't so bad if he took it step by step.

Later, he ran into William Rogers on the street. Rogers commented that he hadn't received any new chapters from him.

"I . . . uh . . . I'm not sure . . . I'll be finishing my project," Rudy said.

Rogers just looked at him, and Rudy thought at once of Master Wang. He hadn't had time to say goodbye to him. There had been too much confusion, and so much he didn't learn.

"I'm . . . I'm registered to begin in law this fall," Rudy said. "So I'll be pretty . . . I'll be busy. And I . . . uh, I've been having a lot of trouble . . . finding an ending. I think maybe . . . probably I should just look at this as a first novel, you know. Most people have a novel that never . . . I mean, it just sits in the drawer . . . "

Rogers continued to look at him.

"Anyway," Rudy said, offering his hand awkwardly. "It's been tremendous working with you and I . . . "

"You've got time," Rogers said.

"Pardon?"

"You've got time," he repeated. "I know you. You've got time to finish your work. And you have something to say, too. Don't turn your back on it. It's just going to follow you."

Rudy nodded, embarrassed and quiet.

"You know what I'm talking about?"

"Yes, sir."

"Then I want to see it when it's done."

Late that summer Rudy had a dream as vivid as any in his life. In the dream he was back in the airport in Lhasa, Tibet, at the end of his visit. He was on the plane already, looking out the window at the guards with their machine guns as the engines sputtered to life. The wind-driven rain looked as if it was freezing to the wings; it wasn't safe to take off, but someone with an army behind him wanted them to go anyway.

Then they were in the air so high that all he could see was the spiny peaks below, which somehow were like those cruel things we live through if we can, and pass over.

And then in his dream he was doing a set of tai chi which he did not know, but somehow his body knew. He was on the rooftop of his building while the sun came up clear and golden over the river, and he watched the first passenger train from Toronto pull into the station in the distance, a silent silver snake, almost too bright to look at. He was doing this strange set of tai chi and thinking about the words that could describe the feeling, the certainty he suddenly felt, and how important it was that he remember this day, the smell of the river drifting to him now on a slight breeze, how small the sun became after it cleared the horizon and sailed higher in the blue, how suddenly warm his body felt.

At first the woman was quite a distance away. She was walking up Bridge Street with too many bags and parcels, having a hard time with the rush of the wind from the traffic. And she was stopping frequently to adjust the loads, and to look at a piece of paper which she held in the fingers of her left hand which was also wrapped around a large package pressed tightly to her. She had to look around the package to see the paper.

He was down the stairs of the fire escape two at a time and running around to the front of the building and dashing right across the street making cars swerve and honk, and then he couldn't see properly because of the tears, he just ran until she became larger and larger.

And then he stopped, and he couldn't speak at all. As if he didn't have enough to cry about — the flash in her eyes and the distinctive pronunciation of his name and the way she stood there grinning, as if she had planned this moment all along — the package in her left arm was not a package, really, it was a child, in a red jacket with blue pants and black eyes and a face that did not look entirely Chinese.

"I am sorry I took so long," she said, like an actress finally able to deliver her line. "But I had to bring you your son."

He awoke with a jolt, the dream upon him in one sudden image and then gone. In his pyjamas he burst out of his apartment and looked at the sun rising over Bridge Street, just like in his dream, and the sky so innocent and blue, the sidewalks clean and fresh and white as bone, with no one on them, no one there.